As Rebe ████████
through the ████ ████ **she stole**
a glance at her unconscious and
unexpected passenger....

Although his color was ashen, his clothes
stained and rumpled, she could tell that he
was handsome in a rugged sort of way. His
strong profile and jaw seemed to speak of
character and integrity. Yet there was a worn
look about his face—a sort of deep weariness
that had nothing to do with his injuries. For
some reason Rebecca had the impression that
he was a man who had seen it all and now
viewed the world with cynicism.

Rebecca's gaze snapped back to the road. She
was letting herself get way too fanciful. Looks
could be deceiving. She knew that from
experience. In a few minutes she'd leave him
at the hospital and probably never see this
man again.

But oddly enough, the thought didn't give her
much comfort....

Books by Irene Hannon

Love Inspired

Home for the Holidays #6
A Groom of Her Own #16
A Family To Call Her Own #25

*Vows

IRENE HANNON

has been a writer for as long as she can remember. This prolific author of romance novels for both the inspirational and traditional markets began her career at age ten, when she won a story contest conducted by a national children's magazine. Presently, her editorial position in corporate communications—as well as penning her heartwarming stories of love and faith—keeps her quite busy.

Irene finds writing for the Love Inspired series especially rewarding because, "Inspirational romances allow me to focus on the three things that last—faith, hope and love. It is a special pleasure for me to write about people who find the greatest of these without compromising the principles of their faith."

The author and her husband, Tom—"my own romantic hero"—reside in St. Louis, Missouri.

A Family To Call Her Own
Irene Hannon

Love Inspired

Published by Steeple Hill Books™

STEEPLE HILL BOOKS

Steeple
Hill™

ISBN 0-373-87025-6

A FAMILY TO CALL HER OWN

Anyone who welcomes one little child like this in my name welcomes me.

—*Matthew* 18:5

To Dorothy Hannon,
my wonderful mother and cherished friend,
who gave me Isabel.

Chapter One

"That's a lie!" Zach Wright shot to his feet and glared at the managing editor, bristling with rage. He leaned on the desk that separated them, palms flat, eyes flashing. "That's a lie!" he repeated furiously.

"I'm sure it is," Ted Larsen replied calmly, not at all intimidated by Zach's threatening posture. "But are you willing to reveal your sources to prove it isn't?"

"You know I can't do that!"

Ted shrugged. "Then we've got to play it their way. For now."

"Why?" Zach demanded hotly. "I'm telling you, this information is solid. I wouldn't use it if it wasn't."

"I know that," Ted conceded. "But Simmons is getting pressure on this—big-time. They're threatening to sue."

"It's just a scare tactic," Zach retorted scornfully, waving the excuse aside dismissively with an impatient gesture. "My information is good."

"You're probably right about the scare tactic. But it worked. For the moment, anyway. It's not easy being a lucrative publisher in this day and age, Zach. You know that. Simmons is just being cautious."

Zach gave a snort of disgust. "I can think of a better word for it."

"Look, we'll work this out. I know your information isn't falsified. We just have to prove it." Ted paused, as if carefully weighing his next words, anticipating the reaction. "And until we do, we're going to kill the series."

With a muttered oath, Zach turned away in frustration, jamming his hands into his pockets as he strode over to the window and stared out at the city streets. St. Louis could be a beautiful city, he thought. But on this dreary February day it was just plain ugly—the same as his mood. This whole experience was leaving a decidedly bad taste in his mouth. "Whatever happened to printing the truth?" he asked bitterly. "I thought that was our job."

"It is," Ted acknowledged. "But Simmons's job is to keep the paper solvent. He's not willing to risk a lawsuit."

"So we just let them get away with it?" He turned back to face the editor, his eyes still blazing. "Ted, the corruption in that office is rampant—misuse of public funds, a rigged bidding process based on nepotism instead of price, blatant bribery—what am I supposed to do, forget about it?"

"No. Just lie low for a while. In fact, why don't you take some time off? How many weeks have you accumulated, anyway? Five, six?"

"Eight."

"When was the last time you took a real vacation?"

Zach shook his head impatiently. "I don't know."

"Maybe you're due."

"I don't want to take a vacation!" Zach snapped. "I'm not running away from this story, Ted! I'll stand behind my coverage even if the paper won't!"

"We're not asking you to run away," Ted replied evenly. "Just give it a little time. If you don't want to take some time off, we can assign you to another story while we straighten out this mess."

"Like what?"

Ted pulled a file toward him. "Looks like the St. Genevieve area is going to get hit with another flood. I need somebody down there to cover it."

Zach stared at the editor as if he'd gone crazy. "You're kidding, right?"

Ted adjusted his glasses and looked across the desk at the younger man, the sudden glint of steel in his eyes making Zach wary. Ted had come up through the ranks, done a stint as an investigative reporter himself before taking over the editor job, and his staff respected his skill and integrity. But they also knew that his usual affable, easygoing manner was quite deceptive. He could be unrelenting and as tough as nails when he had to be. And now, as he fixed his razor-sharp eyes on Zach, it was clear that the conversation was over.

"No, Zach, I'm not," he said, his tone edged with iron. "You're overreacting to this situation, whether you realize it or not. You need some time to decompress. Nobody can maintain the intensity, keep up the pace you set, month after month, year after year, without wearing down. You need a change of scene, a different focus, a fresh perspective. You can do that by taking the flood coverage assignment—or by taking a vacation. It's your choice. But those are the only options."

Zach frowned and took one hand off the wheel to flip on the overhead light, then glanced down at the map lying on the seat next to him. His city beat rarely took him more than a few miles south of town, and this part of the state was totally unfamiliar to him. St. Genevieve must be the next exit, he decided, though it was hard to tell in the dense fog that had reduced visibility to practically zero and obscured most of the highway signs.

Zach tugged at the knot of silk constricting his throat and drew in a relieved breath as the fabric gave way slightly. He didn't like ties. Never had. But dinner with the publisher was definitely a "tie" occasion. Even though dinner had ended late, he'd wanted to get settled in and start his interviews for the flood piece first thing in the morning.

At least Simmons had had the guts to discuss the situation with him face-to-face, he thought grudgingly. The publisher had assured him that the paper stood behind him, that they had confidence in his reporting. But they'd still pulled the series. And as far as Zach was concerned, actions spoke louder than words.

Zach flexed the muscles in his shoulders and glanced at his watch. Ten o'clock. It had been a long day, he thought. A very long day. And the only good moment had been Ted's parting words.

"These setbacks happen to all of us, Zach," he said, laying a hand on the younger man's shoulder. "Don't let it get you down. You're a good reporter. One of the best. We'll work this out."

Ted's compliments were rare, and therefore prized. It had been a satisfying moment for Zach. Maybe the most satisfying in his career for a long time, he realized with sudden insight.

Zach frowned. Maybe he'd just stumbled on the source of the discontent, the restlessness that had plagued him for the last few months. His satisfaction used to come from his work, the feeling that it was making a difference. And that's where it should come from. Not from recognition by his boss. Yet Ted's compliment had given him more satisfaction than any of the work he'd done for the past six months.

Zach remembered his early years as a reporter, when he'd fervently believed that he could make a difference, that his writing could right wrongs and make the world a better place. For the first time in his career he seriously questioned that belief, directly confronting the doubts that he now realized had been growing for quite some time. For fifteen years he'd devoted himself single-mindedly to his work—an insatiable, demanding mistress that took all the passion he had to give. And what did he have to show for his zeal and dedication? A few moments of satisfaction when justice had prevailed. But far more moments of frustration when some scumball short-circuited the system through power, money or influence and walked away, laughing in his face.

And he certainly didn't have financial security. His meager savings were eloquent confirmation of journalism's reputation as a notoriously low-paying profession. He had no home, unless you could bestow that generous title on the sparsely furnished one-bedroom apartment he'd lived in for years. And he had no personal life.

All he had at the moment was a depressing feeling of emptiness.

As his precise, analytical mind clicked into gear, Zach tried to pinpoint exactly when his passion for tilting at windmills began to ebb. It might have been three years ago, he thought, when his story on corruption in the building industry blew up in his face thanks to a well-crafted smear campaign that didn't quite discredit him but hurt his credibility enough so that no one took his coverage seriously. Or maybe it was the story he did on teenage prostitution last year, when he spent too many depressing nights on the streets with kids who should have been at pep rallies or studying for algebra exams, not hawking their bodies.

But it didn't really matter when he'd stopped believing that what he did made a difference. The fact was he had. Maybe it was burnout, as Ted had hinted. Maybe he did need a break. It might not be a bad idea, after all, to take some time off when this assignment was completed.

But why had he burned out? Not everyone did. Josef certainly hadn't. Zach shook his head as he thought of his idealistic journalism school classmate, back home now in Eastern Europe, fighting the good fight, as he called it, trying to make his country safe for freedom. Josef's vision had never faltered, even in the face of setbacks and personal danger, and Zach admired him for that. He wished he had more of Josef's conviction and optimism. But he didn't. Not anymore. He'd seen too much and given too much. The well was dry.

Zach thought back to the last time he'd seen Josef. It had been almost eight years since his friend brought his delicate wife, Katrina, to St. Louis for the birth of their daughter. During their six-week stay with Zach, the two men had spent hours talking, debating, sharing. It had been an energizing, invigorating, renewing experience for Zach. Josef, with his serious nature, deep convictions and passionate feelings had always been an inspiration.

Zach recalled one of their last conversations, when he'd asked Josef how he coped with discouragement.

"But, Zachary, I don't get discouraged," his friend replied, clearly taken aback by the question.

Zach looked at him skeptically. "How can you not? Are conditions any better in your country now than when you started? Have you seen any progress?"

"I have not seen much visible evidence of progress, no," Josef admitted. "But we are making inroads," he stated with conviction.

"How do you know?" Zach persisted.

"Faith," Josef replied simply. "In your country, you expect things to get better like this," he said, snapping his fingers. "Patience is not a virtue in America. But in my country, we are used to waiting."

"But for how long?" Zach asked.

Josef shrugged. "Change is slow. But more and more people are on our side, Zachary, and one day there will be freedom for all. Maybe not in my lifetime. But still, I must do my part. Because, my friend, I believe that everything we do does make a difference. It is just that sometimes we do not see the result right away. But no good work is ever lost."

For a long time after Josef and Katrina returned home, Zach recalled that conversation whenever he became discouraged. It always inspired him. But not tonight. Josef was wrong, Zach thought tiredly, lifting his hand from the wheel long enough to wearily massage his forehead. All his years of personal sacrifice while questing for truth and right hadn't made one bit of difference in the human condition. If anything, crime was worse now than it had been when he was an eager cub reporter, determined to change the world. And that acknowledgment left a bitter taste in his mouth.

Would he feel any different if there had been someone to share his life with, to buoy him up on bad days? he wondered. But his passion had always been directed to his writing, leaving little for anything—or anyone—else. The few relationships he'd indulged in had been brief and sporadic. Either he broke them off when he realized the woman was getting serious, or she did when she realized he wasn't.

As a result there was no one who cared if he ate dinner when he came home late—or even if he came home at all. His family in Kansas City was too far away to keep tabs on his daily life, and his only regular companion for the past ten years—a cat—eventually had her fill of his bizarre hours and crazy schedule. One night she went out and never came back.

But Josef had found time for love, despite the demands of his work and his precarious existence, Zach admitted. Political conditions were extremely unsettled in his country, and from what Josef said, they were becoming more volatile each day. But he was a man of deep faith, who truly put his trust in the Lord and was at peace with his destiny. With his faith as a foundation, he had the courage to create a family in the midst of chaos, to share his life with the people he loved. While Zach had always looked upon a family as a distraction, Josef looked upon it as an anchor, a source of strength.

And maybe that's why he hadn't burned out, why he still had the energy to carry on the fight for his principles, Zach speculated. His family sustained him, and in the atmosphere of love and goodness and faith that pervaded his home, Josef found strength and hope and inspiration. Maybe the lack of those support mechanisms in his own life was the reason Zach now felt so emotionally and spiritually depleted.

In a way he envied Josef's deep faith. Living with the seedy side of life for so long had shaken Zach's belief in a loving, caring God. Yet without that foundation of faith, he felt oddly adrift. And as for a wife and family—it wasn't that Zach *never* wanted those things. It was just that he always told himself there would be plenty of time later. But at thirty-seven, "later" was now, he suddenly realized.

A sign for St. Genevieve loomed out of the mist to his right, abruptly interrupting his reverie, and Zach slowed down. This pea soup would do San Francisco proud, he thought grimly, as he cautiously made his way down the ramp and carefully turned left at the bottom.

As he drove along the two-lane road, visibility was so limited that he actually began to feel somewhat disoriented. It was almost like something in one of those old "Twilight Zone" episodes, he thought. He had the weird sensation that he was the last living thing on earth.

Zach's gaze momentarily flickered to the rearview mirror, confirming the absence of other cars or signs of life. While he might not be alone in the world, he certainly was alone on the ghostly road.

But not quite as alone as he'd thought, he realized, when his gaze returned once more to the pavement in front of him. A deer suddenly materialized from the mist and, startled by the headlights, bolted directly in his path. With a muttered exclamation, Zach instinctively jerked the wheel sharply.

The deer bounded off safely, but Zach wasn't so lucky.

As his lightweight, compact car fish-tailed across the unforgiving fog-slicked asphalt, Zach struggled vainly for control. But the vehicle seemed to have a mind of its own, skidding crazily toward the shoulder. His last thought as the car careened off the edge of the road and plunged down an embankment was that he'd forgotten to buckle his seat belt.

Rebecca Matthews stifled a yawn and reached for the cup of coffee in the holder under the dashboard. She grimaced as the cold liquid sluiced down her throat, but she needed the caffeine. It had been a long day and she was bone weary. She glanced at her watch and groaned. Ten-thirty. Make that a *very* long day, she amended ruefully. Maybe she should have taken her brother up on his offer when he'd walked her to the car.

"I hate for you to drive home alone, Becka," he'd said with a frown, looking down at her worriedly. "Why don't you spend the night? We have plenty of room."

"Oh, Brad, I'll be fine," she assured him. "I've done this drive alone a hundred times."

"I know. I just wish…" His voice trailed off, and he sighed. "I worry about you being by yourself," he admitted quietly.

Rebecca swallowed past the lump in her throat and forced herself to smile brightly. "Worry should *not* be on your agenda today, dear brother," she chided him gently, striving for a light tone. "You have too much to be thankful for. Anyway, save your worry for someone who needs it. I'm busy and happy. Honestly."

He seemed about to say something else, but refrained, bending down instead to kiss her forehead. "Okay. But promise you'll be careful."

"I always am. Besides, you know I could make this drive with my eyes closed," she kidded him with a smile.

And that's about what she was doing, she thought grimly as she peered through the dense, swirling mist, brought on by a combination of damp ground and unseasonably warm weather. So much for her plan to just switch on autopilot for the familiar route from St. Louis to St. Genevieve. For the past twenty miles the weather had conspired against her, requiring every ounce of what little energy and concentration she had left just to stay on the road. And unfortunately tomorrow's schedule wouldn't bend to accommodate her late-night arrival home. She'd still have to be up no later than six to prepare for the Friday lunch and dinner crowd at her restaurant.

Still, the trip had been worth it, she consoled herself. When Brad called earlier in the day to say they were at the hospital, she'd whipped off her apron and left the restaurant in the capable hands of Rose and Frances. That was twelve hours ago. But if it had been a long day for Rebecca, it had been an even longer one for her sister-in-law, Samantha, who had endured a drawn-out, difficult labor, Rebecca thought sympathetically. And poor Brad had been a wreck. But at seven thirty-five, when Emily Matthews had at last deigned to make her entrance, her parents' pain and concern had quickly been supplanted by joy.

Rebecca was happy for Sam and Brad. The tragic death of Brad's first wife seven years before had left him bereft for months, despite his deep, abiding faith and his vocation as a minister. Not only had he lost his closest companion and friend, but Rachel's death had seemingly destroyed his dreams for a family, as well.

Then Sam had come along, unexpectedly infusing his life with love and laughter and hope. And now they had a child. Tonight, as he'd held Emily tenderly in his arms, Brad had referred to her as "our miracle baby," and they clearly regarded this new addition to their life as a gift from the Lord. Rebecca didn't know the story behind that "miracle" reference, but there obviously was one. So it seemed especially appropriate that Emily had been born today, on Valentine's Day. She truly was a product of Brad and Sam's mutual devotion, and she would bring a new dimension to the love they shared as a couple and the love they would create as a family.

Rebecca sighed. Love—at least the romantic variety—wasn't something she knew much about personally, she reflected sadly. And she probably never would. Regrettably, Valentine's Day had never been a holiday she celebrated. Since opening the restaurant three years ago, she'd had little time to indulge in self-pity or dwell on her loneliness, but Valentine's Day always made her sad. And especially so today, when she'd viewed at such close proximity the circle of love shared by Brad, Sam and their new daughter. It had been very hard to hold back her tears as she cradled the tiny new life in her arms, knowing that it was unlikely she would ever repeat the experience with her own child as a loving husband stood by her side.

At thirty-three, Rebecca was still young enough to have the children she'd always wanted. That wasn't the problem. The problem was finding a husband with enough patience to deal with her problem. But patience was a virtue that seemed to be in short supply these days. And any man who was remotely interested in her would have to possess an incredible amount of patience.

Rebecca sighed again. She hadn't met a man yet who was willing to date her more than a couple of times without expecting some physical closeness. While Rebecca didn't believe in casual intimacy, she realized that at some stage in a developing relationship kissing and touching were appropriate. And expected.

But Rebecca couldn't handle that. Even if she liked a man, her only emotion when faced with physical contact was fear, not desire. And no man she'd ever met could deal with that. In fact, she'd stopped trying to find one who could. It was easier this way. Less humiliating. Less stressful. But certainly more lonely.

Yet seeing Brad and Sam together these past few months, and now watching them with their new daughter, made Rebecca yearn for the same things for herself. Surely there must be a man out there somewhere who could help her find a way to express the love she'd held captive for so long in her heart, she thought with a brief surge of hope. A man who could dispel her fear, patiently teach her how to respond, fan into life the flame of desire buried deep in her heart.

With sudden resolve she promised herself that if a man came along who seemed worth the effort, she would make one more attempt to explore a relationship. It wouldn't be easy, she knew. But maybe, with the Lord's help, she could find a way to overcome her fear and create her own circle of love.

And if nothing else, it was a wonderful fantasy for Valentine's Day, she thought wistfully.

But right now she'd better focus on reality, not fantasy, she reminded herself firmly. The fog actually seemed to be growing denser—and more dangerous. It might be better to get off the interstate at the first St. Genevieve exit and take the back road into town, she reasoned. At least there would be minimal traffic, and therefore less chance of an accident. She could barely see ten feet in front of her, and the thought that a tractor-trailer truck could be barreling along only a few feet away, unable to clearly see the lane markings and oblivious to the presence of her older-model compact car, was not comforting.

The exit sign loomed out of the mist unexpectedly, and Rebecca automatically flicked on her blinker, realizing the futility of the gesture even as she did so. She took the exit ramp slowly, with a bizarre sense that the world as she knew it had ceased to exist. Carefully she turned onto the deserted secondary road, her headlights barely piercing the gloom as she crept along. She couldn't remember the last time she'd seen a car, and as she drove through the swirling mist, an eerie feeling swept over her. She didn't spook easily, but the overwhelming sense of isolation was almost palpable. She knew there were homes scattered along the road, but they weren't visible tonight. She had no points of reference with which to mark her progress, and she felt disoriented and vulnerable. Worriedly she glanced at her gas tank, reassuring herself that she had plenty of fuel for the last leg of the trip home. This was definitely *not* the place to get stuck.

Rebecca's gaze flickered back to the road and she gasped as her headlights suddenly illuminated a figure walking slowly along the road, almost directly in front of her car. She swerved sharply to avoid it, then glanced in the rearview mirror in time to catch one final glimpse of the apparition before it was swallowed up in the gloom.

Good heavens, what had she seen? she wondered in alarm, her heart pounding as adrenaline raced through her veins.

Surely not a ghost! Of course not, she admonished herself sharply, stifling her overactive imagination. She didn't believe in such nonsense. She forced herself to take several deep, calming breaths and eased back on the accelerator, frowning as she mentally tried to recreate the image that had briefly flashed across her field of vision.

It was a man, she realized, wearing a white dress shirt and a tie, and carrying a suit jacket. Had he been weaving slightly? Or was that just a trick of the swirling fog? she wondered. And why would he be walking along the road at this hour of the night in this weather? Her frown deepened and she lifted her foot off the accelerator even further, slowing the car to a crawl.

There were only a few possible explanations for the man's behavior. Either he was a lunatic, he was drunk or he was in trouble.

The first two possibilities frightened her. She wasn't equipped to deal with them. Not alone on a deserted road. But if he was in trouble or hurt—she thought about the story of The Good Samaritan, who came to the assistance of the stranger on the road, and bit her lip thoughtfully. There was definitely a parallel here. She couldn't turn her back on someone in trouble. If he needed assistance, she had to provide it. But she wasn't going to take any chances, either. She'd just wait until he appeared and then use her best judgment to determine how to proceed.

Rebecca carefully pulled her car over to the side of the road, double-checked that all her doors were locked and that the windows were tightly rolled up, and waited.

As the minutes ticked slowly by and the man didn't appear, Rebecca began to worry. Perhaps he had become disoriented in the fog and wandered off the pavement. Or maybe he'd fallen into the drainage ditch near the shoulder. Or collapsed in the middle of the road, in the path of oncoming cars. Should she back up and...

Suddenly the man materialized out of the mist immediately

to her left, and Rebecca drew a startled breath. He was less than ten feet away, walking right down the center of the road. In the unlikely event that a car appeared, he would be a sitting duck, she realized. But he seemed oblivious to the danger. He also seemed oblivious to her car. In fact, he didn't seem to notice anything. And he was definitely weaving, she realized. His gait was unsteady, and his head was bowed.

Rebecca lowered her window a mere two inches and called to him. "Excuse me...do you need help?"

The man's step faltered momentarily, and he raised a hand to his forehead, but after a moment he continued to walk without even looking in her direction.

Rebecca frowned and quickly put the car in gear, following along slowly beside him. She lowered her window a little further and tried calling even more loudly. "Hey, mister!"

The man stopped again, and this time he glanced confusedly in her direction. Rebecca studied his face, and though it was mostly obscured by the billowing wisps of fog, she could tell that he was fairly young. Late thirties, maybe. He was also tall. Probably six feet. And he looked strong. Very strong. Which frightened her. She would be no match for someone of his size, and on this deserted road anything could happen, she thought fearfully.

But suddenly, as the opaque veil between them momentarily lifted, she realized that her fears were unfounded. The man was clearly injured. His face was gray, and there was a long, nasty-looking gash at his hairline. He was obviously in no condition to walk, let alone attack anyone. She'd be willing to bet that at the moment her strength far surpassed his.

Feeling a little less frightened, she lowered her window even more. "What happened?" she called.

"Accident," he mumbled, gesturing vaguely behind him.

Rebecca hadn't seen a car, and she looked at him suspiciously. "What kind of accident?"

"Deer," he replied, his voice slurred. He didn't appear to be able to manage answers of more than one word.

Suddenly he started to walk again, but after only two shaky steps his legs buckled and he fell heavily to his knees, palms flat on the pavement.

Without even stopping to consider her own safety, Rebecca unlocked her door and dashed toward him, stopping abruptly when she reached his side to stare down helplessly at his bowed head. What was she supposed to do now? Tentatively she reached down and touched his broad shoulder.

"Look, you can't stay here," she told him urgently. "You're in the middle of the road."

He ignored her, and in desperation she tugged on his muscular arm. "Please, try to get up. It's dangerous here. You could be killed," she pleaded.

Her words finally seemed to penetrate his consciousness, and he tilted his head to look up at her. His brown eyes were clouded and dazed, and he seemed to be having a difficult time focusing.

"Dizzy," he mumbled.

"Look, I'll help, okay?" she offered, tugging more forcefully on his arm.

This time he made an effort to stand. And as he struggled to his feet, she realized just how tall he was. At five-five she wasn't exactly short, but he towered over her by at least six or seven inches. And he was well built. And obviously strong.

A wave of panic washed over her, and for a moment her resolve to help wavered. But when she loosened her grip, he swayed, and she was left with no choice but to guide his arm around her shoulders. Stay calm, she told herself sternly. Think logically. The man is hurt. He does not represent any danger.

She took a deep breath, repeating that mantra over and over again as she slowly guided him to the car. He leaned on her heavily, his breathing labored, and she stole a glance at his face. He looked awful, and she wondered if he might have other injuries besides the deep gash at his hairline. Please,

Lord, help me get him to the hospital as quickly as possible, she prayed.

When they reached the car, she propped him against the front of the hood and backed up, eyeing him worriedly. "Stay put, okay?" she said slowly, enunciating every word. "I'm going to unlock the car door."

Rebecca had no idea if he understood her words—or even if he heard them. In his zombielike state, she doubted whether very much was penetrating his consciousness. She'd just have to work quickly and hope he was able to remain upright until she returned.

She moved rapidly around the car to the driver's side, and with one lithe movement climbed onto the seat and reached across to unlock the passenger door. She lowered the passenger seat to a semireclining position, then backed out of the car.

The whole maneuver took only a few seconds, but when she emerged, the stranger was trying unsteadily to navigate around the car on his own. Her heart pounding, she raced toward him, praying that he wouldn't fall before she reached him. She didn't know whether he'd have the strength to stand up again, and she couldn't lift him.

Just as she reached his side he stumbled, wildly flinging out an arm as he tried to regain his balance. Unfortunately, Rebecca was right in the path of his knuckles.

The backhanded blow caught her on the chin, and she stumbled back, grabbing at his arm to keep from falling. But that only threw him more off balance, and before she knew what was happening he fell against her, pinning her to the hood of the car under his body.

Dazed from the blow, aware only that she was suddenly immobilized and at his mercy, Rebecca panicked as a wave of primitive fear swept over her. With a strangled sob, she struggled to get free, writhing beneath the man's weight. But he was heavy. So heavy! She could hardly move. But she had to get free! She had to! Summoning up all her strength, she shoved him far enough away to tear her body from beneath his.

The stranger seemed stunned by her action, and he staggered back, his eyes glazed. He wavered, then dropped to one knee, groaning as he raised his hands to his bowed head.

Still reeling from his blow, Rebecca reached up and gingerly felt her tender chin. Her chest was heaving as she drew in one ragged breath after another, and she braced herself against the hood, not sure her trembling legs would hold her up. In fact, her whole body was shaking, she realized. As she struggled to control her irrational reaction, she watched the man touch the gash at his hairline, then stare in confusion at the blood dripping from his fingers.

With a sickening jolt, Rebecca realized that the impact of his fall must have opened the cut again, and a pang of guilt swept over her. Dear Lord, what was wrong with her? The man was hurt, for heaven's sake! He was in no condition to attack her even if he wanted to, which was unlikely. He hadn't hit her on purpose. She needed to get a grip.

Rebecca took several more deep breaths, then knelt beside the stranger and scanned his face. Blood was seeping from the gash, his pallor was alarming and his forehead felt clammy to her tentative touch. The man needed medical attention. Immediately. For the first time ever she regretted that she hadn't invested in the cellular phone Brad was always badgering her to get. It would certainly come in handy tonight.

She drew a deep breath and lifted his limp arm, tucking her head underneath. As she draped his arm around her slender shoulders, his hand brushed her bruised chin and she winced. But the condition of her jaw was the least of her problems. She was more worried about getting the stranger upright. Since he probably outweighed her by a good seventy-five pounds, that wasn't going to be easy. But she had to try. She needed to get him into her car before he passed out, which at the moment appeared to be an imminent possibility.

"Okay, can you try to get up?" she asked. "I'll help. Just lean on me."

Rebecca made an attempt to rise, but it was like tugging on a dead weight. He didn't budge.

"Come on, mister, just try. Please!" she pleaded.

This time when she urged him upward he took the cue, struggling to stand as Rebecca tried to assist him. Once he was on his feet he swayed, and she planted her feet solidly, determined to maintain her own footing. She glanced up worriedly, noting the deep grooves of pain etched in his face and the thin, compressed line of his lips. Despite the chilly air there was a thin film of sweat on his brow, and his breathing was labored.

"We're almost to the door," she encouraged him, trying to keep the panic out of her voice. "It's just a few steps. You can make it."

Half dragging, half pulling, she got him into the car, expelling a shaky breath as she shut the door. She retrieved his suit jacket from the middle of the road where he'd dropped it, tossed it into the back seat, and slid behind the wheel. As she put the car in gear, she glanced over at his semisupine form. She wasn't even sure at this point if he was conscious. But at least he was still breathing, she thought with relief, noting the even rise and fall of his broad chest.

As she drove carefully through the swirling, silent fog, she stole an occasional glance at her unexpected passenger. Although his color was ashen, his clothes stained and rumpled and his hair disheveled, she could tell that he was handsome in a rugged sort of way. His dark brown hair was full and slightly longer than stylish, almost brushing his collar in the back but neatly trimmed. Her eyes traced his strong profile and firm jaw, which seemed to speak of character and integrity. Yet there was a worn look about his face—a sort of deep weariness that had nothing to do with his injuries. For some reason she had the impression that he was a man who had seen it all and now viewed the world with skepticism and cynicism. Despite his world-weary appearance, however, there was a feeling of leashed power about him. Even in his present condition he seemed to radiate energy and vitality and...sensuousness.

Rebecca was taken aback by that impression. Yet it was true. The man exuded an almost tangible virility. She stole another glance at him, her eyes lingering for a moment on his firm, strong lips. Her breath stuck in her throat, and she swallowed convulsively, forcing her gaze away from his face and down to his hands. He had nice hands, she thought. They looked...competent. As if they could be gentle or demanding or forceful, depending on the circumstance. The kind of hands that would be equally at home chopping wood—or caressing a woman.

Rebecca's gaze snapped back to the road. She was letting herself get way too fanciful. The man was a stranger! None of her speculations were grounded in reality. For example, just because he looked like he had character and integrity didn't mean he did. Looks could be deceiving. She knew that from experience. Caution was more prudent than curiosity in a situation like this, she warned herself.

Yet she couldn't help but wonder about him. Why had he been driving on this road alone so late at night? She ventured another quick glance at his left hand. No ring. That didn't mean anything, of course. He might be one of those married men who preferred not to wear a ring. But for some reason she had a feeling he was single—and unattached. A surprising little tingle ran down her spine at that possibility.

Which was silly, she told herself sharply. In a few minutes they'd be at the hospital and, her duty done, she could finally go home and catch a few hours of much-needed sleep. She'd probably never see the man again. And that was just as well. For some reason he unnerved her, even in this semicomatose state. He was just so...male.

Rebecca knew that wasn't a very articulate explanation for her reaction, but it was accurate. His mere presence seemed somehow...dangerous...and threatening. Threatening to what, she wasn't sure. Certainly not her physical safety, not in his present condition. It was more insidious than that. It was almost as if he was a threat to her emotional safety, to her peace of mind. Which made no sense at all. She didn't even know the man. And she never would. In a few minutes she'd leave him at the hospital, and that would be the end of this little adventure.

But oddly enough, that thought didn't give her much comfort.

"And you didn't see anything else?" the highway patrolman asked after Rebecca finished her statement.

She shook her head, wrinkling her nose in distaste at the antiseptic hospital smell. "No. Like I told you, he was just wandering down the road. He mumbled something about a deer and an accident. But I didn't see a car."

"Well, we'll check it out." He turned to a new page in his notebook. "Now can I get your address and phone number?"

Rebecca frowned. "Why?"

The officer gave her a quizzical look. "If we have any questions later about the statement, we may have to call you. Is that a problem?"

"I'd really rather keep my name out of this."

"We can mark it confidential, if you prefer. But we do need it for the record."

Rebecca bit her lip. "He doesn't have to know, does he?" she asked, nodding toward the examining room where they'd wheeled the stranger.

"No."

"All right."

By the time they'd finished filling out the report, the doctor joined them in the waiting area.

"So how is he?" the officer inquired. "Can I talk to him?"

"He's still pretty groggy. I'm not sure you'll get much, but you can try if you want to. We're going to keep him here overnight for observation.''

"But he'll be okay?" Rebecca queried.

"Looks like it."

"Is there someone you can notify?"

The doctor nodded. "He gave us the name of a friend in town."

Rebecca sighed with relief, feeling as if a responsibility had been lifted from her shoulders. She was bone weary, and six o'clock was going to roll around way too soon. "So I can leave?" she asked hopefully.

The doctor looked at the officer, and they both nodded.

"He did ask who brought him here, though," the doctor told her. "I guess he'd like to thank you. Do you want me to pass along your name?"

Rebecca shook her head emphatically as she reached down to retrieve her purse from the plastic chair. "No."

The doctor gave her an understanding look. "Okay. We'll just say it was a Good Samaritan. You're probably wise to be cautious. You can't be too careful these days."

Rebecca nodded. Her earlier flights of fancy about the stranger might have been way off base, but she instinctively knew one thing. This man could disrupt her life. She sensed it with a degree of certainty that startled her. Intuitively she knew she would be a whole lot safer if she just vanished from his life.

And as she stepped outside, disappearing into the fog much as the handsome stranger had appeared out of it less than two hours before, she told herself this was the best way for this bizarre episode to end. She'd just pretend it had never happened. She would put the stranger out of her mind, forget their paths had ever crossed.

But for some reason she had a feeling that wasn't going to be easy to do.

Chapter Two

"Hi, Ben."

The rotund man behind the counter turned, wiped his hands on his white apron and smiled at Rebecca as she climbed onto a stool.

"Hi, there. I was beginnin' to think you were going to skip your coffee again this morning. Missed you yesterday."

Rebecca crossed her arms on the counter and rolled her eyes. "I barely made it to the restaurant in time to get lunch going," she admitted ruefully. "I just don't function well on five hours of sleep. And I don't feel a whole lot better today."

Ben looked at her quizzically, his bushy white eyebrows rising. "Late night Thursday?"

"Uh-huh. My brother and his wife had their baby, and I drove up to be with them. I just didn't expect it to take so long. But babies seem to have their own schedules when it comes to making an entrance," she noted wryly.

Ben chuckled. "That's a fact. Everything go okay?"

"Yes. It was a great day—except for driving home in the fog."

"I heard it was bad," he sympathized. Suddenly he peered at her chin and leaned closer. "Say, that's a nasty bruise," he observed, inspecting the bluish patch of skin on her jaw, clearly visible even under makeup. "What happened?"

Rebecca wrinkled her nose and gingerly touched the tender spot. "That, my friend, is a long story."

She was saved from having to explain by the jingling bell on the door, announcing the arrival of another customer. Ben glanced toward the entrance, then poured her a cup of coffee. "This'll wake you up. I'll be back in a minute."

Rebecca took a long, slow sip of the scalding liquid. Ben really did have a knack with coffee, she acknowledged. Of course, she could easily make her own at the restaurant a few doors away. But three years ago, when Ben had been one of the few people to oppose her request for a permit to open a restaurant, she'd gotten into the habit of stopping by every morning. It had taken a lot of talking on her part to convince him that she was no competition, that they would attract a different clientele. But she'd won him over in the end, and now they were the best of friends. Her early trips for coffee, once peace missions, were now simply an enjoyable way to start the day and catch up on town news.

Rebecca glanced affectionately toward the booth where Ben was conversing with another patron, gesturing emphatically over some point. With his bristly white hair framing a swatch of bald head—the fairway, he called it—he could almost pass for Santa Claus. In fact, he played that role every year at a variety of town holiday functions. And he had certainly been good to Rebecca.

By the time he ambled back to the counter, Rebecca's cup was almost empty, and he reached for the pot to give her a refill. She started to protest, but he waved her objections aside. "I know you usually only indulge in one cup, but you'll have a busy day today, bein' Saturday and all. You'll need it." He reached into the toaster oven behind him and plopped a bagel on a plate, adding cream cheese and a pat of butter. "And have this, too. You need to keep up your energy. Running a restaurant is hard work. I know. Although how you manage to stay so skinny in this business is beyond me. Course, I went the other way.'' He patted his generous stomach and grinned. "Too much sampling, I guess," he said with a wink.

Rebecca smiled. "Thanks, Ben. What would I do without you?"

He waved her comment aside. "You'd get along just fine. You've got those two old busybodies dithering over you all day at the restaurant."

"Now, Ben," she admonished him gently. "You know I could never manage without Rose and Frances. They're a godsend."

With a snort he reached for a damp rag and began polishing the sparkling counter. Rebecca stifled a smile as she took a bite of the bagel. The friendly rivalry for her affections between the two camps—Ben in the diner, Rose and Frances in the restaurant—always amused her. But she was grateful to be blessed with such loyal friends.

"Well, all I can say is, you make the best coffee in town," Rebecca declared to appease him. She knew he was mollified when he handed her the morning paper.

"Here. Take a gander," he said gruffly. "Probably be the only time all day you sit down."

"Thanks, Ben." Rebecca took the peace offering and scanned the headlines, her attention caught by a story on area flooding. She didn't even look up when the jangling bell announced a new arrival, at least not until Ben leaned down to give her an update.

"Mark's here. Got a stranger with him, too."

Even before she glanced up at the mirror over the grill and saw his reflection, Rebecca knew with uncanny certainty that the stranger with Mark was the man in the fog. She swallowed her last sip of coffee with difficulty, her pulse suddenly accelerating as she peeked above the paper to surreptitiously survey his image. If she'd had any doubts about his identity, the bandage at his hairline immediately confirmed her intuition. And if she'd sensed a power and virility radiating from him Thursday night when he was half-unconscious, today it was at full strength. His attire—worn jeans that sat well on his slim hips, and a dark green cotton shirt that revealed a glimpse of dark brown hair at the open neckline—only enhanced his appeal.

Suddenly Rebecca felt shaky, and though she made an attempt to control her physical reaction to his presence, it proved futile. She didn't have much time to try, anyway, because Mark immediately walked over to her, the stranger in his wake.

"Hi, Rebecca. Can we join you?"

Rebecca turned slightly at their approach and forced herself to smile at Mark, avoiding the stranger's eyes as she struggled to find her voice. "Of course."

Mark climbed onto a stool and gestured toward his companion. "Rebecca, this is a buddy of mine from way back, Zach Wright. He's a reporter—for that paper, in fact," Mark said, leaning over to tap on the section Rebecca was clutching. "He's here to cover the flood. Zach, Rebecca Matthews."

Rebecca could no longer avoid looking at the stranger, so she took a deep breath and turned to face him. The last time he'd gazed at her his eyes had been glazed, unfocused and dull with pain. Now they were clear and alert and warm. And disturbing. Her pulse went into overdrive.

Zach held out his hand, and short of being rude, she had no choice but to place hers in his firm grasp. "It's nice to meet you, Rebecca." He had a pleasant voice, deep and mellow, with just a touch of huskiness.

"It's nice to meet you, too." She tried to think of something else to say, anything, but her mind suddenly went blank. All she could do was stare into his compelling brown eyes.

Zach was equally captivated by the hazel eyes locked on his. Rebecca Matthews was a beautiful woman, with classic high cheekbones accentuated by the French twist hairstyle of her russet-colored hair. Beautiful and, surprisingly, familiar. He somehow sensed that their paths had crossed before. He had a good memory for names and faces—a skill that was essential in his business—and it rarely failed him. But he came up empty on the woman across from him. Although how he could forget someone who looked like Rebecca Matthews was beyond him.

As the seconds lengthened, Zach realized that they were beginning to draw curious glances, and he reluctantly released her delicate hand with an apologetic smile. "I'm sorry...I don't mean to stare, but...have we met before?" he asked, his eyes probing, quizzical.

Rebecca debated her answer. Originally she'd planned to keep her role in the stranger's rescue a secret because he *was* a stranger. But now that she knew he was a friend of Mark's, remaining anonymous was less important. She'd known Mark for several years, and if this man was a friend of his, he was okay.

She smiled faintly, and a becoming flush tinted her cheeks. "Sort of. Although given the circumstances I'm not surprised you're having a hard time placing me. Between the fog and the accident, I'm amazed you remember anything."

Zach stared at her, the puzzlement in his eyes rapidly giving way to comprehension. "You mean...it was you on the road Thursday night? You were the one who stopped to help and drove me to the hospital?" he asked incredulously.

She nodded and glanced away, reaching for her coffee cup. "Yes."

Mark stared at Rebecca, then at Zach. "Are you telling me that Rebecca is the angel of mercy you've been raving about?"

Rebecca's startled gaze flew to Zach's, and he felt his neck redden. But before he could speak, Mark leaned over to examine Rebecca's chin.

"Wow!" he exclaimed. "I just noticed the bruise! What happened? It looks like somebody slugged you."

Rebecca's gaze flickered to Zach, then skittered away. "It

was an accident,'' she said with a shrug, dismissing his question.

There was a moment of silence, and when Zach spoke his voice was troubled. ''Why do I have a feeling I'm responsible for that?'' he said slowly.

Rebecca turned to find him frowning as he studied the purple bruise shading the delicate line of her jaw. She shrugged again, flushing in embarrassment. ''It was an accident,'' she repeated. ''You were hurt. You lost your balance, and I was in the way.''

He expelled a long breath and ran his fingers through his hair. ''I think I owe you a very big thank-you—and a sincere apology,'' he said quietly, his intense eyes holding hers captive.

Rebecca dismissed his thanks with a shrug. ''I'm glad I could help. And this is nothing,'' she assured him, gesturing vaguely toward her jaw. ''So how are you?'' she inquired, feeling increasingly self-conscious under Zach's speculative gaze.

''Doing better. Thanks.''

''Twelve stitches and a concussion,'' Mark elaborated. ''Go ahead, Zach. Sit down,'' he suggested, indicating the stool next to Rebecca.

Zach hesitated, sensing that for some reason his presence was disruptive to the woman beside him, but she smiled politely.

''Please do,'' she seconded. ''I have to leave, anyway.'' She drained her cup in one long gulp and slid to the ground. ''I hope you recover quickly,'' she said, forcing herself to meet his magnetic eyes.

''Thanks.'' He grinned disarmingly, once more extending his hand, and again she was left with no choice but to take it. As he enfolded her slender fingers in his firm grip, her heart began to bang painfully against her chest, so strongly she was almost afraid he would be able to feel it through the vibrating tips of her fingers. His eyes held hers—curious, questioning, warm…and interested. Which did nothing to slow her metabolism.

"Thanks again for Thursday night." His voice was still shaded by that appealing, husky timbre. "I'm not sure what would have happened if you hadn't come along. I'm just sorry about that." His gaze flickered down to her jaw, and he started to reach up as if to touch the bruise. Rebecca's breath caught in her throat and her heart stopped, but suddenly he dropped his hand, shoving it into the pocket of his jeans instead. Rebecca's pulse kicked back in, then raced on.

"Anyway, I just want you to know that I don't usually go around hitting women," he assured her, his voice even more husky than before.

She cleared her throat, hoping her own voice wouldn't desert her. "I'm sure you don't. I'm just glad you're okay." Carefully she withdrew her hand, and with an effort she tore her gaze from his to look at Mark. "See you later."

"You bet."

"Ben, thanks for the coffee."

"Anytime."

And then she fled.

Zach planted his hands on his hips and watched her leave, a slight frown marring his brow. Clearly she'd wanted to escape from his presence as quickly as possible. But why? It wasn't that she was unfriendly. She just seemed…well, skittish. He reached up and rubbed the back of his neck with one hand. He couldn't recall ever meeting anyone quite like Rebecca Matthews. She was poised and polished, yet she seemed somehow…untouched. Vulnerable. Fragile. Without hard edges or pretense. She radiated an almost innate goodness, an old-fashioned air of shy sweetness. Those weren't qualities he'd run into often, and he was intrigued—and captivated.

He turned thoughtfully and straddled the stool next to Mark, who was watching him with amused interest.

"Forget it, pal," Mark warned with a grin.

"Forget what?" Zach asked coolly, reaching for the mug of coffee Ben placed on the counter.

Mark chuckled. "I've seen that look before. Had it once myself. Just don't get your hopes up. Rebecca's great—but she has no interest in romance."

"Are you speaking from personal experience?"

"Of course! Do you think a single woman who looks like her could come to a small town like this and not be pursued by every eligible man in the county? But she wasn't interested. Period. In anyone. So I didn't take it personally. We all had to settle for being just friends."

"Hmm."

"'Hmm' what?"

"'Hmm' as in, that's interesting but I'm not in the market, anyway."

"Yeah, right."

"Right," Zach repeated firmly. "As my boss told me, I need some time to decompress."

Mark grinned. "I can think of worse ways."

Zach chuckled. "Speaking of which, when do I get to meet your elusive fiancée?"

Mark smiled. "How about dinner tomorrow night?"

"Sounds great."

"Listen, do you mind if I run next door for a minute while you finish your coffee? Then I'll give you the ten-cent tour."

"No problem."

Mark slid off the stool. "Ben will keep you company while I'm gone, right Ben?"

"Sure." A moment later the door jangled to indicate Mark's departure, and Ben ambled over to remove his cup, wiping the counter as he spoke. "Nice girl, Rebecca," he said conversationally.

"Seems to be," Zach agreed.

"Make a good wife for somebody," Ben commented nonchalantly.

"From what Mark says, the lady's not interested in romance," Zach replied, taking a leisurely sip of his coffee.

Ben snorted. "Well, if you ask me, she just hasn't met the right man yet."

Zach had a knack for discreetly ferreting out large amounts of information without people realizing just how much they were divulging. It came in handy in his job—and in situations like this.

By the time he left the diner he knew quite a bit about Rebecca Matthews. She'd moved to St. Genevieve three years before to open her restaurant, "Rebecca's," which was becoming quite popular with both locals and St. Louisans, who often came to the quaint town for weekend getaways. She'd even been written up a few times in area papers—his own included, if Ben's information was accurate. A graduate of the Culinary Institute of America, she'd worked in a couple of prestigious restaurants before striking out on her own. She came from the small town of Jersey, in southern Missouri, where her father still lived. Her brother, Brad—a minister—and his wife, Sam, made their home in St. Louis. She'd been returning from there Thursday night after the birth of their daughter. As far as Zach could tell from Ben's ramblings, Rebecca never dated. And she was apparently doted over by two maiden sisters who worked at her restaurant.

As Mark and Zach started off on their tour a few minutes later, Mark pointed out Rebecca's restaurant. It was a modest building in the historic district, identified only by a discreet awning that displayed the name.

"Rebecca really is a wonderful chef," Mark told him. "The food's great. You'll have to try it while you're here."

"Uh-huh," Zach replied noncommittally. As a matter of fact, he intended to become a regular customer. And not because of the food.

"Rose, have you seen the tube of whipped cream with the star tip?" Rebecca called, her voice muffled as she stuck her head into the restaurant's huge refrigerator.

Rose glanced at the work counter, where the tube lay in clear sight right next to the torte Rebecca was decorating. It was exactly where she'd laid it moments before. Rose glanced at Frances across the counter, and her sister shrugged, mystified. Rebecca was extremely organized, and they'd never seen her flustered. Until this morning.

"It's right here, dear," Rose said, pointing to the tube as Rebecca turned.

"Oh. Well. I guess my brain just isn't in gear this morning. I haven't quite caught up on my sleep since Thursday night," she explained lamely, warm color suffusing her face.

"Frances and I will just finish up in the dining room and leave you in peace to work your magic on that cake," Rose replied, motioning for her sister to follow.

"All right." Rebecca distractedly wiped her hands on her apron and glanced around the kitchen. "Now where did I put that spatula?" she mumbled.

Rose ushered Frances out of the kitchen, and the two older women looked at each other quizzically. With their white hair pulled neatly back into identical soft, motherly buns, the sisters could almost pass for twins, although Rose was the older by two years and stood three inches taller than Frances.

"What do you make of it?" Frances whispered, her voice tinged with concern.

Rose shook her head, frowning. "I don't know," she said slowly, clearly puzzled.

"She almost put cinnamon in the quiche this morning, too," Frances informed her sister worriedly.

Rose considered that for a moment, and then her face grew thoughtful. "Unless..."

"Unless what?" Frances prompted.

"Unless it's a man," Rose replied reverently.

"A man?" Frances repeated, her eyes widening.

"Yes," Rose declared, nodding vigorously, becoming more

certain by the moment. "I'd bet my prize-winning recipe for pickle relish that there's a man behind this!"

"You mean our Rebecca's got herself a man?" Frances said incredulously.

"How else would you explain what's been happening this morning? Have you ever seen her so disorganized or absent-minded?"

Frances shook her head. "No."

"Then there you have it! There's a man behind this, all right," Rose asserted.

"But who?" Frances asked, bewildered.

Rose sighed, her brow knitted in concentration. "I don't know. But maybe that old buzzard, Ben, does. She had coffee there this morning."

"He won't tell us anything," Frances lamented, shaking her head regretfully.

"He will if you drop by with a piece of that torte this afternoon," Rose declared conspiratorially. "He has a sweet spot for you, anyway."

Frances smoothed back her hair and sniffed, pretending indifference. "Well, I suppose I could try."

"It couldn't hurt," Rose agreed.

"So what did you find out?" Rose asked eagerly when Frances returned from her mission later in the day, empty plate in hand.

Frances looked around carefully to make sure they were alone, then leaned close. "There was a stranger in there this morning with Mark," she reported in a hushed voice. "Name of Zach. His car went off the road in the fog, and Rebecca drove him to the hospital. He's a reporter from St. Louis, here to cover the flood. Ben says there was enough electricity flying between the two of them to run his toaster without even plugging it in. Said this Zach seemed like a real nice gentleman."

Rose gave a satisfied nod. "Good job, Frances."

Suddenly the front door of the restaurant opened, and both

women straightened up guiltily. A young man carrying a large vase covered with green florist tissue entered the shop and made his way toward them.

"I have a delivery for Rebecca Matthews," he informed the sisters, consulting the card attached to the tissue.

"I'll get her," Rose offered eagerly, bustling toward the kitchen. She opened the door and stuck her head inside. "Rebecca, there's a delivery here for you."

Rebecca looked up from the soup she was stirring on the stove and frowned. "All our delivery people know to come around back."

"It's not that kind of delivery," Rose replied, her eyes dancing.

Rebecca's frown deepened. "What do you—" But Rose was already gone. Rebecca sighed. She was having a hard enough time concentrating today without all these interruptions, she thought irritably as she pushed through the swinging door.

She stopped abruptly when she saw the young man standing there with what was obviously a vase of flowers, Rose and Frances flanking him on each side like bodyguards.

"Rebecca Matthews?" the boy asked.

"Yes."

"These are for you." He walked over and handed the vase to her. Then, jingling his keys and humming under his breath, he headed back out the front door while Rebecca stared, dumbfounded, at the flowers in her arms.

"Well, aren't you going to open them?" Frances prompted her. "Don't you want to know who they're from?"

Rebecca already knew who they were from. There was no other possibility. Carefully, her heart hammering in her chest, she set the vase down on a convenient table and tore off the green paper to reveal a dozen long-stemmed yellow roses artfully arranged with fern and baby's breath.

"Oh, my!" Frances breathed in awe, reaching out to delicately touch a petal, as if trying to assure herself the roses were real. "Aren't they beautiful?"

"Here's the card, dear," Rose informed Rebecca, extracting it from the flowers and holding it out encouragingly.

Rebecca took it gingerly, suddenly finding it difficult to breathe. She tore open the envelope carefully and slid the card out, taking a deep breath before scanning the message.

"Please accept these with my thanks and apology. It was a memorable encounter. Zach."

For some reason Rebecca suspected that the "encounter" he was referring to had occurred this morning, not Thursday night, and that thought sent a tingle down her spine.

"Well?" Rose prompted.

Rebecca looked up blankly. She'd totally forgotten her audience. "It's just from someone I did a favor for," she explained vaguely, her voice a bit breathless.

"It must have been some favor," Frances commented.

"Yellow roses. Now that's interesting," Rose mused.

Rebecca looked at her curiously. "What do you mean?"

"The language of flowers, dear," Rose replied matter-of-factly. "Yellow roses mean 'I'll never forget you.'"

Rebecca's face flamed and she lowered her head, tucking the note into her apron pocket. "I doubt whether anyone knows that these days," she remarked, striving for an off-handed tone. "It's just a coincidence."

"Maybe," Rose replied, her eyes twinkling. "And then again, maybe not."

"Well, I don't have time to speculate about flower messages," Rebecca declared briskly. "There's too much to do." She picked up the vase and, without a backward look, headed for the kitchen.

The two sisters watched until the door swung shut behind her. Then Frances turned to Rose.

"Do you think they're from him?" she asked eagerly.

"Absolutely. Who else would be sending Rebecca flowers?"

"So our Rebecca really does have a beau," Frances breathed in awe.

"Looks that way," Rose affirmed. "Now let's just hope she gives him a chance."

"Rebecca, some friends of yours are here," Frances announced as she came bustling into the kitchen to pick up the salad course. "That nice couple from St. Louis."

"Nick and Laura?" Rebecca said in surprise, turning from the stove where she was stirring the sauce for chicken Madeira. Normally she checked the reservations, but she simply hadn't had time today.

"Mmm-hmm," Frances confirmed.

"Tell them I'll stop by and say hello at dessert, would you?" Rebecca asked over her shoulder.

"Of course."

Rebecca smiled as she added some lemon juice to the sauce. She didn't get to see her childhood friend often enough. Laura's business as a landscape architect was booming, and her free time was pretty much devoted to Nick, "the man of her dreams," as she called him. And Rebecca couldn't blame her. Nick Sinclair would make any woman's heart beat faster. Rebecca didn't know much about Laura's first marriage, but apparently there had been serious problems of some sort. Serious enough that Brad, who was not only Laura's friend but her minister, had once told Rebecca that he doubted whether Laura would ever remarry. But then along came Nick, who somehow convinced Laura to take a second chance on love.

Rebecca was happy for her. She remembered that even as children, Laura, who was several years older than Rebecca, had always taken it upon herself to watch out for her younger friend and make sure she was included in the games and activities. Rebecca never forgot her kindness, and she was truly happy that Laura had found her own Prince Charming. And she also had Laura to thank for getting Sam and her brother together. If Sam hadn't been Laura's maid of honor, Sam and

Brad might never have found each other. The Lord really did work in mysterious—and wondrous—ways, Rebecca reflected with a smile.

An hour later, as Rebecca put the finishing touches on the chocolate mousse with zabaglione, she was glad once again that she limited dinner service to a single seating on Friday and Saturday nights. Until she could afford to hire another chef, one seating was all she could manage. And when she had a full house—as she did more and more often lately—she was a zombie by Saturday night. But it was satisfying to know that her efforts were paying dividends, and not a day went by that she didn't give thanks for her success.

Rebecca stepped back and surveyed the forty servings of dessert, nodding in approval. They were picture-perfect. She shrugged out of her apron, and as Rose and Frances entered the kitchen with two of the high school students who helped out on weekends, she picked up two servings of dessert and stepped into the dining room. Her gaze immediately went to Nick and Laura's "special" table, the same one they'd sat at on their first visit, in the early stage of their relationship. They always asked for it when they made reservations.

As she joined them, Nick rose and pulled out a chair for her.

"Thanks," she said with a smile. "But I'm not staying long. I don't like to intrude on my guests' dinner."

"Oh, Rebecca, we want to visit a little," Laura assured her. "We hardly ever get to see you anymore."

"Life is busy. What can I say?" she replied with a grin. "And I'm not complaining. In this business, busy is good."

"Mmm, I can see why you're busy, with desserts like these," Laura complimented her, closing her eyes as she savored the rich, creamy confection.

"I'll second that," Nick added appreciatively.

"It's a good thing we don't come here too often, though, or my figure would certainly suffer. Not that it will matter soon, anyway," Laura said, smiling tenderly at Nick, who took her hand in a gentle clasp, his eyes warm and caressing as he gazed at her.

Rebecca glanced from one to the other as suspicion turned to certainty. "Does that mean what I think it does?" she asked with a smile.

Laura looked back at Rebecca, her eyes shining. "Yes," she replied softly. "Our first little one is on the way."

Rebecca reached over and took Laura's free hand. "I'm so happy for you," she told her sincerely, her gaze encompassing them both. "When's the big day?"

"October 4, according to the doctor. It seems like such a long way off, but I know the time will fly. And I can't wait to decorate the nursery!"

Rebecca felt her throat constrict at the glow of happiness on Laura's face, and she blinked rapidly. She was thrilled for Laura, of course. Just as she had been for Sam. But once again, being in the presence of such a committed, loving couple only served to remind her of her own solitary life. She forced herself to smile, and with one final squeeze of Laura's hand, she stood up. She needed to escape to the kitchen, take a moment to compose herself.

"Well, I'll leave you two alone to celebrate. You obviously have lots of exciting things to discuss."

Nick stood up, as well, and took Rebecca's hand. "It was wonderful seeing you again," he said warmly. "And the food, as always, was superb."

"Thank you, Nick."

"Keep in touch, okay, Rebecca?" Laura requested.

"Of course. And if nothing else, I'm sure I'll get regular updates from Brad and Sam. Good luck, Laura. I'll keep you in my prayers."

"Thanks, Becka," Laura replied warmly, reverting to her friend's childhood nickname.

Rebecca turned away and walked unseeingly toward the kitchen, struggling to hold her tears at bay, berating herself for indulging in such blatant self-pity. She had so much to be thankful for. It was wrong to feel sorry for herself. Just because she'd never found someone who had the key to unlock her heart didn't mean…

"Hello, Rebecca."

Rebecca stopped abruptly and glanced toward the voice that had haunted her dreams for the past week. Zach Wright was sitting alone at a secluded corner table. She swallowed and brushed her hand across her eyes before moving toward him, trying to compose herself and discreetly erase evidence of her teary state. Which was difficult to do when her respiration had suddenly gone berserk and her eyes still felt misty.

Zach watched Rebecca approach, his discerning eyes missing nothing as they raked over her face. She was upset. Almost in tears, in fact, although she was struggling mightily to conceal that fact. He'd watched her interacting with the couple at the table across the room, and she'd been smiling and happy then. Their parting had been warm and amicable, as well. But something had prompted this sudden change of mood. He rose as she approached, and indicated the extra chair.

"Could you join me for coffee?"

Rebecca ran her damp palms down the front of her simple, tailored black skirt, trying to still the erratic beating of her heart. Now she was doubly sorry she hadn't taken the time to check the names on the reservation list. It would have been nice to have some warning of Zach's presence. She knew he'd come in for lunch several times since arriving a week ago, but she'd gone out of her way to avoid him, much to the dismay of Rose and Frances. The simple fact was he made her nervous.

Rebecca knew, instinctively, that Zach was way out of her league in the arena of man/woman relationships. Smooth, fast, a man of strong passions—those were the words that came to mind when she thought of him. And she simply wasn't equipped to deal with someone like that. Especially not now, when her emotions were so near the surface. She'd just have to find an excuse of some sort to decline his offer.

"Thank you," she said, her voice sounding shaky even to her ears. "But there's so much to do in the kitchen that—"

"Nonsense, my dear," Rose declared briskly, pausing to refill Zach's coffee cup as she bustled by. "Everything is under control. You sit down and have some coffee with this nice young man. You've been on your feet all day."

Rebecca looked at Rose in dismay, then turned to find Zach watching her expectantly.

"I won't take up much of your time," he promised with an engaging smile.

Rebecca sighed. She might as well give in. Rose had invalidated her best excuse to decline his invitation, and nothing else came to mind. "All right. For a few minutes."

Rose waved to Frances, who hurried over to place a cup of coffee in front of Rebecca. "Now isn't this cozy?" she asked with a satisfied smile.

Rebecca gave the hovering sisters a withering look, but they seemed oblivious.

"If you need anything else, you just let us know," Rose told Zach.

Zach watched them depart, then turned to Rebecca. "They seem very nice," he remarked, his eyes glinting with amusement.

"Oh, they are. Just a little too motherly at times," Rebecca replied wryly. "For two women who have been single all their life, they take an inordinate interest in my—" She started to say "love life," but caught herself, a flush creeping across her cheeks as she gazed at Zach. She had the uncomfortable feeling that he knew exactly what she was going to say, but at least he didn't pursue it.

"Well, I like them," he declared. "But I do feel a little guilty. I didn't mean to railroad you into having coffee with me. I hoped you might *want* to, but I have a feeling I may have caught you at a bad time." He paused and stirred his coffee, frowning slightly. "I hope you won't think I'm being too personal, but you seemed…upset…when I stopped you. I thought maybe you had some bad news from that couple over there.'' He nodded toward Nick and Laura.

"Oh, no, not at all," Rebecca assured him. "Just the opposite, in fact." She gazed back at her friends, who seemed oblivious to their surroundings as they sat close together, talking and laughing softly. "I just found out they're expecting their first child, and I'm very happy for them."

"I see." Zach thought there was more to it than that, but he wasn't going to push. Rebecca struck him as a very private person who might easily back off if she felt he was encroaching on her turf.

When her gaze returned to his she found him studying her speculatively, and she dropped her eyes self-consciously, tracing the rim of her coffee cup with one finger. "I'd like to thank you for the flowers," she said softly. "They were beautiful. But it wasn't necessary."

"I wanted to do it. You took a risk, stopping to help a stranger, and I appreciate that. Besides, I still feel badly about the bruised jaw. Sending flowers was the least I could do."

Frances was walking by at just that moment, and she stopped in her tracks. "So those beautiful roses were from you!" she exclaimed. "Rebecca just loved them! She even kept one to dry."

"Frances!" Rebecca rebuked the older woman, blushing furiously.

"Oh, my, I guess I shouldn't have said anything, should I?" Frances murmured contritely. "You're always supposed to keep the gentleman guessing, aren't you? Well, I'll just leave before I put my foot in my mouth again."

Zach chuckled as he watched her hurry off. "I see what you mean about the sisters," he acknowledged.

"Listen, I'm really sorry about that," Rebecca apologized, her face flaming. "Just because a man sends me flowers and then asks me to have coffee, they're jumping to all sorts of conclusions. Most of which are wrong."

Zach took a sip of his coffee, carefully set the cup down and leveled a direct look at her. "Are they?"

Rebecca stared at him. "What...what do you mean?" she asked, her voice quavering.

Before she could anticipate his intent he leaned forward and laid his hand over hers. "Exactly what you think I mean," he said evenly.

Rebecca swallowed with difficulty. She'd never met a man quite this...frank...about his interest. It was just as she suspected. He was fast moving...and smooth. "Look, Zach, I...I don't date, if that's what you're after."

"That's exactly what I'm after," he confirmed. "Why don't you date?"

For a lot of reasons, she thought silently. None of which she wanted to go into, especially with a man she hardly knew. "I just don't."

"Well, I'm not the kind of guy who gives up easily. Do you mind if I keep trying to convince you to make an exception in my case?"

Rebecca glanced down at the strong, tanned hand, flecked with dark brown hair, that covered hers. She'd like to get to know him better, actually. There was something about him that she found appealing. But despite the promise she'd made to herself on Valentine's Day—to allow the possibility of romance into her life—she wasn't yet ready to deal with someone of Zach's determination and almost tangible virility. It frightened her. Besides, getting involved with a man who was just passing through wasn't at all wise. She could be too easily hurt.

"You'll be wasting your time," she told him with a soft sigh, keeping her eyes downcast.

Zach squeezed her hand, then leaned back and picked up his cup. "Well, I must admit that this isn't exactly great for my ego. You avoid me whenever I come in for lunch, and you won't go out with me. Don't you like me, Rebecca?"

"You seem nice," she hedged.

"'Seem.' An interesting choice of words," he mused. "Do I detect a note of caution in that comment?"

She shrugged. "You know what they say. A woman can't be too careful these days."

"Unfortunately, that's true." He paused and took a sip of his coffee. He sensed there was more behind Rebecca's wariness than mere caution, and he was determined to get the whole story before he gave up on her. "Well, we could bring along a chaperone. How about Rose or Frances?"

Rebecca smiled despite herself. "Now that would be something, wouldn't it?"

"Hey, if it makes you more comfortable, I'm game."

For a minute she was actually tempted. But the fact remained that soon he would be returning to his life in St. Louis, and while St. Genevieve wasn't that far away in distance, she suspected that once enmeshed in his life in the city, it would seem like another planet to Zach. He would forget the small town—and the woman named Rebecca who had simply provided a pleasant diversion while he was stuck there.

Regretfully she shook her head. "I don't think so, Zach."

He looked at her, letting a few moments of silence pass before he spoke. "I'd still like to keep trying."

"Why?" she asked curiously. The man certainly didn't discourage easily, she'd give him that.

"Because I find you attractive. Appealing. Interesting. And very intriguing. And I'd like to get to know you better. So…do you mind if I keep at this for a while?"

Rebecca couldn't help but be flattered—and a little overwhelmed—by his compliments and his determination. "Does it matter if I do?" she asked faintly.

He looked surprised. "Of course. I'm not into harassing women. If you want me out of your life, I'll be gone. But I think there's a spark between us. I sure feel it, and I suspect you do, too, whether you're willing to admit it or not," he said frankly. "I'd like to see where it leads. And I'd like to keep trying to convince you to do the same."

This was her chance. She could just tell him to get lost, and he would. He'd said as much. And she suspected he would honor his promise. She opened her mouth to decline his pursuit, but to her surprise different words came out instead. "I just hope you're not disappointed."

Zach smiled, and though his posture had seemed relaxed throughout their conversation, she could feel an almost palpable easing of tension. "I'll consider that a green light. And as for being disappointed—well, let's just say I'm not worried."

"Maybe you should consider it a yellow light," Rebecca countered, "as in 'proceed with caution.'"

"Okay, a yellow light then," he said, laughing.

Rebecca looked into his warm and insightful eyes, and felt her heart stop, then rush on. Zach said he wasn't worried. And she believed him. She just wished she could say the same about herself.

Chapter Three

Zach turned up his collar and took another sip of steaming coffee from the paper cup. The Red Cross tent offered an oasis of light but only marginal protection from the cold drizzle and bone-chilling wind that sliced through the darkness. It had been raining steadily for the past three days, and the river was rising ominously, edging precariously close to danger levels. An urgent call had gone out two days ago for volunteer sandbaggers, and it seemed just about everyone in town had turned out to help with the hard, messy work. Zach had interviewed a number of volunteers as well as National Guard and Red Cross spokespeople, and he was just about to call it a night.

But though he was tired and cold, he was also impressed by the spirit of generosity and selflessness he'd discovered during his ten days in the small community. Having dealt for so long with the selfish, unethical side of human nature, he'd almost forgotten there was a generous, moral side. His experience in St. Genevieve had certainly given his faith in humanity a much-needed boost.

Zach drained his cup, then turned to toss it into a trash container, colliding with a passing volunteer in the process.

His hand instinctively shot out to steady the middle-aged man, who was wearing horn-rimmed glasses.

"Sorry about that," Zach said contritely.

The man waved aside the apology. "I'm sure it was my fault. These glasses are so fogged up and wet I can hardly see where I'm going." He took them off and carefully wiped them on a handkerchief, then reset them on his nose and grinned at Zach. "That'll help—for about two minutes."

Zach's mouth twisted into a wry smile of acknowledgment. "Nasty night."

The man looked out into the darkness and nodded. "It sure is. I just hope we can keep up with the river." He turned back to Zach and held out his hand. "I'm Phil Carr. English teacher at the high school."

Zach returned the man's firm grip. "Zach Wright from St. Louis. I'm a reporter, here to cover the flood."

"Oh, yes, Mark Holt mentioned your name."

"You know Mark?"

Phil smiled. "This is a small town. I know a lot of people. Besides, Mark lives down the street from me." He hesitated and looked at Zach earnestly. "I was actually hoping I might run into you."

Zach's eyebrows rose quizzically. "Why is that?"

"Well, I hope you won't think this is too much of an imposition, and I'll understand if you can't do it, but I teach composition and it would be a real treat to have a reporter from St. Louis talk to one of the classes. Do you think you might be able to spare an hour or two before you head back?"

Zach considered the unexpected invitation thoughtfully. He hadn't done anything like that for a long time, and his classroom skills were probably pretty rusty. But it might be fun. "Sure. As a matter of fact, I've always been interested in teaching. I even double majored in college—journalism and education. I just couldn't make up my mind between the two. But I got a good newspaper offer when I graduated, so that sealed my fate. It would actually be nice to get into a class-room again,'' he mused, warming to the idea as he spoke.

"Great! I'll give you a call. Are you staying in town?''

"Yeah. Let me jot down the information for you.'' Zach scribbled the name of his motel, as well as his work number on a piece of paper and handed it to Phil. "If I'm not at the motel, just leave me a voice mail at the office.''

"I'll do that. And thanks again. The kids will really enjoy this.'' He tucked the slip of paper carefully into his pocket and rubbed his hands together. "Well, back to the trenches,'' he said with a smile.

Zach watched him leave, then turned to survey the scene once more. The ranks were thinning a bit, but it was nine o'clock, after all. Most of these people had put in a full day at work and would have to do the same tomorrow. It was really amazing, he thought. The vast majority of the volunteers weren't personally threatened by the flood, yet they were still willing to help out, even under these miserable conditions. He almost felt guilty for heading back to his warm, dry motel room. But he did have to put this story together and E-mail it to the paper, so he still had a long night ahead of him.

Zach stepped out from under the tent and slowly made his way past the line of sandbaggers, shivering despite his sheep-skin-lined jacket. The cold rain was already working its way insidiously down his neck, and his boots made loud sucking sounds as he trudged through the mud. He glanced again at the tired faces as he passed. Sandbagging was backbreaking work, as he'd come to learn in the past couple of days, yet people of all ages and sexes were here to help, from high-schoolers to grandfathers to—

Zach stopped abruptly and stared at a slight figure up ahead in one of the sandbag lines. He could swear that was—

"Zach!''

With an effort Zach pulled his gaze away from the figure and turned. "Hi, Mark.''

"Working late?''

"Yeah. But I'm about to call it a night. Listen, tell me I'm wrong, but—" he glanced back with a frown toward the figure that had caught his attention "—is that…"

"Rebecca?" Mark finished. "Yeah. She's been helping every spare minute since the call went out for sandbaggers. I've been trying to convince her to go home for the last hour. I even offered her a ride, but she said she wanted to stay."

"How long has she been here?"

Mark shrugged. "I don't know. But she was here when I showed up three hours ago."

Zach felt a muscle clench in his jaw, and he jammed his hands into his pockets. "She must be frozen. Not to mention exhausted."

"Well, why don't you try to convince her to leave?" Mark suggested. "Maybe you'll have better luck. I sure didn't get anywhere. Say, Joe!" he called to a figure in the distance. "Wait up! Zach, I'll see you later."

Zach watched Mark disappear into the darkness, then looked back at Rebecca. Her motions were robotlike, as if she was operating on adrenaline and nothing else. Which was probably the case, he thought grimly. She was too delicate for this type of heavy work, anyway. Couldn't whoever was in charge see that? In sudden decision, without stopping to consider how his actions might be interpreted, he strode over and laid his hand on her shoulder.

She turned, her eyes dull with fatigue, and frowned up at him in confusion. "Zach?"

One searching sweep of her face was all it took for Zach to assess her physical condition—absolute exhaustion—and he glanced around, signaling to a passing National Guard member who held a clipboard.

"Zach, what is it?" Rebecca asked, her voice so scratchy and hoarse it was barely recognizable.

"Hang on a sec, okay?" he replied curtly.

The uniformed man joined them, and Zach nodded toward

Rebecca. "Do you have someone who can fill in here? She's had all she can take," he said tersely.

The National Guard member gave Rebecca a quick but discerning glance and nodded. "No problem." He turned and scanned the group on the sidelines, motioning to another uniformed Guard member. "Dave, take over here for a while, okay?" he called.

Zach took Rebecca's arm and gently drew her away from the line. Her legs felt stiff and shaky when she tried to walk, and she stumbled, grateful that Zach reached out to steady her, his hands firm on her shoulders. But why was he bothering her, when there was so much urgent work to do? She looked up at him, still frowning. "What are you doing?" she demanded.

"You're going home, Rebecca."

She stared at him, and even through the haze of her fatigue she was aware of the rigid set of his jaw and the steely determination in his eyes. On one hand, she was touched by his concern. More than touched, actually. No man had ever taken such an active interest in her well-being. On the other hand, she wasn't accustomed to being ordered around. Even if it was for her own good. She straightened her shoulders and glared at him. "Excuse me?"

Zach saw the sudden, stubborn tilt of her chin, heard the indignant tone in her voice, and sighed. *Wrong move, buddy,* he admonished himself. Rebecca was not the type to respond to high-handed tactics. And he wasn't the type to employ them—socially, at least. But for some reason, seeing Rebecca cold and tired and wet had awakened a sort of primal, protective urge in him, and he'd reacted instinctively. And obviously inappropriately. Giving orders was clearly *not* the way to convince her to go home.

A sudden harsh gust of wind tugged several strands of wet hair out of Rebecca's French twist and whipped them across her face, and a visible shudder ran through her body as she reached up to brush them aside. Before she could lower her hand Zach captured it in a firm grip, silently stripping off her wet glove and cocooning her fingers between his palms. Her hand felt like ice, and a spasm once more tightened his jaw. He took a deep, steadying breath, and when he spoke he made an effort to keep his tone gentle and reasonable, though neither of those emotions accurately reflected his mood at the moment.

"Rebecca, Mark says you've been out here at least three hours. You're chilled to the bone, you're wet and you're exhausted. You need to go home where it's warm and dry and get some rest. You won't help anyone if you stay here till you get sick."

Rebecca looked into Zach's concerned eyes, and her protest died in her throat. She couldn't argue with his logic. And he was right about her physical condition. Her legs were shaky, her back was stiff, and her hands and feet were numb with cold. She'd put in a full day at the restaurant, and she had to be up at six tomorrow. It probably made sense for her to call it a night.

With a deep, weary sigh she gave in, her shoulders suddenly sagging. "I guess you're right," she admitted, her voice flat and lifeless with fatigue as she brushed a hand tiredly across her eyes. "Mark said he'd give me a lift a little while ago. I just need to find him."

"I'll take you home, Rebecca."

Her eyes flew to his in surprise. "You?"

"I was leaving, anyway. In a town this size, your place can't be that far out of my way."

Rebecca never took the risk of putting herself in a situation where she was alone with a man she barely knew. But Zach was a respected journalist. He was a friend of Mark's. Ben liked him. So did Rose and Frances. Surely a simple ride home would be safe. Besides, she was just too tired to worry about it tonight. She felt strange—unsteady and shaky—and she knew that if she didn't sit down soon, she was going to fall down.

Zach watched her face, prepared to argue the point if she protested. Under normal circumstances he knew she'd flatly refuse his offer of a ride. But in her state of near collapse he hoped that instead of trying to analyze his motives, she would simply accept them at face value. He cared about her and simply wanted her safe and warm and rested. It was as simple as that. He wasn't sure himself *why* he cared so much about a woman he hardly knew. But he did.

He watched her face, trying to anticipate her response, but before he could come to any conclusions she surprised him by acquiescing.

"All right, Zach. Thank you," she accepted wearily.

He felt a tension he hadn't even realized was there ease in his shoulders, and silently he took her elbow and guided her toward his car. The fact that she didn't protest this protective gesture told him more eloquently than words that she was about ready to drop. He could sense that every step was an effort for her, and when she stumbled a couple of times on the uneven ground he was tempted to just pick her up and carry her. But he knew beyond a shadow of a doubt that the lady *definitely* wouldn't put up with that. A hand at her elbow was one thing. Holding her in his arms was another—even though the idea was suddenly immensely appealing, he realized. In fact, he'd like to do a whole lot more than that. But he quickly—and firmly—reined in his wayward thoughts. Now was not the time to indulge in romantic fantasies.

When they reached his car he pulled open the passenger door, but Rebecca hesitated, glancing down at her muddy, wet clothes and shoes. "Zach, I'll m-mess your c-car up," she protested, trying unsuccessfully to keep her teeth from chattering.

"Don't worry about it," he said shortly, dismissing her concern as he urged her gently into the car.

But she held back stubbornly, resisting his efforts. "Don't you have a blanket or a towel in the trunk that I can sit on?"

He gave her an exasperated look. The last thing he cared

about at the moment was soiled upholstery. After all his car had been through in the past ten days, a little dirt wasn't going to hurt anything. But rather than argue the point, he left her standing by the door to quickly rummage through the trunk, emerging a moment later with a rug he kept handy for tire changes. Wordlessly he laid it over the passenger seat, and Rebecca finally slid into the car. *Collapsed* was actually a better word, Zach thought grimly, as he shut the door and strode around to the passenger side. She was all in.

She somehow summoned up the energy to direct him to her apartment, and within a few minutes they pulled up in front of her building.

"I appreciate the l-lift, Zach," she said, her teeth still chattering as she reached for the handle.

"I'll walk you to your door."

She thought about protesting, but by the set of his jaw she knew it would be useless. Besides, she was too tired to argue anymore.

He took her elbow again for the short walk, and this time the protective gesture registered in her consciousness—and also tugged at her heart. Rebecca wasn't sure why Zach continued to bother with her. He'd made no secret about wanting to date her, true, but she'd given him virtually no encouragement. Yet still he'd taken the time to see her home tonight, and she somehow sensed that for whatever reason, he cared about her well-being.

Her door was sheltered by a small porch, barely large enough to accommodate the two of them, and Rebecca was acutely aware of Zach's presence just a breath behind her as she withdrew the key from the pocket of her coat. Her numb fingers fumbled as she attempted to insert it in the lock, and it slipped from her fingers, clattering to the concrete.

With a weary sigh, she started to bend down, but Zach restrained her with a preemptive hand on her shoulder, retrieving the key himself in one smooth swoop. Then he reached past her to insert it in the lock, his other hand still resting lightly on her shoulder. He was only a whisper away now, and Rebecca caught the scent of his distinctive aftershave as he leaned close. When his arm brushed her chest, a surge of yearning unexpectedly swept over her, and she drew in a sharp breath.

Zach turned to her immediately, his concerned eyes probing her face. "Are you all right?" he asked with a frown.

She nodded jerkily, not trusting her voice.

He looked at her appraisingly, noting that she'd wrapped her arms tightly around her body in a protective gesture that said, "Stay away." But, surprisingly enough, her unguarded eyes said something entirely different. They reflected a combination of emotions—longing, fear, uncertainty, confusion, yearning. He doubted whether she realized just how eloquent they were. Rebecca definitely did not have a poker face. She wore her emotions too close to the surface, and her eyes were a window to her soul, communicating clearly what was in her heart.

Zach wanted to respond to the longing he saw, wanted to reach out and gather her into his arms, but he stifled the urge and drew in an unsteady breath. His self-control had never been taxed as much as it was around this woman, who brought out a protective instinct in him that he thought had died years ago. She was the kind of woman who should be cherished and loved and always treated gently, in keeping with her gentle nature.

Unfortunately, Zach didn't have much experience dealing with women like that. Suddenly, desperately, he wished he did, wished he knew how to make Rebecca relax with him, to trust him, to give it a chance. He honestly didn't know where a relationship with her might lead. The physical attraction was definitely there. And maybe that's all there was. But he didn't think so. His gut told him there could be a whole lot more, and he'd learned to trust his instincts. They ought to explore their attraction. But first he had to convince *her* of that.

However, now was not the time. She was cold, aching, tired

and wet. What she needed was a dry, warm bed. And rest. And peace of mind. Which—unfortunately—was his cue to exit.

Rebecca was caught in the spell of Zach's magnetic eyes as they held hers captive. He had wonderful eyes, she thought. Trustworthy. Caring. Insightful. Vibrant. Passionate. Very definitely passionate, she realized with a start. She might want rest. He clearly wanted something else—something she couldn't give. Certainly not now. And maybe never. The simple fact was, Zach was a man of intense passions. Rebecca knew that as surely as she knew her reaction to passion. And the two were not a promising combination, she thought bleakly.

Zach saw the sudden melancholy steal into Rebecca's eyes, and without stopping to consider the consequences he slowly reached over and laid his hand against her cheek, brushing his thumb gently over her soft, silky skin. He felt her quivering beneath his touch, but she didn't pull away as he'd half expected. She just stared up at him with wide, vulnerable eyes.

Get out of here before you do something you'll regret, an inner voice ordered. *Now!*

"Take a hot bath, okay?" he suggested.

"Okay," she whispered.

"And get some rest."

"I will."

It would be so easy to just pull her close, to taste her lips, to demonstrate the depth of his attraction to her. It was what he *wanted* to do. Even with her hair in disarray and darkened by dampness, her classic features tinged with fatigue and wiped free of makeup, wearing mud-caked boots and an oversize parka, she did more for his libido than any woman he'd ever met. It didn't make any sense. And if he was confused, she surely would be, too.

Zach didn't usually waste time analyzing his reaction to a woman. He just listened to his hormones and went after what he wanted. But he knew instinctively that Rebecca wouldn't respond to his usual direct approach. And he also recognized that tonight was not the time to explore their attraction. She was too tired and too vulnerable.

Regretfully, summoning up the last reserves of his self-control, he let his hand drop from her cheek and removed his other hand from her shoulder. "Good night, Rebecca."

"G-good night. And thank you."

He hesitated one more second, then, with a last lingering sweep of her face, he turned and strode away into the rain.

Rebecca rose on one arm to peer at the bedside clock, reading the digital display with a groan. One in the morning! She thumped her pillow and flopped onto her back, cringing as her aching muscles protested the abrupt movement. After the last couple of days of backbreaking work she needed rest desperately, but sleep was proving to be elusive tonight. Her sore muscles were just making it too difficult to get comfortable.

But so were thoughts of Zach, she admitted. Tonight she was sure he had been thinking about kissing her. But then, in her exhausted state, maybe she'd misread his eyes. It wasn't as if she had a whole lot of experience to draw on. But there had definitely been...vibrations, she thought, for lack of a better word. Surely she wasn't mistaken about that. Yet, in the end, he'd simply walked away.

Rebecca stared at the dark ceiling and tried to think logically. Despite his restraint earlier in the evening, she knew he was interested. He'd made no secret of the fact. He'd been angling for a date ever since their "official" meeting in the diner. She'd put him off, but he didn't seem discouraged. Just more determined. Which made her nervous.

But what made her even more nervous was her interest in him.

Rebecca closed her eyes and drew a deep, quivering breath. She didn't want to be interested in Zach. She didn't want to feel nervous and unsettled every time she was in his presence. She didn't want to wait anxiously every day to see if he'd stop in for lunch so she could at least catch a glimpse of him. But she was and she did. And that scared her. Because she knew that deep in her subconscious she was starting to consider going out with him.

It wasn't that she didn't want to date him. She did. She found him attractive, was flattered by his attention, impressed by his apparent character and integrity. But she was so afraid of what would happen if he... A choked sob cut off her thought in mid-sentence. She didn't have to wonder what would happen. She *knew*. Physical closeness freaked her out. Period. She'd embarrass both of them. He might even be angry. She didn't know him well enough to be able to judge his reaction. But based on past experience with other men, it wouldn't be pretty. No, dating Zach would be a mistake.

Besides, she consoled herself, he'd be leaving soon. This was just a temporary beat for him. He was a city man, used to lights and action and excitement. And he sure wouldn't find those in St. Genevieve. She was better off sticking to her original decision.

But if that was true, then why didn't she feel better off? she cried silently.

Zach typed in the final line of his story, then leaned back and wearily massaged his temple. It had been a long, cold, wet night, and it had taken him what seemed like hours to warm up after he dropped Rebecca off. But at least he had a good story to show for his discomfort, he thought in satisfaction. It uplifted. It reaffirmed. It found goodness even in the midst of chaos and tragedy. It was the kind of story Josef would like, he realized suddenly, a faint smile touching his lips as he thought of his friend.

Zach pulled out his wallet and flipped through the plastic holders, stopping at one that contained a photo taken at Isabel's christening, nearly eight years before. Josef and Katrina had insisted that Zach be the godfather, though he'd protested that the honor should go to a relative. He still remembered Josef's response to his reaction.

"Sometimes ties of the heart are the strongest of all, stronger even than blood, Zachary. You are my best friend, and you would honor us by becoming part of our family in this way."

And so, of course Zach had agreed. He recalled clearly the day the picture was taken. It was right before Zach and Katrina went home, an unseasonably warm late-May afternoon even for St. Louis. They asked him to hold Isabel for the picture, and then stood on either side of him while the minister snapped the photo. Zach had no experience with babies and was almost afraid to grasp the tiny, fragile bit of life, with her flailing arms and kicking legs. But Josef laughingly assured him that Isabel wouldn't break, and in fact she lay quietly in his arms as the picture was taken, staring up at him solemnly with big blue eyes.

Zach glanced at the facing picture, a slightly fuzzy shot taken when Isabel was six. Almost two years ago now. She had turned into a beautiful child, with her mother's long brown hair and Josef's inquiring eyes. Josef and Katrina had gone out of their way to treat Zach as one of the family, despite the distance that separated them, and Zach always remembered Isabel's birthday with some sort of stuffed animal or toy. It would be nice to see them all again, he thought wistfully. He glanced down at the molded pewter ring on his finger that had been their parting gift to him, and recalled the inscription: Friends—Always. And they would be, he knew.

On impulse, Zach leaned forward and checked his E-mail. He hadn't heard from Josef in over two weeks, and he was starting to worry. Though Josef never said it in so many words, Zach knew he was growing increasingly concerned about the deteriorating conditions in his country. He and Katrina rarely went out anymore with friends, and Isabel spent most of her time indoors for safety reasons. Josef's powerful, persuasive writing was also attracting more and more attention from opposing factions, and Zach had begun urging him to use caution. But that word wasn't in Josef's vocabulary, not when he felt he was doing the right thing. Although Zach suspected that there was a very real danger for his friend, Josef downplayed it.

This time, when Zach opened his mailbox, he was rewarded with a note from his friend, and he eagerly scanned it. But it wasn't the kind of message he had hoped for.

Things are not very good for us right now, Zachary. Katrina has had a miscarriage and is very ill. I wish we could be in St. Louis, with good Dr. Anderson, who took such fine care of her when Isabel was born. But that is not the Lord's will, it seems. We must stay here and hope that He will watch over us.

I cannot write much now, my friend. It is not safe here at the newspaper office. We will be moving again soon. It seems that our talk of freedom is causing much distress to the powers that be. But still we persevere, for the torch must be carried.

I hope, Zachary, that all is well with you. I think often of our happy days at Mizzou. It was a good time, was it not? So much hope and enthusiasm and optimism. We were going to change the world, you and I. Remember? And we are, you know. It is just very slow work. But I carry on, firmly believing that this is what the Lord intends me to do.

I will write again when the opportunity arises, my friend. Now I must return to Katrina, who gives my life so much joy. I pray that she will quickly be well again. And I pray also that peace will soon return to our troubled country.

Zach rested his elbows on his desk and steepled his fingers, a frown creasing his brow as he scanned Joseph's message a second time. He hadn't even known about Katrina's pregnancy. He assumed it had been by accident, not design. After her first difficult pregnancy and delivery, the doctors had warned her that attempts to have more children could be extremely dangerous. And Josef loved her too much to risk that.

Zach wished there was some way he could help his friend. Long ago he and Josef had promised each other that should either ever be in need, the other had only to ask and help would be on the way. But Josef hadn't made such a request. Probably because he knew there was nothing Zach could do. Except maybe pray.

But unlike Josef, who was a religious man, Zach's once-solid faith had withered and died in the alleys and slums of St. Louis. Yet he took a moment now, in case there really was anyone listening upstairs, to ask for protection for his friend and his family. Because Zach was beginning to suspect that only a Higher Power would be able to keep them safe.

Chapter Four

Rebecca sighed and reached up to secure a wayward pin in her French twist. The last few days had been tough. She was putting in her usual long hours at the restaurant, then spending every spare minute sandbagging. The rain hadn't abated, and despite the diligent efforts of the townspeople and the National Guard, it appeared that the flooding would be severe and widespread. Rebecca hadn't been in town during the last flood, several years before, but stories of the horror survived. Families homeless, businesses ruined, hundreds of lives turned upside down. She paused for a moment and closed her eyes. Please, Lord, keep everyone safe, she prayed. And help us all realize that lives are more precious than things.

Rebecca opened her eyes and glanced at the clock, sighing once again. Ten at night was not an ideal time to be getting ready for tomorrow's scheduled bridal shower in the restaurant. But the work had to be done, even if she was bone weary after sandbagging for three hours earlier in the evening. Thank heavens Zach had more or less dragged her off that sandbag line two nights ago! Even though her sleep had been restless that night, disrupted by both sore muscles and conflicting emotions about her "rescuer," at least her body had gotten some much-needed rest. That had helped carry her though the next couple of days. But the reserve was starting to wear thin. Maybe if she worked quickly tonight, she'd get home before midnight, she thought hopefully.

Rebecca checked the consistency of the potato leek soup and, with a satisfied nod, turned off the blender. Now she just had to finish up a couple of special items for the shower and she'd be done.

As she walked toward the refrigerator, a sudden knock on the back door startled her, and she stopped abruptly, glancing toward the door with a frown. Who in the world could be here at this hour?

Leaving the chain firmly in place, she opened the door an inch or two and peered out into the rainy darkness, her eyes widening when she recognized the visitor. "Zach! What are you doing here?" she asked in astonishment.

"I was driving by and thought I saw the light on back here. I just wanted to make sure everything was all right."

"Oh. Yes. I'm fine. Thanks. Just catching up on a few things."

He turned his collar up and dug his hands into the pockets of his coat, propping one shoulder against the door frame as he sniffed appreciatively. "It sure smells good in there."

Rebecca frowned. "Didn't you have dinner?"

He shrugged. "I've been working. And I pitched in for a little while with the sandbagging. Can't you tell?" he asked with a crooked grin, glancing down at his mud-splattered jeans. "Fortunately someone loaned me a slicker, or I'd look a whole lot worse than this."

Rebecca scanned his form in one swift glance. He looked cold and wet and—as her eyes came back to rest on his face— tired. There were lines at the corners of his eyes, furrows on his brow. And his mouth looked strained, as if he was in pain. She frowned and bit her lip. "Do you think you should be sandbagging, Zach? It's been less than two weeks since you had the concussion. Didn't the doctor tell you to take it easy for a while?"

He dismissed her concern with a shrug. "I feel okay. At least I did until a little while ago, when I started to get a headache. I just need some rest and I'll be fine. I'm just going to grab a bite somewhere and call it a night." He straightened up and smiled. "Well, I'll see you around."

"Zach…" She couldn't just let him walk away. Not when he was cold and hungry and in pain. It wasn't right. Besides, he'd gone out of his way for her two nights ago and spent this evening helping with the sandbagging. She could at least offer him some soup. It would be the kind thing to do—even if it wasn't the smart thing, she acknowledged. Not when her heart went into overdrive every time she was in his presence. But her conscience prickled, telling her she was being self-centered. With a sigh of capitulation, she shut the door and slid the chain free, then swung the door open. "Would you like a bowl of soup?"

He frowned and dug his hands deeper into the pockets of his coat. "I wasn't angling for a meal, Rebecca," he said slowly. "I just wanted to make sure everything was okay."

"I know. And I appreciate that. I also appreciated the lift home the other night."

"I'm glad. I was afraid you'd think I was a little too heavy-handed."

She shrugged, smiling faintly. "I did," she admitted. "But you were right. Anyway, I just made some soup, and you're welcome to a bowl."

"Well…" He hesitated for another moment, then sniffed appreciatively. "Okay. I can't resist that aroma."

She moved aside to allow him to pass, then shut the door and slid the chain back into place. She watched him shrug out of his jacket and hang it on a hook by the door, then rake his fingers through his wet hair. As he did so, she saw the angry red welt near his hairline. It was obvious that the stitches had only been recently removed.

"It's not as bad as it looks," he assured her with a smile.

Her gaze dropped from the injured area to his eyes, and she flushed. "I didn't mean to stare."

He shrugged. "That's okay. I realize it's not a pretty sight. So much for any hopes I might have had for a modeling career," he joked good-naturedly.

The scar didn't mar his rugged appeal one iota as far as Rebecca was concerned, but she decided it was safer to make a quick comment and then move on. "It will fade in time. Why don't you go ahead and sit down while I get the soup."

"I threw a spare pair of shoes in the car before I left the motel, so at least I won't track mud on your floor," he told her with a grin, strolling toward the center island. "But I'm starting to run out of dry clothes."

"Aren't we all," she empathized, heading for the stove. She ladled a generous serving of soup into a bowl, then added a couple of pieces of homemade bread and some butter. When she turned he was sitting on a stool at the counter, and he grinned disarmingly as she set the food in front of him.

"Well, this is a first," he noted.

"What do you mean?"

"Eating in the kitchen. I have to say, I prefer the atmosphere in the dining room, but the company's better here."

Rebecca flushed and turned away to fiddle with a pot on the stove.

"So what are you doing here at this hour, anyway?" he asked, attacking the soup with vigor.

"I'm running a little behind," she explained, reaching up nervously to secure another hairpin. "Frances has the flu, so I'm shorthanded. And I have a special party tomorrow—a bridal shower—which is extra work, too." She was babbling, and she knew it.

Zach paused and studied her with a frown. "Are you still sandbagging?"

She turned to look at him in surprise. "Of course."

"That kind of work is too hard for you, Rebecca," he said quietly.

She shrugged dismissively, though she couldn't so easily dismiss the tingle of pleasure that ran through her at his concern. "I can manage. Besides, every pair of hands helps."

"But do you really have to go every night, after putting in a full day here?"

"These are my friends and neighbors, Zach," she said with quiet sincerity. "This is how life is in a small town. We help each other. It's the best way I know of to put The Golden Rule into practice."

Zach didn't have a rebuttal for that comment. Rebecca clearly took her faith seriously and believed in living the principles, not just talking about them. He admired her for that. But she was pushing herself too hard. "Isn't there some other way you could help that isn't so physically taxing?" he persisted.

"Sandbagging is where the hands are needed," she replied lightly, still touched by his concern. "Besides, it's good for the waistline."

His eyes dropped automatically to the referenced part of her anatomy, then quickly returned to hers. Even under a voluminous white apron, it was clear that her waistline was already in great shape. It was also clear that he wasn't going to be able to convince her to cut back on her volunteer efforts. Nevertheless, he tried once more. "Rebecca, whether you realize it or not, you need more rest."

"I'll be done here soon."

A flash of inspiration suddenly hit, and he smiled. "Well, you'll be done even sooner if I help," he said determinedly.

"Help?" she parroted blankly.

"Sure. I don't mind. What do you want me to do?" He set his spoon down and loosened his cuffs, rolling up his sleeves to the elbows.

"Really…you don't have to do that," she protested faintly.

"Oh, give me a chance," he cajoled, his eyes twinkling.

"I'm not the world's greatest cook, but I can do simple stuff. I promise I won't poison any of your customers."

"It's not that…"

"Look, think about it while I finish the soup, okay? I'm sure you can find something for me to do."

"But you're tired, too. And you haven't fully recovered from the concussion. You admitted you have a headache. You need some rest, Zach."

"The headache's much better now. I think the soup did the trick. Besides, if I help, you can get home a little bit sooner."

When he put it that way, the offer *was* tempting. And why not? she thought. He was already here, anyway. In sudden decision she walked over to the refrigerator and withdrew a bowl of crab salad and some Belgian endive.

"Okay. I just need the endive leaves filled. Here, I'll show you how," she said, deftly demonstrating.

He watched her for a moment, then nodded confidently. "I can handle that," he assured her, taking the spoon out of her fingers. "You go ahead and do whatever else needs to be done."

Rebecca focused on chopping the green part of the leek for the soup garnish, stealing occasional glances at Zach as she worked. His brow was knit in concentration, but he was doing well, she thought, her gaze dropping to his hands—strong, capable, confident. She'd noticed his hands that night in the car, and she remembered her summation at the time—that they would be equally at home chopping wood…or caressing a woman.

"So how am I doing?"

Rebecca's startled gaze flew to his, and she flushed guiltily, turning away quickly to hide the telltale blush. "Fine, great," she mumbled, trying to quiet her rapid pulse. Change the subject, she told herself. Get your mind on something else. "I hear you're going to lecture at the high school," she remarked, striving futilely for a casual, conversational tone.

If he noticed that her voice was slightly breathless, he made no comment. He just shook his head and grinned. "I'd say the grapevine is alive and active in St. Genevieve."

Rebecca smiled. "Word does travel fast in a small town. Mark lives on the same street as Phil Carr, who told him, and Mark told me. Being in a classroom will be quite a switch for you, won't it?"

"Mmm-hmm. But believe it or not, I almost became a teacher. In fact, I double majored in college. But when I graduated I was offered a newspaper job that was too good to pass up, so my teaching career ended before it began."

"You usually do investigative work, right?"

"Mmm-hmm."

"That must be pretty exciting."

He shrugged. "It used to be," he replied, methodically working his way through the crab salad as he spoke. "But I was never in it for the excitement. I did it because I thought I could make a difference, change the world for the better. But as I've recently come to realize, that was a pretty naive attitude. The truth is I spent fifteen years tilting at windmills. Nothing I did made any difference," he said, a trace of bitterness creeping into his voice. "I'm actually thinking of taking some time off to reevaluate whether I want to spend the rest of my life doing something that really doesn't seem to matter."

Rebecca frowned. "I have a feeling you're being too harsh on yourself, Zach. I think everything we do makes a difference, even if we don't see the results right away. I really believe that good work is never lost."

Zach sent her a startled look, a strange expression on his face. "That's odd," he remarked softly.

She tilted her head and looked at him quizzically. "What?"

"What you just said. I have a friend who used almost those same words once."

"Really?"

"Uh-huh. He's a reporter, too. In Eastern Europe. Despite

the chaos in his country, and the setbacks and lack of visible progress, he still believes his efforts are making a difference."

"He sounds like a man of faith," Rebecca surmised.

"Yeah, " Zach replied with a nod. "He is."

"Faith can be a great source of encouragement."

Zach gave her a skeptical look. "Maybe. But somewhere along the way mine evaporated. I guess I dealt with the seamy side of life for too long. There was very little evidence of God on my beat."

"I suppose working in that environment could put your faith to the test," Rebecca conceded slowly. "But you know, that's the beautiful thing about God. We may abandon Him, but He never abandons us."

Zach studied the woman across from him. He admired her faith. Even envied it a little. Much as he envied Josef's. He wished he had their conviction, their certainty. But he didn't, not anymore, and it was too late tonight to even think about it. He reached for a towel and wiped his hands, then stood up and rolled down his sleeves. "Well, are you about ready to call it a night?"

Rebecca nodded. "I just need to turn out the lights."

He picked up the tray of endive. "Where do you want this?"

She opened the refrigerator door. "In here. Top shelf."

As he slid the tray in, his glance fell on a decorated cake on the counter. Although several pieces were missing, enough of the greeting remained to indicate that it had contained a birthday message for Rebecca. "Is today your birthday?" he asked in surprise.

She flushed. "Yes. Frances and Rose brought the cake in, which was very sweet. But to be honest, with everything going on I only had time for a quick sample. Would you like to take a piece with you?"

"No, but thanks." He looked at her thoughtfully. "So what did you do to celebrate?" he asked, knowing the answer even before she spoke.

Other than a phone call from her father, and one from Brad and Sam who invited her up for a belated birthday dinner when things settled down with the new baby, it had been a day like any other. Special days didn't mean a lot when you lived alone. But she'd successfully kept that thought at bay throughout the day, and she wasn't going to start feeling sorry for herself now.

She forced herself to smile brightly as she answered Zach. "I was way too busy," she replied, striving for a careless, it-doesn't-matter tone. She wasn't sure if she fooled him, so before he could pursue the subject, she hung her apron on a hook and reached for her purse. "Listen, thanks a lot, Zach. I'll just turn out the lights and lock up. Go on home and get some rest yourself."

"I'll walk you to your car first."

Rebecca opened her mouth to protest, took one look at his determined face and closed it. She recognized that look from the other night. "Okay. Give me a minute."

It took less than that, and as she locked the door she nodded toward her older-model compact car parked a few feet away. "I'm right over here," she told him. "And thank heavens it's finally stopped raining!"

"We could do with some dry weather," he agreed.

Rebecca was tinglingly aware of him close behind her as she walked to her car and fumbled with the key. When she at last fitted it into the lock and swung the door open, she breathed a sigh of relief. In a few moments she could drive away, escape from this man who always made her heart behave erratically.

But instead of leaving, as she expected, Zach leaned on top of the door and looked at her, his face deeply shadowed and largely unreadable in the dim light. There was silence for a moment, and although he didn't move, Rebecca intuitively knew that he'd like to touch her. Her nerve endings started to sizzle, and her breath lodged in her throat.

"You know I'd still like to take you out," he said at last, without preamble, his voice deep and husky.

Rebecca dropped her gaze. "I don't date, Zach," she reminded him, her voice uneven. "I told you that."

"And I told you I was going to try and change your mind. You even gave me a yellow light. Remember?"

"Yes," she whispered.

"You do like me, don't you, Rebecca?" he asked gently, his voice soft and coaxing.

She nodded mutely.

"Then why don't you let me in on your secret?"

Startled, her gaze snapped to his and she frowned. "What secret?"

"About why I make you so nervous."

To deny it would be foolish, so she didn't try. "It's getting late," she replied instead.

He sighed heavily. "I guess that's about the response I expected. But I figured it wouldn't hurt to ask."

"Why don't you just give up, Zach?" she asked with a dispirited sigh.

He shook his head slowly. "That's not my style."

Rebecca dropped her gaze and fidgeted with the door lock. She'd assumed as much. Zach was a man of determination and action, who clearly liked challenges. And that was probably all she was to him, she thought bleakly. Which was one more reason *not* to get involved, she told herself firmly. Okay, so she'd promised herself on Valentine's Day that if a man came along who seemed worth taking a chance on, she would risk opening herself to a relationship one more time. And Zach seemed like such a man. But circumstances were against them. First of all, she suspected their natures were quite different. She was slow, cautious and timid. He was fast, impetuous and brash. Patience was not a virtue she would ascribe to him. But it was a virtue that any man truly interested in her would have to possess. Besides, Zach would only be in town for a brief time—not a good omen for a long-term relationship. No, he was wrong for her, she thought resolutely. It was as simple as that.

But his expression when she looked back at him to say good-night was anything but simple, and her words died in her throat. His eyes held hers with fierce intensity, reflecting a myriad of emotions. Hunger. Frustration. Passion. Tenderness. Confusion. And though the parking lot was only dimly lit, she could also tell from his faint frown that some sort of internal debate was taking place.

Suddenly, with a jolt, she had a feeling she knew exactly what that debate was about. She swallowed convulsively and nervously licked her lips.

Zach's gaze dropped to their ripe fullness, and now it was his turn to swallow with difficulty. Actually, kissing Rebecca wasn't something he'd seriously considered tonight. At least not until now. Sensing that she'd respond best to casual, nonthreatening behavior, he'd made an effort to keep things pretty lighthearted.

But suddenly he decided to throw caution to the wind, to give her some concrete evidence of his attraction. Words were getting him nowhere. Maybe action was the answer. At least enough action to let her know in no uncertain terms that he was serious in his intentions to get to know her better.

Slowly he moved out from behind the car door until he was standing directly in front of her. His eyes still locked on hers, he reached over and traced a gentle finger across her eyebrow and down her cheek. Then his hand dropped to the side of her neck, his thumb gently stroking the remnants of the bruise on her chin.

Rebecca knew exactly where this was leading. Zach was going to kiss her. She ought to pull away before she freaked out. But for some strange reason she didn't feel threatened. Yes, they were alone. Yes, Zach was a lot bigger and stronger than she was. Yes, he could easily overpower her. But Rebecca didn't sense any ill intent in his touch. It was gentle and caring and tender. Still, she ought to back off, for all the reasons she'd mentally ticked off just moments before. Except that she suddenly couldn't remember even one of them.

Zach studied her eyes, trying to decipher the conflicting emotions in them, attempting to determine if desire was stronger than uncertainty. He couldn't tell for sure. And there was only one way to find out. Slowly, his gaze riveted on hers till the last possible moment, he leaned toward her, his eyes telegraphing a message that even in her agitated state Rebecca couldn't miss. *Don't be afraid,* they said. *I won't hurt you. Trust me. Everything will be all right.* Then, letting his hand drift to her nape, he slowly lowered his mouth to meet hers.

It was a simple kiss, as light as a drifting leaf, a gentle, uncomplicated connecting of lips. But Rebecca's reaction wasn't uncomplicated in the least. A thousand sensations washed over her, and she felt caught in a riptide of sweeping emotion. There was so much to take in! Zach's hand cradling her head, his touch sure and confident. His warm lips, undemanding and gentle, moving over hers, awakening a response that sent her world spinning out of orbit. The woodsy scent of his aftershave wafting around her, and the distant, plaintive echo of a train whistle.

Rebecca knew, deep in her heart, that every time she heard that mellow sound for the rest of her life she would remember this moment. Not just because of the sensory overload that left her breathless and trembling, but because she wasn't afraid. For whatever reason, by some miracle, she didn't panic! She felt shaky and off balance, true, but it was an unsteadiness born of yearning, not fear. It was a new, heady experience for Rebecca, and she did what she never thought she'd be able to do. She responded, returning his kiss as best she knew how.

Zach had imagined how Rebecca's lips would feel against his. But nothing had prepared him for their innocent sweetness. At her age most women generally had plenty of practice in the art of romance. But not Rebecca, whose simple, straightforward kiss was that of a schoolgirl, reflecting absolute inexperience. Zach was stunned—but not displeased. He found her almost-timid shyness refreshing—and extremely appealing.

Other than the soft meeting of their lips and his hand on her neck, Zach didn't touch her. He left his other hand in his pocket, somehow sensing that was the right thing to do. He just savored the moment. At last, with reluctance, he released her.

For several moments she kept her eyes closed, too lost in the magic of his touch to tolerate the intrusion of reality. But finally, with a wistful little sigh that caught at his heart, she opened her eyes and gazed up at him in wonder.

A tender smile tugged at the corners of his mouth. "Happy birthday, Rebecca," he murmured, his voice strangely hoarse.

His hand was still at her nape, his fingers gently stroking the back of her neck, and she was finding it extremely difficult to breathe. "Th-thank you," she stammered softly, her own voice uneven.

"You know, I have an idea," he said softly. Actually, he had plenty of ideas at the moment, only one of which he intended to discuss. "Since you really didn't get to do anything special for your birthday, how about having dinner with me Sunday? Sort of a belated celebration. We could drive up to St. Louis, maybe go to the Hill, if you like Italian. Do you?"

She was staring at him, mesmerized by the tender light in his deep brown eyes. "Do I what?" she asked, trying to follow the conversation, but having a difficult time concentrating on anything but his eyes.

"Like Italian food."

"Oh. Sure."

"Then you'll go?"

Tell him no, her mind instructed firmly. *Think, don't feel. Be rational.* But her heart had other ideas. "Uh-huh."

His smile broadened, and the warmth in his eyes took her breath away. "Great! I'll call to set it up, okay?"

"Okay."

He hesitated for a moment, his eyes caressing her face. Then he leaned forward and once more brushed his lips over hers, the brief contact leaving her yearning for more.

"Good night, Rebecca. Sweet dreams."

She slid into her car, then turned to watch him stride toward his as she sighed contentedly. *No problem, Mr. Wright*, she thought. Sweet dreams are a guarantee.

"My goodness!" Rose said, glancing around the kitchen in surprise. "We came in extra early to help you get ready for that shower, but you've got everything done!"

"Yes. It didn't take as long as I thought," Rebecca replied vaguely, turning to Frances. "How are you feeling?"

"Right as rain," she declared. "Nasty bug, though. I'm glad it's over. Did you work late last night?"

"Mmm-hmm."

"Say, what's this?" Frances asked in surprise.

Rebecca turned. The woman was examining a ring—Zach's ring, to be exact. He must have taken it off when he was helping last night and then left without it, she realized in dismay. Rebecca's face turned bright pink, and she reached for it, dropping it into the pocket of her apron. "It's Zach's. He stopped by last night while I was working," she said shortly.

Rose sent Frances a knowing glance, which Rebecca intercepted. "Now don't you two get any matchmaking ideas," she warned.

Rose smiled at her innocently. "Of course not, dear. Just because the man sends you flowers, comes in three times a week for lunch and happens to drop by late at night—why would we get any ideas?"

Rebecca's flush deepened. "Well, it doesn't mean anything," she stated dismissively. "He's new in town and he doesn't know that many people yet. I'm just a familiar face."

"I'd say that 'familiar' is exactly what he'd like to be," Frances remarked pertly.

"For heaven's sake, you two are hopeless!" Rebecca declared in exasperation.

"Well, that young man is going to start feeling pretty hopeless himself, if you don't give in and go out with him soon," Rose told her.

Rebecca turned away and stirred the soup. It was useless to try and hide the fact that she'd accepted his dinner invitation. People would find out somehow. They always did in a small town. So she might as well be up-front about it, pretend it was no big deal. "Actually, I'm having dinner with him Sunday," she informed the sisters, striving to keep her tone light, hoping to make the date sound inconsequential. But the dead silence that met her revelation told her that she wasn't fooling anyone. Taking a deep breath, she looked over her shoulder to find them both beaming at her approvingly.

"Well, it's about time!" Frances declared. "I'm glad that poor boy's persistence finally paid off. Such a nice young man!"

Rebecca set down the ladle and turned to face Rose and Frances, her hands on her hips, her gaze stern. She needed to stop any rumors before they even started. "Before you get too carried away, remember that Zach and I are just acquaintances. Period. So you better just get these romantic notions out of your heads right now."

"Of course, dear. We certainly will," Rose promised agreeably.

Rebecca congratulated herself, convinced that she'd succeeded in dampening their enthusiasm—until Rose stopped to toss a prediction over her shoulder as she headed for the dining room. "But I don't think it will be easy to convince that young man to do the same."

Rebecca didn't reply. What was the point—when she knew Rose was right?

Chapter Five

Rebecca eyed her reflection critically in the full-length mirror behind her bedroom door and frowned. Was she overdressed? she wondered worriedly. Except for the night in the fog, when he'd been wearing a suit, she'd never seen Zach in anything more formal than khaki slacks and a cotton shirt. He hadn't told her where they were going on the Hill, St. Louis's well-known Italian neighborhood, and the restaurants ranged from corner pizza parlors to elegant gourmet eateries. If they ended up at the pizza end of the spectrum, her beaded white angora sweater and slim wool burgundy skirt were definitely going to be out of place. But worrying wasn't going to solve the dilemma, she thought with a sigh as she reached up to tuck a couple of stray strands of hair into her French twist. If she was dressed inappropriately, she'd find out soon enough.

The more important question was why she'd even agreed to this date in the first place. Logically, it was the wrong thing to do. She knew that. But somehow, in her heart, it *seemed* right. And her heart, rather than her mind, had guided her decision, she admitted. Even now, as she recalled the tender feel of Zach's lips on hers, his hand cradling her neck as he kissed her, a surprisingly intense surge of longing swept over her. She closed her eyes and slowly exhaled a shaky breath. Yes, accepting the date felt right. Because for some reason his touch hadn't frightened her. It was almost like a sign, she thought, an indication that she should give this relationship a chance. Maybe the Lord was trying to nudge her forward. She *had* asked for His help, after all. Perhaps Zach was—

The sudden ringing of the doorbell made her eyes fly open, and she turned with a start toward the sound, her pulse accelerating as she reached up with trembling fingers to nervously smooth her hair one final time. With a silent plea for courage, she drew a long, steadying breath and moved toward the door, turning the dead bolt and unhooking the security guards at the top and bottom with trembling hands.

As she swung the door open, she realized instantly that she was *not* overdressed. Zach wore a charcoal gray suit, which sat well on his broad shoulders and emphasized his muscular physique, and a burgundy-and-silver-striped tie rested against the crisply starched white shirt that hugged his broad chest. He looked impressive, distinguished, suave, incredibly handsome—in other words, absolutely fantastic, she thought appreciatively, her heart banging against her rib cage as she gripped the edge of the door.

While Rebecca completed her perusal, Zach did his own in one swift, comprehensive glance that missed nothing—the glitter of beads on her sweater; the pulse beating in the delicate hollow at the base of her throat; her beautiful eyes, wider than usual tonight as they gazed up at him with a touch of trepidation; and the classic bone structure of her face, highlighted by her sophisticated French twist.

His gaze lingered for a moment on her hair. The style suited her, but he'd love to see what her hair looked like loose and free, the russet highlights glinting as the waves tumbled around her shoulders. He imagined what it would be like to run his hands through those burnished tresses, feel their softness against his fingertips…

"Hi," Rebecca said timidly, abruptly interrupting his fantasy.

"Hi," he returned huskily, firmly reining in his wayward thoughts. He let his gaze travel over her once more, not even attempting to hide the appreciation in his eyes. "Has anyone told you lately that you look lovely?"

She flushed and turned away on the pretext of retrieving her purse. "Not that I recall," she replied, striving for a light tone yet secretly pleased by his compliment. "You look very nice tonight, too."

"I don't wear suits often," he admitted as he strolled into the tiny foyer behind her. "Only on special occasions."

So he considered tonight a special occasion, she thought, a delicious tingle running down her spine. *But it could be just a line,* she reminded herself. *Don't get carried away.* She knew he was smooth, practiced, probably very accomplished in the art of seduction. He was the type of man who would know exactly what to say to please a woman. She shouldn't take it too personally.

"Nice apartment," he commented, his gaze traveling around the living room. Chintz-covered couches and chairs, lace curtains, a heart-shaped dried flower wreath on the wall and family pictures artfully arranged in a collection of frames on an end table all combined to give the room a warm, homey feel.

"Thanks. It will do for a while, but eventually I'd like to get a house with some land at the edge of town. My dad is a great gardener, and he got me hooked on the hobby. I miss not being able to work with flowers."

"It doesn't seem as if you have much time for that sort of thing, anyway."

She gave him a rueful smile. "That's true. The restaurant is pretty demanding."

"Speaking of food," he said with a smile. "I have reservations for seven-thirty, so if you're ready we might as well head out."

"Okay. Is it cool enough for a coat?" The weather had been unseasonably mild for the past day or so, providing a much-needed glimpse of spring to the winter-weary, flood-exhausted residents.

"I don't think so. It's a nice night, and that sweater looks pretty warm." And *very* attractive, he acknowledged silently. But he needed to keep such thoughts on ice, he told himself firmly as he stepped aside for her to pass. Later, if things went well, maybe he could allow them to resurface. And perhaps even pursue them.

As they drove into the city, Zach purposely kept the banter light. He knew Rebecca was uncomfortable with this date, had half expected her to cancel. His goal for the moment was to get her to relax, to enjoy his company. Because he didn't want this to be a one-time event.

By the time they arrived in St. Louis, she did seem to be more at ease, but as they pulled up in front of the restaurant her voice died in mid-sentence even as her eyes widened in surprise. He had chosen one of the finest, priciest restaurants on the Hill for tonight's dinner date.

"Zach! I never expected anything like this," she exclaimed, completely taken aback.

He smiled, pleased at her reaction. "I hoped you would like it."

"Like it! That's an understatement! I only know this place by reputation, but I've always wanted to eat here. It's just too expensive." Suddenly she frowned and turned to him. "Zach, this will cost a fortune! I can't let you spend that kind of money on me. We hardly know each other!" she protested.

"Well, I intend to remedy that. Starting tonight. Just think of this as a birthday gift, Rebecca. And I'll let you in on a little secret," he added with a smile, leaning closer to drape an arm casually across the back of her seat, his fingers brushing her shoulder. "It may not be my birthday, but I definitely consider this date a gift. Thank you for coming tonight."

Rebecca was too stunned by his candor to reply. Fortunately

she didn't have to. Just then the valet opened her door. Zach winked at her before removing his arm from the back of her seat, and it was all she could do to keep her thoughts coherent as she stepped from the car. He joined her immediately, his hand resting lightly but proprietarily against the small of her back as they walked toward the restaurant, and somehow she knew that no matter what happened in the future between them, she'd always remember this birthday celebration as one of the most special of her life.

The dinner was everything Rebecca had expected—and more—and she even drank a little wine, a rare indulgence for her. But tonight it seemed appropriate, and as the meal progressed she grew mellow and relaxed, smiling and laughing freely. Zach was an ideal dinner companion—witty, well-read, an excellent conversationalist, moving with ease from one topic to another. She found herself telling him about her hometown, about Brad and Sam and their new daughter, about the satisfaction of making her dreams of owning her own restaurant a reality. Zach skillfully drew her out, asking all the right questions, until finally she paused to laugh.

"What's so funny?" he asked with a smile, his fingers idly playing with the stem of his wineglass as he gazed at her quizzically.

She shook her head and grinned ruefully. "I have a feeling you're *very* good at your job."

"What do you mean?"

"You've managed to find out an awful lot about me in a very short time. That skill must come in handy in your work."

He grinned. "I suppose so. But tonight my questions are motivated purely by personal interest," he replied candidly. What he *didn't* tell her was that he hadn't found out the one thing he was most interested in—why she rarely dated. He'd tried a couple of subtle probes, but she'd adeptly sidestepped them. And he didn't think pressing the issue was a good idea.

"So tell me about you, Zach," she said, interrupting his thoughts.

He shrugged. "Not much to tell, really. I grew up in Kansas City, and my mom still lives there. So does my older brother and his family. I went to Mizzou, became a journalist and *voilà!* Here I am."

"Talk about a condensed version of a life story!" she protested. "I guess I'll just have to ask a few questions of my own. What brought you to St. Genevieve? I don't know much about the newspaper business, but a flood doesn't seem like the usual sort of thing an investigative reporter would cover."

"You're right," he acknowledged. "I've been working on a series on corruption in city government, and a couple of the people implicated got wind of it. They claimed I was using falsified documents as a basis for my coverage and threatened to sue the paper if the series ran. So the publisher put a hold on the story while they look into the charges, and sent me off to St. Genevieve for the duration. Mostly to keep me out of the way, I assume."

Rebecca frowned. "No wonder you sounded so burned out about reporting when we talked the other night."

He shrugged. "It wasn't just that. There have been lots of instances through the years when a piece has blown up in my face, or people have found a way to work around the system and get away with murder. Sometimes literally. I think this was just the proverbial straw that broke the camel's back. To be honest, my editor actually realized before I did that a break from investigative work would be good for me," he admitted.

"How do you know?" Rebecca asked curiously.

"At our last meeting he said I needed some time to decompress and regain my perspective. I didn't buy it then. But now that I've been away for a couple of weeks, I have to admit that he's right. In fact, since I talked to that class at the high school on Friday, I'd go even further. I don't just need time away from investigative work. I need time away, period."

"It sounds like a good idea," Rebecca agreed. "Can you manage it?"

He nodded. "I have quite a bit of vacation accumulated. It

shouldn't be an issue. In fact, when Ted—my managing editor—called yesterday, I told him that I'm thinking about taking some time off when this assignment is over. Being in the classroom with those kids was a catalyst, in a sense. It reminded me why I was attracted to teaching in the first place—and also that there's a whole world out there apart from journalism and a lot of ways to make a difference in the human condition. I'm going to think about it for a couple more days, but I've pretty much decided that a long vacation would be a good idea.''

"It does seem to make sense," Rebecca concurred. Then she propped her chin in her hand and tilted her head as she studied him. "You know, I imagine you'd probably be a really good teacher."

He smiled. "Why do you say that?"

She considered the question seriously, frowning slightly. "Well, you've been out in the real world. You talk from experience. Kids respect that. And you have an intensity...a commitment, I guess is the right word...plus a real sense of integrity, that would be inspiring to young people. Not to mention the fact that you're obviously an intelligent, well-read, articulate person."

Zach was taken aback by her unexpectedly flattering assessment, and he felt his neck redden. He wasn't a man who handled praise well. It made him uncomfortable. "Well, I think you're being too generous, but I do appreciate the kind words."

She gazed at him speculatively, an idea forming in her mind. "Did you know that Phil Carr hurt his back sandbagging last night?" she asked suddenly.

Zach frowned. "No."

"I found out this morning at church. It sounds like he'll be out of commission for the rest of the semester. They'll be looking for a replacement to come in when spring break ends next Monday."

Zach digested that piece of news in silence for several seconds. When he spoke, his tone was thoughtful. "That suggests some interesting possibilities," he mused. On a lot of fronts, he added silently. A trial run at teaching appealed to him. So did staying close to Rebecca. And he could use some time not only away from reporting, but away from the city, when this assignment was finished. Which would be soon, given that the flood waters had crested. But the teaching slot was probably a long shot. "I'm sure they have people in mind already," he said.

Rebecca shook her head. "I don't think so. At least not on such short notice—*and* for a several-week stint."

"Hmm. Well, I'll have to give that some thought," he said noncommittally. Then he placed his napkin on the table and smiled. "So…are you ready to head back?"

Not really, she thought. The evening had been so enjoyable that she hated for it to end. But she couldn't think of any reason to delay the inevitable, so she summoned up a smile. "If I can move, after all that food," she joked. "It was wonderful, Zach. Thank you."

"It was my pleasure."

The ride back was pleasant. The conversation flowed naturally, punctuated by periods of comfortable, contented silence that allowed time for reflection. Zach had proven to be a wonderful companion, Rebecca thought. She couldn't remember the last time she'd been out with a man socially and felt so relaxed.

But relaxation slowly changed to anticipation as they approached St. Genevieve. Would he kiss her good night again? she wondered, her nerve endings beginning to tingle. She had enjoyed their last kiss, much to her surprise, and she wasn't averse to repeating the experience. No, that wasn't quite accurate, she admitted honestly. She *wanted* to repeat the experience. She wanted him to touch her in that gentle, nonthreatening way, wanted to savor the tender feel of his hand on her cheek. She found it hard to believe, after years of avoiding that type of experience, that she was now looking forward to it. She only hoped Zach was, too!

When they pulled up in front of her apartment, he turned off the engine and angled himself toward her, draping his arm across the back of her seat. "Home safe and sound," he announced lightly.

Rebecca tried to smile, but suddenly her lips felt stiff. She had very limited experience in this good night business, and she suddenly wondered if she was supposed to invite him in. But that scared her. It was too…intimate. For all she knew, inviting a man in also implied an invitation for more, and she figured she'd better not take the risk. "I had a great time, Zach," she offered, her voice quavering slightly.

"So did I."

His fingers were brushing her shoulder lightly now, back and forth, back and forth, and she suddenly found it difficult to breathe. She tried to discern the intent in his eyes, but in the dim light his expression was unreadable. She dropped her gaze, playing nervously with the clasp of her purse as she searched for something else to say, anything, to break the electric silence between them, but her mind went blank.

Zach knew Rebecca was nervous. It would take a total clod to miss the signs. But he also knew he was going to kiss her. She'd been nervous the last time, too, but she'd responded once he'd initiated the kiss. He hoped she would do the same tonight. Because for the last twenty minutes that had been the only thing on his mind. He wanted to feel her soft, pliant lips against his, wanted to run his fingertips across her silky skin, wanted to hold her so close that he could feel the thudding of her heart against his chest. And Zach was a man used to getting what he wanted. Not that he ever had to push. He had learned through the years to accurately assess a woman's interest and he didn't waste time and energy pursuing unwilling partners. Though he knew Rebecca was nervous, he also knew she was willing. And interested. She just seemed to need a little coaxing.

Zach didn't much relish the idea of kissing Rebecca in the car, however. There was too much in the way. For example, the gearshift would definitely hamper his style, he thought wryly. But she hadn't said anything about coming in. His gaze flickered away from her momentarily to scan the surroundings, coming to rest on a secluded bench discreetly tucked between two pine trees. Thank goodness it was a mild, dry night, he thought in relief.

Slowly he withdrew his arm and smiled at Rebecca. "If you're not in a hurry, we could sit for a while," he suggested casually, his tone giving away none of the anticipatory tension that was slowly beginning to build inside him. "It's a nice night, and there's a convenient bench right over there," he noted, nodding toward the pine trees.

Rebecca swallowed. This was what she wanted, wasn't it? So why did she suddenly feel so nervous and uncertain? Everything would be fine. She was only a few steps from her door, not trapped at a secluded scenic overlook or miles from help, should she need it. Which she wouldn't. *Take a deep breath and relax,* she told herself.

"Okay," she agreed, trying to steady the tremor in her voice.

Zach gave her shoulder an encouraging squeeze, then got out of the car in one lithe movement and came around to open her door. He took her arm as they walked across the uneven ground, the warmth of his fingers penetrating the soft wool of her sweater. When they reached the old-fashioned park bench, she perched stiffly on the edge while he leaned back, draped his arms across the back and stretched his legs in front, crossing his ankles. He seemed totally relaxed and at ease, Rebecca thought enviously. Of course, he probably had a whole lot more experience at this than she did.

Rebecca wasn't sure why she felt so uncomfortable. Maybe because the last time, things had seemed to evolve naturally, spontaneously. She certainly hadn't expected to be kissed that night. And she'd be willing to bet that Zach hadn't planned to kiss her, either. It had just happened. Tonight was different. Tonight she felt intent in Zach's actions. And for some reason that scared her. She shivered suddenly, hoping vainly that Zach wouldn't notice, but she should have known better. His perceptive eyes never missed a thing.

"Are you cold?" he inquired solicitously.

"N-no."

"Well, you *look* cold. Why don't you lean back and I'll warm you up." He reached forward and gently drew her into the protective curve of his right arm, draping it around her shoulder and urging her close. She followed his lead numbly, simply because she didn't know what else to do. And it *was* warmer here—although his proximity did nothing to quiet her pounding heart. She gripped her purse tightly in her lap, aware of their thighs only a breath apart, inhaling the distinctive scent of his rugged aftershave, feeling his warm breath on her temple. She was getting in over her head here and she knew it. But she wanted so desperately to give this a chance! Please, Lord, help me find the courage to at least *try* to relate to this man on a physical level, she prayed fervently.

Zach knew Rebecca was skittish, but he attributed her nervousness to inexperience. She was probably embarrassed by her lack of sophistication, he reasoned. But if he was reading her signals correctly, she did like him. And she'd had a good time tonight, he could tell. He wanted to tell her to relax, to forget about her lack of experience because it didn't matter to him. But maybe, instead of telling her, he needed to show her.

Slowly but very deliberately he let his hand wander from her shoulder to her neck, his thumb playing gently with the lobe of her ear. She went absolutely still, almost as if she was holding her breath, but she didn't protest, he noted with relief. When he lowered his head to nuzzle her neck, he heard her swiftly indrawn breath, could feel the pounding of her pulse against his lips.

"You look very lovely tonight, Rebecca," he murmured softly, his voice husky.

She swallowed with difficulty. "Th-thank you."

He pressed his cheek to hers. "You taste good, too," he whispered, his breath warm against her skin.

This time Rebecca didn't even try to answer. The touch of his lips was now making skyrockets go off.

Gently, he cupped her chin to turn her face toward his. His lips traveled up the slender column of her throat, which she involuntarily arched to meet his kiss, then across her cheek, up to her forehead. Her eyelids drifted closed, and she sighed with pleasure as he kissed each one very gently.

Zach tried to quiet the thudding of his heart, but when he spoke, his voice was hoarse with emotion. "Oh, Rebecca..." Without giving her a chance to respond, he cupped her face with his hands and tenderly claimed her lips.

Rebecca found herself responding tentatively to his touch. Her hand crept around his neck and, without consciously deciding to do so, she turned into the embrace, tunneling her fingers through the soft hair at the base of his neck and pressing herself closer. Caught in his spell, she relaxed in his arms as his kiss worked its magic.

Zach felt her trusting response, her willingness to explore their attraction, and with a groan he deepened the kiss. If he felt her sudden surprise, her hesitation, he was too caught up in the moment to notice.

Zach drew her even closer. He shifted so that she was leaning against the back of the bench as he continued to kiss her.

Rebecca didn't know at exactly what moment she panicked. All she knew, quite suddenly, was that she had. The old feelings of terror resurfaced with an intensity that took her breath away. She felt powerless, helpless, suffocating as his pressing weight immobilized her. The kiss that had started out so welcome had suddenly become a thing to be feared; his lips, once seeking now seemed demanding as they imprisoned hers; and his arms felt like steel cables holding her in place. She couldn't breathe, and she clawed at his shoulders desperately as her heart thudded painfully in her chest, hot tears stinging her eyes. But still he seemed oblivious to her distress. Finally, with one last, desperate, superhuman effort she wrenched her lips free, turning her head aside as she gasped for air, struggling to push him away.

Only then did Rebecca's ragged breathing and the frantic pressure of her hands against his shoulders penetrate Zach's consciousness. He hesitated, backing up far enough to look into her face.

That was the only opening she needed. With a strangled sob she broke free of his arms and jumped unsteadily to her feet, dashing blindly for her apartment as tears streamed down her face. She stumbled once, her heels sinking into the rain-soaked earth, but she quickly regained her footing and continued her irrational flight, her thoughts a chaotic jumble, her emotions tattered. She groped desperately for her key, her fingers closing around it reassuringly as she reached her porch. In a moment she would be safe!

But just as she stepped up a hand shot out and grasped her wrist, throwing her off balance. She gasped, teetering precariously on the edge of the concrete stoop, until another hand reached out to steady her.

Once more Rebecca felt trapped, and she tried to shake off the hands, her heart clamoring in her chest. "Let me go, please!" she pleaded, twisting in Zach's grasp.

"Rebecca, calm down!" he said tersely, alarmed at her near-hysterical state.

"Please," she repeated, her voice breaking on a sob. "Just let me go!"

"Not until you tell me what this is all about," Zach said, his voice quiet but touched with steel.

Rebecca could hear the contained anger in his voice as she averted her face. But she missed the underlying concern and confusion as she struggled to control the irrational fear that held her in a vise. *Stay calm,* she told herself. *Get a grip. You're two steps from your front door and a single scream will bring a dozen people running. You're safe.* She forced herself to take deep breaths, fighting the sudden wave of blackness that swept over her, willing her heart to slow down.

"Rebecca, answer me," Zach demanded, gripping her wrist.

"Please—just let go of me," she said brokenly, turning at last to face him.

Zach took one look at her tear-streaked face, at the almost-wild fear in her eyes, and automatically loosened his grip as her sheer panic finally registered. Tension was radiating from every pore of her body, and she was shaking. Badly. Something was very wrong here, he realized with a frown. Okay, so maybe he'd come on a little too strong. But his overzealous ardor shouldn't have induced this frenzied response. There was something else going on, something that had made her freak out at what essentially was just a kiss. And his caveman reaction to her panic certainly hadn't helped the situation, he thought, silently cursing his insensitivity.

Zach released her wrist, jamming his hands into his pockets. He figured that was the safest place for them, considering that his instinct was to reach over and frame her face with them, erase her tears with the gentle brush of his thumbs over her cheeks, taste the salt on her lips as he kissed away her hurt and fear. But he instinctively knew that touching her in any way whatsoever was *not* a good idea. He'd already made a major mistake tonight, it appeared, and he was not about to make another one. He was playing it safe from here on out.

"Rebecca, what's wrong?" he asked softly, gentling his voice considerably, striving to keep his posture nonthreatening.

She shook her head jerkily. "Please, Zach. J-just go. You w-wouldn't understand."

"Would you at least give me a chance to try?"

She shook her head and attempted to swallow past the lump in her throat, praying that he would just leave her alone to mourn the death of her dream of a normal relationship with a man. She had hoped—prayed—that this time it would be different. But it wasn't. And it never would be.

Zach gazed at her, trying to probe her eyes, searching for answers she clearly wasn't going to give. But all he saw reflected in their depths was abject misery, absolute loneliness and utter despair. His gut wrenched painfully as he looked at her, wanting desperately to ease her distress but not knowing how. There were larger issues at work here, issues he couldn't hope to uncover tonight in her present state. All he could do was try to calm her, make her feel safe. But that was going to be a monumental task in itself, judging by her body language. She was poised for flight, hovering only inches from her door, ready to bolt at the slightest provocation.

"Look, Rebecca, I'm sorry," he apologized huskily, trying to communicate with his eyes that he would never purposely hurt or frighten her. "I guess I just got carried away. I scared you, didn't I?"

She hesitated, but finally she lowered her gaze and nodded. Denying the obvious would be foolish. "Y-yes."

"I'm sorry," he repeated, the warmth and tenderness in his voice acting like a balm on her frayed nerves. "That was certainly not my intent. I find you attractive, and I thought the kiss was an appropriate way to demonstrate that. Obviously it wasn't, because you reacted almost like I was attacking you. I want you to know that was the last thing on my mind, Rebecca. I would never force my attentions on any woman."

She knew that, now that the rational side of her brain was finally kicking in. But she also now knew with absolute certainty that she wasn't equipped to deal with a man of strong passions—like Zach. She was sure that any other woman would be flattered by the advances of such a handsome, intelligent, caring man, would welcome his ardor. But Rebecca wasn't like other women. And even though she'd followed through on her Valentine's Day promise to give a relationship one more chance, she'd failed miserably, just as she'd feared.

Much to her embarrassment, a tear silently rolled down her cheek, and she reached up to brush it away with shaking fingers, turning toward the door as she spoke. "It's not your fault, Zach,'' she told him, her voice catching on a sob. ''Just don't waste your time on me anymore, okay?''

''Rebecca…'' He wanted to reach out and restrain her, and it took every ounce of his willpower to keep his hands in his pockets, balled into fists of helpless frustration.

She finished fitting the key into the lock, then half turned, waiting for him to continue. Except he didn't know what else to say. He wanted to ask her why she was so afraid, but he knew she'd just shut down even more. Yet there was no way he could fight her fear if he didn't know its source. All he could do at the moment was let her know how he felt.

''Rebecca, I care about you,'' he said slowly, deliberately. ''I don't know exactly what went on here tonight, except that I upset you very badly. But I don't want things to end like this. We need to talk about it. Not tonight, I know, but how about tomorrow, in the daylight, somewhere you feel safe? Just name the place and time.''

Rebecca's eyes misted again. He was trying, she'd give him that, exhibiting more patience than she had a right to expect after the way she'd rebuffed his embrace, surely denting his ego in the process. But it wouldn't work. Zach didn't strike her as a man who was used to waiting, and she knew his patience would quickly wear thin. To continue to see him would only delay the inevitable.

''I'm sorry, Zach,'' she whispered, her voice quavering. ''It's no use. But thank you for offering. And for not being angry about tonight.''

''Rebecca, please let me—''

''Goodbye, Zach,'' she said, opening the door and slipping inside as she struggled to control the sobs begging for release. ''You're a very nice man, and I-I'm sorry,'' she finished helplessly, her voice breaking as she shut the door with a quiet but decisive click.

Zach stared at the closed door, frowning in confusion and frustration, at a loss for one of the few times in his dating career. He had absolutely no idea how to proceed. But as he turned and slowly made his way to his car, he knew one thing with absolute certainty. He wasn't going to let this intriguing woman slip out of his life so easily. *She* might think their relationship was over, but *he* had other ideas. He hadn't lied to her about not forcing his attentions on uninterested women. But she *was* interested, he'd bet his life on it. Whether she was willing to admit it or not, there were good vibrations between them. Certainly on the physical level, despite what had happened tonight. And on other levels as well. At dinner this evening he'd glimpsed a number of fascinating aspects of her personality that left him hungry to learn more. She had wit and charm and a great sense of humor, and he'd delighted in the sound of her carefree laughter, in the way her eyes sparkled in amusement and deepened with conviction as their discussion ran the gamut from old movies to her strong faith.

Zach had met a lot of women in his life. He'd even been halfway serious about a couple. But none of them had ever sparked his interest in quite the way Rebecca Matthews did. Perhaps it was the combination of social innocence and professional savvy; poise and uncertainty; strength and vulnerability. But whatever the reason, something told him that if he walked away, as she'd asked, he'd spend the rest of his life regretting it. Because he had a feeling that Rebecca was a once-in-a-lifetime kind of woman. And he intended to check out that theory.

Now he just had to convince her.

Chapter Six

~◆~

Zach stared in shock at the message on his computer screen, trying to absorb the words as a cold knot formed in his stomach, then tightened painfully. Katrina was dead.

He closed his eyes and rested his elbows on the desk, steepling his fingers. A muscle clenched in his jaw as he slowly exhaled an unsteady breath, his mind in denial. He couldn't believe Katrina was gone. It just didn't seem possible. Or maybe he just didn't want to believe it, he thought bleakly. Because although the news might *seem* unreal, the words that stared back at him from the screen when he reluctantly opened his eyes were real enough. He forced himself to read Josef's message again, more slowly this time, finding the content even more jolting—and more final—the second time through.

I do not know how I find the strength to write these words, my friend. Though the outside world goes on around me, my own world seems to have ended. Katrina died two days ago, Zachary. The miscarriage depleted her strength, and infection set in. She was never physically strong, as you know. But she had such inner strength that I thought her light could never be dimmed, that it would always burn brightly to light my way. Yet the Lord has chosen to take her from me, leaving my world in darkness.

I write to you now to request a very great favor. Do you remember the promise we made to each other, Zachary, so many years ago? A promise to help each other should the need ever arise? I hope that you do, my friend, because the time has come when I must make such a request. I do so with full understanding of the burden it will impose. But if you take the sabbatical you mentioned in your last correspondence, perhaps it will not be so difficult.

Things are not good in my country, as you know. They are especially not good right now. I do not care much for myself, but I worry about Isabel. She is all I have left now, Zachary, Katrina's legacy to me, and I must keep her well. But that is not easy to do. It is no longer even safe for her to go out and play. There are too many random acts of violence and bombings. My work is also putting me at more risk right now. If something should happen to me, I do not know what would become of my precious child. I would turn to my family for help, but my mother is too old and frail to care for her, and my sister can barely put enough food on the table for her own six children.

So, my friend, I ask you from my heart to take Isabel for a few weeks, until things settle down here and it is safe for her to return to me. I know it is a great favor, one I should probably not impose on you. But I do not know where else to turn. There will surely be many details to work out, arrangements to make, red tape to cut through. But I am confident that with your help, we can accomplish this and keep my Isabel safe.

I will wait anxiously for your reply, Zachary. And may God be with you.

With a heavy sigh Zach rose slowly and walked over to the window, folding his arms on the sash and staring pensively out into the darkness, his brow deeply furrowed. It had been quite a night, he thought grimly. First he'd frightened Rebecca. No, more like traumatized her, he corrected himself harshly. That incident had thrown him off balance, leaving him with equal measures of guilt, confusion and compassion. And then he'd come home to be hit with this devastating news. With sudden anger, he slammed his fist against the sash, making the glass rattle, as he railed silently against any Higher Power that might be listening.

Dear God—if You're even up there—how could You do this to Josef? he demanded. *Katrina was everything to him. He's a good man who doesn't deserve to be hurt. He's always lived by Your rules, done the right thing even in the face of personal danger and sacrifice, and how do You reward him? You deprive him of the wife he loved beyond all measure, and You deny his daughter the mother she so desperately needs. It just isn't fair!*

Even as that last thought flashed across his mind, Zach sighed. It didn't do any good to complain that life wasn't fair, he thought resignedly. It was just a fact, plain and simple. He saw proof of it every day in his job. But the truth had just never hit quite so close to home before.

Wearily he walked back to the computer and printed out Josef's message. Somehow it seemed even more real when he held the hard copy in his hands, the black words stark against the white paper. Josef's request seemed more real, too, and more urgent. And therein lay a problem.

Zach remembered their promise, of course. And they'd both meant it, with every fiber of their being, during those heady years in J school that now seemed a lifetime ago. But promises made in the optimism and fervor of youth weren't always easy to keep years later, he now realized. Circumstances changed, life became more complicated. Yet a promise was a promise, a sacred trust not to be treated lightly. His father had always told him that a man was only as good as his word, and Zach believed that. Without integrity and honor, a person was nothing. Zach knew beyond the shadow of a doubt that if circumstances were reversed, Josef wouldn't hesitate to keep their promise. Could he do any less for this man who was closer to him even than his brother?

The answer, of course, was no. Zach stared down again at the letter as he considered the situation. The logistics could be dealt with, that wasn't a problem. He had plenty of contacts from his years of reporting, colleagues all over the world who knew how to cut through red tape. No, that would be the easy part, he thought dismissively. But how on earth would he, a man who had virtually no experience handling young children, cope with a little seven-year-old girl who had just lost her mother and was being sent far away from her beloved father and the only home she'd ever known?

Zach didn't have the answer to that question. And he wasn't sure where to find it.

Rebecca hooked the pepper spray onto her belt, pulled a sweater over her head, secured her long hair loosely with a barrette and locked the car. A good long walk in the fresh air and quiet woods, next to a bubbling brook, would lift her spirits, she told herself resolutely, though in her heart she wasn't convinced it would help. But at least it couldn't hurt. Her spirits were so low right now that the only place for them to go was up.

She struck out purposefully on the state park trail, determined to return to her apartment with some sense of perspective. She'd spent a sleepless night staring at the ceiling, going over and over last night's disaster in her mind. And the more she thought about it, the more she empathized with Zach. *What must he think of her?* she wondered, her face flushing even now. She had overreacted—dramatically—to what, for him, was probably the standard way to end an evening with a woman whose company he had enjoyed.

In retrospect she realized that her attempt to fight off a non-existent attack had probably not only hurt his ego, but insulted him, as well, by implying that she thought him capable of such an act. Dear Lord, she had really messed things up! If only she could relive that moment! But with a profound sense of discouragement, she admitted in her heart that it would probably end the same. Here, alone, in the fresh air and sunshine, she could think rationally, logically analyze her reaction. But in his embrace, held captive by the strength of his arms and the pressure of his lips, she would panic. It had become an instinctive response through the years, until now it was a self-fulfilling prophecy. She could no more control her irrational panic in that situation than she could stop the flood waters that had slowly but powerfully risen to threaten the town.

Rebecca wished with all her heart that there was some way to overcome her problem. But her hopes seemed doomed and, as a result, so did her dreams of a husband and family.

She trudged along, her gaze fixed on the trail to avoid stumbling over the protruding rocks, so lost in her misery that for once she was oblivious to the beauty of nature around her. In fact, so deep was her introspection that when she glanced up and saw Zach it took a moment for his presence to register.

She stopped abruptly, certain she must be hallucinating. He was just off the trail, sitting on a large flat boulder by the stream, arms around his bent knees. But what on earth was he doing on this secluded nature trail? she wondered in confusion. The state park was usually deserted this time of year on weekdays. She hadn't expected to see anyone, let alone Zach. But it was definitely him, she realized as she stared at the pensive figure not more than twenty feet ahead.

Rebecca considered beating a quiet—and hasty—retreat, but before she could make a move he glanced up, as if sensing a presence, and their eyes connected.

Zach's reaction was much the same as hers—a double take, followed by an ''am I imaging this?'' look. But he recovered quickly, greeting her in weary voice. "Hello, Rebecca. Fancy meeting you here."

"Hello, Zach."

"Nice day," he commented, tilting his head to look up at the cobalt blue sky, the canopy of branches above him exhibiting the first tender buds of spring.

"Yes, it is. But..." She stopped uncertainly, still bewildered by his presence in this unlikely place.

He looked back at her, his lips curving up into the semblance of a smile. "What am I doing here?" he finished for her.

"Yes."

He turned back to gaze down into the stream. "Mark told me about this place a while back. It sounded like a good spot to think."

His face looked haggard, Rebecca thought, as she inched cautiously closer. She knew he was upset about last night's fiasco, but for some reason she had a feeling his subdued mood today wasn't caused by that incident alone. Maybe the much-creased sheet of paper in his hand was the key to his uncharacteristic melancholy, she thought. But whatever the reason, he didn't seem anxious to discuss it with her. Not that she could blame him, considering her behavior last night. Yet she couldn't just walk off and leave, when she sensed that he needed someone to talk to.

"Zach...is everything okay?" she asked tentatively, trying to give him an opening.

He turned back to her once more. She had moved close enough now for him to see the dark circles beneath her eyes, eloquent evidence of her sleepless night, and he knew with a pang of guilt that he was to blame. But much as he wanted to work out the situation between them, it wasn't his priority at the moment. He had a more urgent problem to resolve. He glanced back at the letter in his hand and sighed. "Not really. I got some bad news last night."

"A letter?"

"E-mail. It was waiting when I got home."

"Something to do with your family?" She was only a few feet away now, and she paused uncertainly, still unsure of her welcome.

"You might say that." He turned to gaze at her, his eyes troubled. "Look, Rebecca, you don't need to keep me company. You obviously came out here to be alone. I'll work this out myself."

She bit her lip. Was he trying to tell her to get lost? Or just being considerate of her needs, trying not to intrude on her day? There was only one way to find out. "I can be a good listener, Zach, if you want to talk about it," she offered quietly.

His gaze dropped to her belt and he gave a mirthless chuckle. "Well, at least you're prepared today. A blast of that pepper spray should keep me in line."

In the instant before she turned away, Zach saw the shaft of pain shoot through her eyes at his rebuke, and he felt like someone had kicked him in the gut. *Of all the stupid remarks!* he berated himself. Just because he was upset about Josef's situation was no excuse to take it out on this gentle woman who had just offered him a much-needed sympathetic ear.

He rose in one swift movement to follow her, reaching her just as she stumbled on a rock. His hand shot out to steady her, and she reached up to swipe at her misty eyes, trying to clear her clouded vision.

"Rebecca, please forgive me," he implored, his voice raw with pain. "That remark was totally out of line and completely insensitive. My only excuse is that I've had a really lousy twelve hours. Look, stay awhile, okay? I could use the company."

Rebecca held herself stiffly, blinking back the tears still welling in her eyes. She'd always been overly sensitive, wearing her feelings so close to the surface that they were easily hurt. In her heart she knew Zach wouldn't have made that remark under normal circumstances. Something must be terribly wrong. Refusing to forgive him would only add to whatever trauma he was trying to deal with. Rebecca struggled with forgiveness sometimes, often finding it hard to forget callously inflicted hurts. But she needed to learn to let go, and this was a good chance to put that lesson into practice.

She let her shoulders relax and reached up to wipe away the last traces of her tears before she turned to face him. "Are you sure you want me to? I didn't mean to force myself on you."

Zach's own shoulders sagged in relief. He knew his curt remark could have alienated her permanently, considering that they were on shaky ground already. Thank God she was willing to give him another chance! he thought gratefully.

"Believe me, you're welcome," he assured her, the husky timbre of his voice more pronounced than usual. "Come on, let's go back and sit on the rock." He took her arm protectively as they made their way over the rocky ground, releasing it as they sat down on the large boulder. Glancing down at the letter, he drew a deep breath. "Do you remember the friend I mentioned once, the one in Eastern Europe?"

"Yes."

"We went to journalism school together. Mizzou. I can't think of anyone in this world I admire more than Josef. He's a man of deep conviction, impeccable character and great faith. He's always been an inspiration to me when things got tough." Zach paused and picked up a pebble, fingering it absently as he continued, his eyes fixed on a spot across the stream, but his gaze clearly turned inward. "We've kept in touch all these years, despite the distance. About eight years ago he and his wife, Katrina, came to the States for the birth of their daughter, Isabel. Katrina had a problem pregnancy, and was always a little frail, anyway, so Josef didn't want to take any chances. They stayed with me for six weeks, and I was even Isabel's godfather at her christening.'' He paused to pull out his wallet, flipping to a photo before handing it to Rebecca. ''This picture was taken that day.''

Rebecca took the wallet and examined the shot. She saw a much-younger Zach, gingerly holding a tiny bundle in white, flanked by an attractive, delicate-looking woman and a slender, dark-haired man with compelling eyes. ''They look like a nice family,'' she said softly.

''Yeah, they were,'' Zach replied. ''That's a more recent picture of Isabel up above.''

Rebecca's gaze flickered up to examine the solemn face staring back at her, framed by long dark hair, the delicate bone structure mirroring that of her mother. But it was Isabel's eyes that held her. They were Josef's eyes, no question. But they were also eyes that had seen too much for someone so young, she thought, her heart aching with compassion. No child's eyes should look that wary and vulnerable, so old for their years.

''I got this last night,'' Zach said quietly, handing her the paper before turning away.

Rebecca looked at his rigid back, knew that whatever this letter contained had brought him great anguish, and wanted to reach over and comfort him. But she held back, not sure that he would welcome her sympathy, and forced herself to read the words on the sheet instead.

As her eyes scanned the page, and the horror of the situation unfolded, she felt her stomach clench, and by the time she reached the end, she wanted to cry. She didn't know Josef or Katrina or Isabel. But in the brief, eloquent note Josef had written she could feel the love and devotion, pain and loss, desperation and fear that now consumed his life. Her heart went out to this grieving man and his cherished child, and she felt suddenly guilty and small for spending so much time agonizing over a personal trauma that paled into insignificance compared to what this family had endured.

"Oh, Zach," she murmured at last, her voice choked. "I'm so sorry. Poor Josef! And Isabel...no wonder he's concerned. The conditions sound so awful! And terribly dangerous!"

"Yeah," Zach replied, a muscle clenching in his jaw.

"What are you going to do?"

He sighed and raked a hand through his hair. "I'm going to take Isabel, of course. How can I not? Josef has always prided himself on taking care of his family himself, so I know he would never ask me to do this unless the situation was desperate." He sighed and threw the pebble into the stream in frustration. "But I don't have any experience with children. Especially girls. Then there's the teaching job. I was going to approach the school about it, but I really can't take it if I have Isabel here. I'd like to bring her to St. Genevieve, though, because I think it would be good for her to spend time in a place like this after the environment she's been in. But I can't afford to keep an apartment here and in St. Louis unless I take the teaching job, and it's not worth closing my apartment in the city for just a few weeks."

The words came out in a long, almost stream-of-consciousness data dump that clearly reflected his turmoil. He paused for a moment and expelled a long breath before finishing. "That's why I came out here today, to try and work things out in my mind."

Rebecca bit her lip and stared down at the letter, an idea slowly forming in her mind. "Zach."

He turned to her, realizing suddenly that for once she hadn't pinned her hair up. Instead, it tumbled freely to her shoulders, held back loosely by only a barrette, the russet strands glinting in the sun just as he'd imagined them. It was a measure of his distress that it had taken him this long to notice the soft waves cascading down her back, he thought wearily.

She looked up at him, her face thoughtful, oblivious to the direction of his wayward thoughts. "Zach, I could help you with Isabel," she said impulsively.

That jolted him back to reality, and he stared at her, taken aback. "But...but why would you want to get involved in this?"

"Because these people need help."

"You don't even know them."

"It doesn't matter. I can't turn my back on someone in need."

Zach studied her face, knew she was absolutely sincere in her offer. For her, it was simple. She saw a need, and she offered to help. Period. That was why she'd stopped for him that night on the deserted highway, why she'd pitched in with the sandbagging.

What a remarkable woman, he thought in awe, his admiration for her increasing tenfold. She was completely selfless, more giving and generous than anyone he'd ever met. He knew, if he accepted her offer, that she would throw herself into the care of Isabel, heart and soul. But she had enough to do with the restaurant, he reminded himself. She often seemed to be running on pure adrenaline as it was, and this would be just one more burden on her already-taxed energy and time.

"I appreciate the offer, Rebecca. More than I can say. But you're too busy already."

"But you said yourself that you have limited experience with children. I don't have much more, I'll admit. But together I think we could pull this off. I can watch Isabel at the restaurant while you teach—if you get the job. And I'm off on Monday, so it's really only four days a week that I'd have her. And just during school hours. I don't mind, really. I love children, Zach. I always wanted..." She cut herself off sharply, glancing down at the stream as a flush tinted her cheeks. "Anyway, I'd be glad to help."

He looked at her speculatively. It didn't take a genius to fill in the blanks. She'd always wanted children of her own. And she was the type of woman who should have a houseful of children, he realized. With her warm, compassionate nature, she would make a wonderful mother. Yet she'd never married. And after last night, he was beginning to understand why. Which reminded him...

"You realize this will put us in close contact, don't you?" he pointed out slowly, loath to bring up the subject but feeling compelled to make sure she understood the implications. "I got the impression last night that was the last thing you wanted."

He was right. Last night, being together *was* the last thing she wanted. But circumstances had changed. A little girl needed their help, and as far as she was concerned, that took precedence over her own wants. She'd just have to deal with their proximity. But maybe *Zach* didn't want to deal with it, she thought suddenly, glancing down with a frown. "I wasn't being very rational last night," she admitted slowly, her voice subdued. "I'm willing to give it a try, though, if you are. But I wouldn't blame you if you didn't, not after what happened."

A large hand entered her field of vision, gently covering her own. "Rebecca, I told you before. I care about you. What happened last night didn't change that."

She risked a glance at him then, and the warmth and caring in his deep brown eyes made her breath catch in her throat. "It isn't that I don't like you, you know," she told him shyly, a blush creeping onto her cheeks.

He smiled and gave her hand a gentle, encouraging squeeze.

"I'm glad to hear you say that. I'll admit I was beginning to wonder."

"What happened was…I can't— It had nothing to do with you personally," she said disjointedly. "It's…it's a long story."

"Maybe someday you'll share it with me."

She looked at him steadily, knowing that she had to be honest. "I can't make any promises."

He returned her look just as steadily. "I'm not asking you to. How about if we just take it a day at a time? Besides, I have a feeling that one little seven-year-old girl is going to require most of our attention and energy in the next few weeks." He tilted his head and looked at her quizzically. "Are you absolutely sure you want to get involved?"

She glanced down at the letter and pictures she still held. "I think I already am. Besides, I have a feeling the Lord wants us to work together to help this family."

Zach wasn't so sure that divine intervention was involved. Then again, maybe it was, he reflected, considering that after last night he figured it would take a miracle to bring Rebecca back into his life. It seemed that such a miracle had just been wrought. He just wished it hadn't come at the expense of his friend.

"How on earth did you manage to arrange everything so quickly?" Rebecca asked in amazement as Zach turned the van onto the highway, heading south.

He grinned. "Chalk it up to my charm and persuasive powers."

Rebecca looked at him speculatively, half believing his explanation. In the past three days he'd interviewed for, and been offered, the job at the high school; arranged to take all eight weeks of his accumulated vacation, plus an additional four-week personal leave; found an apartment in St. Genevieve and signed a short-term lease; and cut through the red tape to get Isabel's paperwork in order. He'd also arranged with a foreign-correspondent colleague who was returning from Eastern Europe to courier Isabel as far as New York and put her on a plane to St. Louis. She would arrive Sunday.

"So what's left to do?" she asked.

"Move some of my stuff from St. Louis. That's on the agenda for tomorrow. And pick up your old bedroom furniture today. The loan of which I greatly appreciate, in case I haven't already thanked you."

"You have," she assured him. "And it's my pleasure. It's just sitting there gathering dust at the house. Dad never even goes into my room anymore, and Brad and Sam use his old bedroom when they visit. By the way, how did you talk Mark into letting you borrow his new van to haul everything?"

He grinned again. "I told you. Charm." When she shook her head and laughed, he sent her a crushed look. "I think I'm insulted," he declared, feigning indignation. "Are you implying that I lack charm?"

On the contrary, she thought, eyeing his strong profile as he turned his attention back to the road. The man had plenty of charm. In fact, it oozed out of every pore in his body.

"No-o-o," she replied with exaggerated thoughtfulness. "I guess not."

"Well, don't be so enthusiastic in your denial," he retorted wryly, then turned to her with a grin. "Speaking of charm, you must have used some yourself to get Rose and Frances to agree to handle the lunch crowd this afternoon."

"They offered," she told him. "Since we didn't leave till noon, most of the prep work was done. It's mostly just a matter of serving and cleanup, and they said they didn't mind." Actually, they'd said a whole lot more, Rebecca thought, a flush rising to her cheeks. At least half a dozen times this morning they'd reminded her to give "that nice young man," as they referred to Zach, some encouragement, waving her off and telling her to have a good time when she left. Even though she'd explained the businesslike purpose of their trip—twice—she knew the sisters remained unconvinced, certain that *Zach's* purpose was romance.

Actually, since the night of their dinner, romance seemed to be the *last* thing on Zach's mind, she reflected. He was attentive and considerate, but she noticed that he not only kept their conversations impersonal and lighthearted, he kept his distance as well. Which was fine with her. She felt safer this way. And she'd actually begun to enjoy their congenial, teasing banter. If the gleam of romantic interest in his eyes had dimmed, she was grateful. Wasn't she?

"So what did your dad say about this?"

Her glance returned to Zach, and she forced her attention back to the conversation. "He thought it was a very nice thing for you to do," she replied. He'd also asked far too many questions about Zach, which Rebecca had sidestepped as much as possible, telling her father only that Zach was an acquaintance she was helping strictly out of Christian charity. She wasn't sure her father bought that explanation, but at least he'd eventually stopped quizzing her. Either he'd lost interest, she'd convinced him, or he was biding his time. Knowing her father, however, she had a sinking feeling it was the latter. He'd always had a propensity for prying into the lives of his children, though always with the best intentions. Maybe she had better warn Zach to expect the third degree.

"Um, Zach, one thing about my father. He's a great guy and all, but...well, he tends to ask a lot of questions, and I haven't brought many men to the house through the years, even for an innocent reason like this, so he's apt to jump to a few wrong conclusions and…probe…a little. I just don't want you to be surprised.''

"You mean he's going to ask me about my intentions?" Zach teased her.

"Well, I don't think he'll be quite that direct," she replied, color stealing onto her cheeks.

"So what do you want me to tell him?" Zach asked easily.

She looked at him in surprise. "The truth, of course," she replied. "That we're friends, and I'm just helping you out in an emergency. I've already told him that myself, but he gets these ideas into his head and…" Her voice trailed off and she shrugged helplessly.

"Hmm," was Zach's only reply.

Rebecca squirmed uncomfortably, suddenly suspecting that her explanation for Zach's intentions was way too simplistic. But it was the only one she wanted to deal with at the moment.

Fortunately he didn't pursue the subject, and by the time they pulled into the driveway of the two-story frame house with the lattice-trimmed front porch, she was feeling more relaxed again.

"On a day like this Dad's probably in the garden, getting everything ready for spring," she informed Zach, opening her door and sliding to the ground as soon as the van stopped. "I'll let him know we're here."

"Okay." Zach got out more leisurely, watching as Rebecca disappeared around the side of the house, her snug jeans hugging her narrow waist, slim hips and long, shapely legs. Her hair was in its customary French twist today, but for a moment he allowed himself to imagine how it would look cascading down her back. Then he jammed his hands into the pockets of his jeans with a frown. Now was not the best time to be having those kinds of thoughts, he told himself sternly.

He followed Rebecca slowly, reminding himself of the resolution he'd made to bide his time. Now that she had agreed to help with Isabel, he had weeks ahead to woo her, to slowly build her comfort level. He just needed to be patient. Except patience had never been his strong suit, he admitted wryly. But he knew time and patience were the essential ingredients in a successful campaign to win this woman's confidence, and he was determined to give her both. Even it if killed him. Which it very well might, he thought ruefully, as he rounded the corner of the house and another surge of desire swept over him at the sight of her slender, appealing figure.

She was talking animatedly to a spare, wiry man with fine gray hair and a slightly angular nose, who was leaning on a shovel. As Zach made his way toward them, the man glanced his way, said something quietly to Rebecca, then laid down the shovel.

Rebecca turned as Zach joined them. "Dad, this is Zach Wright. Zach, my father."

The older man, who was several inches shorter than Zach, wiped his hand on his slacks, then held it out. Zach took it in a firm grip as their eyes connected, and Rebecca's father gave him a shrewd, assessing look, which Zach returned steadily. When the older man smiled at last, Zach had an odd feeling that he'd just passed some sort of test.

"It's nice to meet you, Mr. Matthews," Zach said.

"Call me Henry. Makes me feel younger. And I'm pleased to meet you, too," he replied cordially.

"We don't want to keep you from your garden, Dad. We'll just go up and sort things out."

"Garden will always be here," he replied with a dismissive wave. "But I don't get that many visitors. Besides, I'd like to get to know your young man a little while you're here."

Rebecca's face turned beet red, but Zach just grinned, proprietarily draping an arm around her shoulders as he spoke. "I'd like to get to know you better, too, Henry."

Rebecca shot him a startled look at the unexpected gesture, shrugging off his arm as she spoke. "This isn't a social visit, Dad. We just want to pick up the furniture."

"That won't take long. Zach and I will have it loaded in no time. I thought you'd at least have time for a glass of lemonade and some German apple spice cake. I picked one up at the bakery this morning."

"That does sound good," Zach injected hopefully before Rebecca could refuse, as he suspected she was inclined to do.

She planted her hands on her hips and stared from one man to the other. "Why do I have a feeling there's a conspiracy here?"

"Oh, come on, Rebecca. We can spare half an hour to visit. We'll get back in plenty of time. What do you say?" Zach cajoled. He sensed an ally in Henry, and he intended to use that to his advantage with Rebecca.

With a sigh of capitulation, she gave in. Arguing the point would only make her father even more inquisitive. "Okay. Fine."

"Good, good," Henry approved heartily. "You two go on up and decide what you want to take. I'll just wash my hands and follow you in."

Rebecca strode silently toward the house and up the stairs, turning to face Zach with an accusatory frown when they entered her childhood bedroom. "Why did you do that?" she demanded, keeping her voice low and a watchful eye out for her father.

"Do what?" Zach asked innocently.

"Put your arm around my shoulders."

He shrugged, giving her a bewildered look. "It just seemed

like a...friendly...thing to do. After all, we are friends, aren't we? That's what you told your father.''

She eyed him suspiciously, suspecting an ulterior motive. But he *looked* sincere. ''That's not the way my dad will interpret it. I told you, he jumps to conclusions.''

''Stop worrying, Rebecca,'' Zach chided her gently. ''Your father seems like a reasonable man. I'm sure his perceptive powers are right on target.''

That's what she was afraid of, she thought in dismay, as she turned to fold up the bedspread. She wasn't exactly sure of Zach's feelings at this point. But she was very sure of her own. She liked this man. A lot. Despite the disastrous end to their date, she was still attracted to him. And she had a feeling her father knew it, whether Zach did or not.

''Are you sure you don't mind, Rebecca? I hate to ask, but I'm all thumbs with a needle and thread.''

''No problem, Dad.'' Rebecca reached for the suit coat and inspected the spot where the lining had come loose. ''This will only take a few minutes.''

''Thanks, honey. Listen, Zach, while Rebecca takes care of that, why don't I give you a tour of my garden?''

''I'd like that,'' Zach replied, depositing his lemonade glass on the wicker table and rising to his feet.

Rebecca glanced up from her seat on the porch swing and gave her father a suspicious look. ''There's not much to see yet, Dad.''

''The perennials are all coming up,'' he replied promptly. ''And Zach strikes me as a man with imagination. I bet he'll be able to picture what I describe.''

She watched them walk down the porch steps, conversing companionably, and frowned. She fervently hoped her father was talking about flowers.

"So you're taking charge of a little girl, I hear," Henry remarked as he led the way toward the rose garden.

"That's right."

"Mighty nice thing to do."

"Josef, her father, is like a brother to me. Considering the situation over there and the loss of his wife, it's the least I can do."

"Pretty bad in some of those places, from what I see on the news."

"I can't even imagine living like that," Zach remarked, shaking his head.

They paused on the edge of the rose garden. "I've got thirty-two bushes," Henry said proudly, nodding toward the bed. "Quite a sight in the summer when they're in full bloom."

"Must be impressive," Zach concurred. "I don't think I've ever seen thirty-two bushes all in one place, except at Shaw's Garden."

Henry beamed with pride at the comparison to St. Louis's well-known botanical garden. "Sam was surprised when I told her how many I had, too," he recalled with a chuckle. "Sam's my daughter-in-law. Married to my son, Brad. They just had a little girl."

"So I hear. Which makes you a proud grandpa now, I guess."

He nodded vigorously, his eyes sparkling with enthusiasm. "Cutest little thing you ever saw. Big blue eyes and a fuzz of the softest reddish hair. Gonna be a carrottop, like Sam, I suspect."

"They sound like a nice family."

"They are," he confirmed. "Course, I never thought it would happen. Brad was married before, you know. First wife died years ago. A real tragedy,'' he reflected, shaking his head. ''I didn't figure he'd remarry. You ever been married, Zach?''

Henry didn't waste any time, Zach thought in amusement, suppressing a chuckle. ''No. Never found the time. Or the right woman.''

''Hmm,'' Henry ruminated. ''Seems to me like you have to *make* time for some things. Course, you can't be too careful. You sure don't want to make a mistake, pick the wrong partner. That's what I always tell Rebecca. Not that she seems to be looking, anyway. Always been kinda prickly around men.''

''I noticed,'' Zach admitted. ''I wonder why?''

''Can't say,'' Henry replied, shaking his head. ''Always wondered about that myself. She's a fine woman. Make someone a good wife. But seems like she needs special handling. Sort of like a skittish colt. Gotta approach her gentle-like, let her get comfortable around you. No sudden moves to spook her, you know what I mean?''

Zach stifled a smile, not at all sure Rebecca would appreciate being compared to a horse. But he got the drift of Henry's comment. And it confirmed the conclusion he'd already come to. ''I think you're right. Reminds me of that old saying—good things come to those who wait.''

Henry turned and looked up at Zach, placing a hand on the younger man's shoulder as he gazed at him appraisingly. ''I know waiting can be hard sometimes,'' he acknowledged. ''I was young once myself. But some things are worth it.'' He dropped his hand and nodded back to the porch. ''Looks like Rebecca's done with that jacket. Let's head on back.''

As they waved goodbye to Henry a few minutes later and climbed into the van for the trip home, Rebecca turned to Zach curiously. ''What did you two talk about, out there in the garden?''

He chuckled. "Let's just say your dad missed his calling. He'd have made a great investigative reporter."

Rebecca bit her lip and frowned. That's what she'd been afraid of.

Chapter Seven

Rebecca scanned the crowd emerging from the plane's exit ramp, her heart pounding in her chest, her palms clammy. What on earth had she gotten herself into? she wondered in silent panic. When she'd offered to help Zach with Isabel, her heart had certainly been in the right place. But what did she know about taking care of a child? Especially a child who was not only grieving, but had just been sent to live with strangers in an unfamiliar land! She could be in way over her head here. Suddenly, without even consciously realizing what she was doing, Rebecca reached for Zach's hand, seeking courage in the strength and comfort of his touch.

He looked down at her in surprise, hesitating for only the briefest second before willingly enfolding her seeking hand in his warm clasp. "This is pretty scary, isn't it?" he empathized, as if reading her mind.

She looked up at him with a worried frown. "Honestly? Yes."

He gave her hand an encouraging squeeze. "Well, if it makes you feel any better, I'm just as nervous as you are," he admitted.

"Zach—I just thought of something!" Rebecca exclaimed in sudden alarm. "Does Isabel speak English?"

He smiled reassuringly. "Yes. That's one problem we won't have to deal with. Josef is fluent, and he made sure Isabel was bilingual."

Relief flooded her eyes. "Thank goodness! I don't know why I didn't think about that before!"

"You've had a few other things on your mind. Like running a restaurant and decorating a little girl's room. Quite charmingly, I might add," he said with a smile.

Rebecca smiled as she thought about the way she'd transformed the bare, sterile bedroom in Zach's apartment, hanging frilly lace curtains at the window to complement the pale pink eyelet bedspread, decorating the walls with colorful posters from popular animated children's movies, and attaching fanciful mobiles to the ceiling. She'd even brought along her favorite music box from childhood, a statue of Cinderella that played "Someday My Prince Will Come," to decorate the top of the dresser. "I just hope she likes it."

"I can't imagine any little girl who wouldn't."

As the last of the passengers disembarked, a stewardess appeared in the doorway holding the hand of a petite dark-haired child who was clutching a very raggedy Raggedy Ann doll. Zach drew a deep breath and gave Rebecca's hand another encouraging squeeze. "We're on," he said.

In the brief seconds it took to reach the pair, Rebecca studied Isabel. She wore a pink sweater and a pink and beige striped skirt, and her white ankle socks were edged with lace. Rebecca had a feeling that Josef had dressed his daughter in her "Sunday best" for the trip. Her hair was parted in the middle, pulled up and back on each side, and secured with a pink ribbon that had probably started out crisp but now lay limp and bedraggled. She was smaller than Rebecca expected, pale and thin and delicately boned, and she looked bleary-eyed from fatigue, which wasn't surprising, given the length of her trip and the emotional trauma she had endured.

Isabel watched them approach with large, solemn eyes, looking very much like a little girl who was frightened but trying mightily to be brave, and Rebecca's heart ached for her. As soon as she reached her side, Rebecca dropped to one knee while Zach talked with the stewardess.

"Hello, Isabel," she said softly, giving the waiflike little girl a warm smile. "I'm Rebecca. Zach and I are so glad you came to visit us. Is this Raggedy Ann?" She reached over and touched the obviously much-loved doll.

Isabel nodded. "She's tired now."

"I'm sure she is," Rebecca sympathized with a nod. "It was a long trip, wasn't it?"

"Yes. My papa's far away now, isn't he?" A tremor ran through her voice and her eyes filled with tears.

Rebecca's throat contracted, and she reached over to gently smooth some wayward strands of hair back from the wan little face. "Not if you keep him in your heart," she replied gently.

"That's what he said about my mama, too."

Rebecca swallowed with difficulty. "He's right. The people we love are always with us in our hearts."

Zach knelt down beside Rebecca then, and he smiled at Isabel. "I guess you don't remember me, do you, Isabel?"

Silently she shook her head. "I was just a baby when I saw you the last time," she pointed out matter-of-factly. "But my papa told me all about you. He and my mama talked about you a lot. And I liked the presents you sent me for my birthdays."

"Well, it seems you like that one especially," he noted, reaching out to touch the Raggedy Ann doll he'd sent her two years ago.

She nodded. "I do." She tilted her head and looked at him quizzically. "Are you really my uncle?" she asked suddenly.

"Is that what your papa told you?"

She frowned. "He tried to explain it to me. He said you were his friend, but really more like a brother, so that made you my uncle."

Zach cleared his throat, and when he spoke there was an odd catch in his voice. "That's right."

"So should I call you Uncle Zach?"

"That would be fine."

Isabel turned to Rebecca with a puzzled frown. "But you're not my aunt, are you?"

"No. I'd like to be your friend, though."

"Can I call you Rebecca, then?"

"I think that would be just right."

"Well, why don't we collect your luggage, and then we can all go home?" Zach suggested, standing up.

Rebecca rose, as well, then reached down and took Isabel's hand, giving it a reassuring squeeze. "That's a good idea. Raggedy Ann is tired," she told Zach with a wink. "It's past her bedtime."

By the time they collected Isabel's two suitcases, made their way to the car and buckled the little girl into the back seat, she was fading fast. Her eyes kept drifting shut, though she was trying hard to stay awake.

As Zach slid behind the wheel he glanced back at his new charge. "Are you hungry, Isabel?" he asked.

"No."

He looked at Rebecca, raising an eyebrow quizzically.

"How about a hamburger?" Rebecca suggested, with sudden inspiration.

"A hamburger?" Isabel echoed, her interest piqued. "My papa told me about American hamburgers. He said they were good."

"Well, why don't we let you decide for yourself?" Zach replied.

Fifteen minutes later, as Isabel polished off the hamburger and fries from the drive-through fast-food restaurant, Zach grinned at Rebecca. "Good idea," he complimented her in a low voice.

"Sheer luck," she said with a small smile. "I figured she needed to eat. But actually—" she glanced toward the back seat, in time to catch Isabel yawning hugely "—I think she's more exhausted than anything else. Talk about a day of emotional overload! She just needs to go to bed."

"I appreciate your offer to keep her overnight tonight," Zach said. "I wish I had one more day before school started, but that's just not how things worked out."

"I don't mind," Rebecca assured him. "I'm off, and it will give us a chance to become acquainted. I'll get her unpacked and settled in at your place, too, if you like."

He sent her a grateful look. "That would be great! I'll give you my spare key before I leave tonight."

Rebecca glanced out the window, trying to work up the courage to ask her next question. She'd been thinking about it ever since they decided she would keep Isabel the first night. "Um, Zach, I was wondering...since you'll probably be tired after your first day at school, and not in the mood to cook...well, Isabel does need to have balanced meals, you know, so I...I wondered if you might want to come over for dinner tomorrow night."

He turned to look at her, but she kept her face averted and he couldn't discern her expression in the darkness. To say he was surprised at the invitation was an understatement. But he was also immensely pleased—and touched. "That would be wonderful, Rebecca," he replied, his voice tinged with that husky timbre she found so appealing. "But I feel like I've imposed too much already. Besides, the last thing you need to do on your day off is cook."

"I don't mind, really," she assured him quickly. "And it would probably be good for Isabel to sit down to a nice meal with us her first night in town. It would make her feel more at home and welcome than if you two just grab a bite on the run."

Was concern for Isabel Rebecca's only motivation for the invitation? Zach suddenly wondered with a frown. He tried to read her expression, but again the darkness was her ally. Whatever her motivation, however, she'd made the offer, and he wasn't about to look a gift horse in the mouth. "Well, if you're sure you don't mind."

"Not at all."

"Okay. And thank you. For everything."

Rebecca felt a tingle run down her spine at the intimate tone in his voice. If he was willing to come for dinner, he must not be holding her bizarre behavior the night of their date against her, she thought in relief, saying a silent prayer of thanks. And a "family" type dinner would be good for Isabel. But Rebecca was honest enough to admit that her motives weren't entirely altruistic. Deep in her heart she thought the dinner would be good for her, too. It would give her a chance to be with Zach in a safe, comfortable environment, with Isabel acting almost like a chaperone. And maybe, if she got accustomed to being with him in that kind of setting, without all the pressures incumbent on "dating," she might eventually feel comfortable enough to give a romantic relationship one more try.

If he was willing to take a second shot at it. And that, of course, was a big *if,* she knew. He said he still liked her. But *like* and *attraction* were two different things, she realized. She just hoped she hadn't killed the latter by her performance the other night. But only time would tell.

When Rebecca opened the door in answer to Zach's ring the next night, her eyes widened in surprise at the bouquet of pink tulips, daffodils and baby's breath that he held out to her.

"I thought you might like these," he said with a disarming grin. "You mentioned once that you enjoyed gardening, so I figured you must like flowers."

She reached for the bouquet, smiling in pleasure even as she protested. "Oh, Zach, this is too extravagant!"

"Hardly. Consider it a thank-you for dinner—and for everything you're doing to help with Isabel."

"Well...thank you," she said, a delicate flush tinting her cheeks. "Come on in. Dinner's almost ready."

"Can I do anything to help?" he asked as he followed her inside.

"No, thanks. Isabel and I took care of everything, didn't we, sweetie?"

Isabel looked up from the table, which she was setting with great precision and care. "Yes. We're having spaghetti," she informed Zach.

"Mmm. That sounds good."

"I haven't had spaghetti before, but Rebecca says I'll like it," she informed him.

"I think Rebecca is right."

Half an hour later, after watching her demolish a salad, a hearty helping of spaghetti and four pieces of garlic bread, Zach turned to her with a chuckle. "So what did you think?"

She considered the matter seriously. "I think Rebecca cooks real good."

Zach smiled. "I'll second that."

Rebecca's face flushed at the compliments, and she stood up to clear the table. "Well, I'd say it's time for some brownies," she remarked. "Isabel helped me make them," she informed Zach over her shoulder as she headed toward the kitchen to put on the coffee.

"I didn't know you knew how to cook, Isabel," Zach said in mock surprise, turning to the little girl.

"I'm not very good yet," she replied seriously. "But Rebecca said she'd teach me. She has a restaurant, you know."

"Yes, I know."

"She's also very nice," she added in a conspiratorial whisper, leaning close.

"I know that, too," he replied, also lowering his voice. "And I know something else. See that bag over there by the door? I think there's something in it for you."

She looked at him wide-eyed. "For me?"

"Uh-huh. Why don't you go over and take a look?"

She jumped up and scampered toward the door, peeking into

the bag eagerly, her eyes lighting up as she withdrew a video of a popular animated children's film. "Is this really for me?"

"It sure is."

She hugged it to her chest, her eyes awed. "Oh, thank you, Uncle Zach. Can I watch it now?"

Zach sent a quizzical look to Rebecca, who was depositing the plate of brownies on the table.

"Well, if your Uncle Zach says it's okay, I guess you can take your brownie into the living room just this once."

"Can I, Uncle Zach?"

"I don't see why not," he agreed. "I'll get it started for you."

By the time he returned to the table, Rebecca had poured their coffee and was sipping hers leisurely. "That was a nice thing to do."

He glanced at the small figure, already enthralled with the video. "I just feel so sorry for her," he admitted helplessly. "I know you shouldn't spoil children, but she's had such a tough time I didn't figure a few indulgences would hurt."

"I agree."

"So how did it go today?"

"That was going to be my next question for you," she replied with a smile.

"You first."

"She slept like a log last night, which I expected. We had pancakes for breakfast, went over and met Ben, stopped for burgers at lunch, then went to your place and got her settled in."

"I bet she liked the room."

Rebecca smiled, a flush of pleasure stealing over her cheeks. "Yes, she did. In fact, she asked me if I could come over tonight and tuck her in. I...I didn't think you'd mind, this first night," she said, her eyes anxious and uncertain as they met his.

He reached over and covered her hand with his, his eyes tinged with an intimate warmth that made her tingle all over as they locked on hers. "Rebecca, you are always welcome at our place."

She blushed and looked down, toying with her spoon as she surreptitiously looked at his tanned, lean-fingered hand covering hers. She liked his touch—a lot—in this no-risk setting. Maybe she could eventually learn to enjoy it when they were alone, as well. But in the meantime it was better to move on to safer subjects. "So tell me about your day," she prompted.

He removed his hand, and she missed his touch immediately. "It was good. But a bit overwhelming," he admitted. "The academic world is very different from what I'm used to. I'm glad Phil Carr filled me in a little. And I picked up quite a bit in the teachers' lounge, too. Everyone was very nice and went out of their way to be helpful."

"How were the kids?"

"A little wary. Scoping out the new teacher, getting the lay of the land. But they seem like good kids—in general."

"Why the qualifier?"

He frowned and took a sip of his coffee. "I'm teaching a creative writing class, and I had one kid who didn't turn in the homework. I mentioned his name in the lounge, and it seems he's somewhat of a troublemaker. Rarely does his homework, so his grades are marginal. But he aces out on tests, so he's obviously bright. It's a shame for potential like that to be wasted."

Rebecca frowned. "What's his name?"

"Pete Cramer."

She shook her heard slowly. "Doesn't ring a bell."

"I got the impression that he comes from a broken home. Lives with his father, I think, who works at the plant."

"Maybe no one's ever really encouraged him," Rebecca speculated.

"How do you mean?"

She gazed at him earnestly. "Well, if someone took a real interest in him, *made* him do the work, he might blossom."

Zach frowned. "How do you *make* a seventeen-year-old boy do anything?"

"Long-term I guess it's a matter of finding a way to make him *want* to do it," she said thoughtfully. "In the meantime, though, some discipline might do the trick."

He gave her a rueful grin. "Not a popular word in this day and age."

"Maybe not," she agreed. "But being an authority figure isn't always a popularity contest," she pointed out. "I really believe that even though kids may *act* like they resent discipline, they respect it when it's administered by someone who is genuinely concerned about them. And I also think it boosts their self-esteem to know that someone cares enough to take that kind of interest."

Thoughtfully he took a sip of his coffee and eyed her speculatively. "You could be right."

"Well, I certainly don't have any great experience to draw on," she admitted. "But it might be helpful to be firm and set the rules right up front."

"I'll give that some thought," he promised, before turning the conversation to less serious topics.

By the time the video ended, Isabel's eyelids were drooping, and Zach glanced at Rebecca with a smile. "I think it's somebody's bedtime."

"It will take her several days to get over the jet lag," Rebecca replied sympathetically. "I'll just follow you home and get her settled for the night."

An hour later, as Rebecca leaned down to hug Isabel's thin shoulders and place a kiss on her forehead, the little girl clutched at her hand, her eyes wide and imploring.

"Couldn't you stay tonight?" she pleaded.

Rebecca regretfully shook her head. "I'm afraid not, Isabel. This is Zach's apartment."

"I bet he wouldn't mind if you stayed," she tried again, her bottom lip starting to quiver.

Would he? she wondered wistfully, then quickly squelched

that wayward thought. "But I don't live here, Isabel," she gently reminded the little girl. "I'll see you in the morning, though. Zach will drop you off at the restaurant on his way to school."

"I...I miss my m-mama," Isabel said in a barely audible voice that was tinged with tears, gripping her Raggedy Ann doll fiercely.

With difficulty, Rebecca swallowed past the lump in her throat. "I know, sweetie."

"My papa says I have to be brave and not be sad, because now Mama is with God and she's happy and well again. But I still miss her."

"My mama is with God, too," Rebecca told Isabel, once more hugging her close. "And I still miss her every day, just like you miss your mama. But try not to be sad. I'm sure your mama would want you to be happy. You still have your papa, who loves you very much. And now you have Uncle Zach and me, too."

"W-will you stay till I f-fall asleep?"

"Of course I will. I'll even sing you a little song, how would that be?"

Rebecca didn't know any children's lullabies, so she chose a familiar hymn instead. By the time she sang it through twice, Isabel had drifted off, too worn out to stay awake, despite her best efforts. Gently Rebecca extricated her hand, and once more lightly brushed her lips across Isabel's forehead before rising.

Zach was waiting on the couch in the living room when she emerged, but he'd discreetly eavesdropped on the scene in the bedroom a couple of times. He'd heard enough to realize that Isabel was both homesick and grieving. And enough for his heart to be touched by Rebecca's tender, compassionate interaction with the frightened little girl. He wasn't surprised at the sheen of tears in her eyes when she finally appeared.

"Pretty tough situation for a little kid," he commiserated.

"Yeah." She blinked rapidly, trying to compose herself.

"It's hard sometimes to understand why the Lord lets things like this happen."

"It's not just hard, it's impossible," Zach replied, a touch of bitterness in his voice.

"I guess that's true," she admitted. "But it's because we're trying to understand with our finite human intellect. It's almost a sin of pride to even suppose we could understand the ways of God."

"So you just accept everything?"

"Is there any other choice?" she asked quietly.

Zach rose and strode over to the window, staring out into the darkness just as he had the night he received Josef's letter. He jammed his hands into his pockets and sighed. "You sound a lot like Josef. He always accepted everything that happened as the Lord's will, even when he didn't see the reason for it. I guess that's what faith is all about."

"That's part of it, anyway," she concurred.

He continued to stare out into the darkness for a few moments, his brow knit pensively, but finally he expelled a long, weary breath and reached up to massage the back of his neck with one hand. "Listen, I want to thank you for coming over to get Isabel settled, Rebecca. You seem to have acquired an avid fan. I only hope I'll be as lucky." His tone was less than confident as he cast a worried glance toward the half-shut bedroom door.

"You will," she replied reassuringly. It would be hard for anyone not to like Zach, she thought silently—adult or child.

"I E-mailed Josef last night to let him know she arrived, so maybe at least now he'll have some peace of mind."

"That reminds me." Rebecca rose, speaking over her shoulder as she walked toward the coat closet. "I found something you need to see when I was unpacking Isabel's suitcases." She opened the door and withdrew a bulky parcel from the top shelf. "There's a letter taped to it that's addressed to both of us," she told him as she handed over the package and they sat down on the couch. "I was surprised to see my name on it. Did you mention me to Josef?" she asked quizzically.

He'd done a lot more than that, Zach reflected. Josef and he always shared important events in their lives, and meeting Rebecca certainly fell into that category.

"Yeah. I thought it might make Josef feel better to know that a woman would also be watching over Isabel." Which was true. But he'd mentioned Rebecca to Josef long before this situation came up. "Why don't we read it together?" he suggested.

He carefully pulled the white envelope free, then slit it open. As he unfolded the single sheet of paper, Rebecca scooted closer, and the room became silent as they both scanned the contents.

My Dear Zachary and Rebecca,

I address this note to you both because it seems you will share in the care of my precious Isabel. Rebecca, even though we have never met, I feel I know you from Zachary's letters. I am grateful that such a fine, generous and loving woman will be helping watch over my daughter, and I thank you most sincerely for your kindness. Since she just lost her mother, it will be good for Isabel to have a woman's care and special touch.

Zachary, this package is only to be opened in the event something happens to me while Isabel is with you. Otherwise, please return it unopened when Isabel comes home to me. Remember how you always used to tease me about being "buttoned down" when we were in school, about never leaving any loose ends hanging? (See? I have not forgotten my American slang!) Well, I am still that way, planning ahead for all possibilities.

My dear friends—and I now count you among those, Rebecca—I will never be able to repay the great favor you are doing for me. I send you my heartfelt thanks and eternal gratitude. Please know that in the weeks ahead you will be prominently in my prayers. And I ask that you keep me in yours as well. God bless you both.

Rebecca blinked back her tears as she finished reading the note, and Zach's ragged sigh told her he was equally moved. If Isabel's small hand so trustingly placed in hers at the airport yesterday had dispelled most of the doubts Rebecca harbored about the wisdom of her offer, this note banished any that lingered. For reasons of His own, the Lord had put her in a position to offer assistance to this traumatized family. Maybe she wasn't the best-qualified person for the job. She certainly didn't have any experience with children. But she did have a great capacity to love, and perhaps that, more than anything, was what was needed in this situation.

Rebecca thought again about the tragedy and heartbreak endured by the grieving, vulnerable child who now slept peacefully in the next room and by her loving father, driven to extreme measures by their desperate plight, and her heart ached. She couldn't even imagine how difficult it must have been for Josef to put his child, who meant more to him than anything else in the world, on that plane and send her thousands of miles away. His sacrifice was a true measure of the depth of his love, and Rebecca vowed to do everything in her power to give Isabel the comfort and love and stability she so badly needed.

Slowly Zach folded the letter and silently replaced it in the envelope. Rebecca studied his profile, the familiar elements of strength, character and integrity now underlaid with pain, sadness and worry. She had never been blessed with a friendship like Zach's and Josef's, but she realized that the ties that bound them truly were stronger than blood. Strong enough for Zach to feel Josef's pain almost as keenly as if it was his own. Her instinct was to reach over and comfort him, to lay a gentle hand on his arm, but she was afraid to initiate even such an innocent touch. So she let her hands rest motionless in her lap.

As if sensing her scrutiny, Zach turned to look into her

sympathetic eyes. "I wish there was—" He stopped to clear his throat. "I wish there was more I could do."

"You're doing everything you can, Zach," she consoled him.

He glanced back at the package in his lap. "Yeah, I guess so," he replied wearily.

"Josef did ask for our prayers. That's something else you could do," she offered quietly.

He shook his head. "I think I'll have to let you do the praying for both of us, Rebecca. I'm sure God will be more likely to listen to a firm believer like you than a wayward soul like me. I haven't prayed with any real conviction in six or seven years."

"It's not too late to start again," she reminded him softly, wishing he would. Because she had a feeling that if he did, much of the restlessness, the searching, she sensed in him would ease.

"It is tonight. I'm beat. It's been a long day for you, too. We both ought to just go to bed."

At another time, under different circumstances, Rebecca might have sensed an innuendo in that remark. But not tonight. It was a simple statement of fact, and judging by the lines of fatigue on his face, Zach really was all in. She was fading fast herself. "You're right," she agreed, rising to retrieve her purse. "I'd better take off."

Zach rose and followed her to the door, still subdued. As she turned to say good-night, she wanted to reach over and smooth the twin furrows in his brow, which spoke more eloquently than words of his troubled thoughts and deep concern. But again she held back.

"Good night, Zach," she said softly.

"I'll walk you to your car."

"I'm right here." She pointed to her older-model car just steps from his door.

"Oh. Well, I guess I'll see you tomorrow morning, then. Is eight-thirty okay? My first class is at nine."

"That's fine. And don't worry about breakfast for Isabel. I'll give her something when you drop her off."

"Are you sure?"

"Absolutely. I'll be cooking, anyway. And Zach," she paused and glanced down shyly. "Thanks again for the flowers."

He smiled, and the concern in his eyes gave way to an intimate warmth that made her pulse take a sudden leap. "I'm glad you liked them."

She looked up at him, her eyes suddenly filled with a wistful yearning that he knew she wasn't even aware of. It made him want to pull her into his arms, to let his lips say good-night in a way that expressed more clearly than words both his gratitude for her support during this difficult time, as well as the depth of his attraction to her. Somehow, the latter had been relegated to the back burner in the past week as they'd both prepared for Isabel's arrival and he'd prepped for his new job. But he didn't intend for it to stay there much longer. Now that he'd settled into his apartment, started his job and Isabel had safely arrived, he could turn his attention back to the most important thing in his life at the moment. Rebecca.

Except that he still needed to be patient and move slowly, he reminded himself, recalling Henry's sound words of advice. So though his hands longed to pull her close, he stuck them into the pockets of his slacks instead and drew a long, shaky breath. "Drive safely, okay?"

With difficulty, she pulled her gaze away from the compelling intensity of his eyes. "Sure. It's not like I have far to go." She tried for a joking tone, but her voice sounded breathless.

"Will you call me when you get there?"

She looked at him in surprise. "Why?"

"I'll just feel better knowing you're home safe and sound."

She was touched by his concern, and a flush tinted her cheeks. "If you want me to," she agreed. "Good night."

As she turned and walked away, her heart felt lighter than

it had in years. For the first time ever, she had a man in her
life who cared about her and a child who needed her. The
circumstances weren't exactly what she'd imagined years ago,
when she'd dreamed of a husband and family. But it felt good
nonetheless. And right.

Rebecca knew this idyll was only going to last a few weeks.
But she resolved to make the most of her time with this special
man and charming child. And when it was over…well, for
once in her life she would follow Scarlett O'Hara's advice.
She would worry about that tomorrow.

Chapter Eight

Zach wasn't sure what woke him in the predawn hours. A noise of some sort, he assumed, listening as intently as he could manage in his half-comatose state. But the apartment was absolutely still. With a sigh he turned on his side and hitched the sheet up higher on his bare chest, drifting back to sleep even as he did so. But he was still awake enough to feel the sudden slight jolt, almost as if someone had bumped into his unfolded sleeper sofa bed.

His eyes snapped open and he rose on one elbow, squinting into the dimness as he made a rapid three-hundred-and-sixty-degree scan around the bed. But there was nothing. He frowned. How bizarre! Could that gentle shake, almost like a nudge, have been caused by an earth tremor? he wondered. He knew this area was prone to them. Yet somehow he felt that wasn't the explanation.

Perplexed, he glanced down at the floor—and got his first clue. A blanket trailed along the floor, disappearing from his sight as it reached the bed. He inched closer to the edge and cautiously looked down, his throat contracting at the sight that met his eyes.

Isabel was curled into a ball on the floor, wedged as close

as possible next to the bed, her doll clutched to her chest. One bare foot peeked out from beneath the trailing blanket, and even as he watched she scooted closer still to the couch, making it vibrate ever so slightly.

Zach didn't have any experience with children. Had never *wanted* to have any. The idea of being responsible for some little person who was totally dependent had never appealed to him. But the pathetic sight of this tiny, frightened child seeking the comfort of mere human proximity just about did him in.

Moving with extreme care so as not to disturb her, he swung his feet to the floor, then bent down and scooped her up, cradling the reed-thin body in his arms. There was nothing to her, he thought in shock, her featherlike weight hardly registering. She felt like…like a wisp, and he was once again struck by her vulnerability. Isabel whimpered slightly, and he held her closer, instinctively rocking her gently in his arms, murmuring soothing sounds as he made his way back to her room. But when he tried to lay her down, her thin little arms snaked around his neck and she held on fiercely, showing remarkable strength for someone so tiny. Short of prying her arms away—and waking her up in the process—there wasn't much choice but to take her back to bed with him, he realized.

He retraced his route, easing himself down and stretching out carefully, Isabel still in his arms. She burrowed next to him as he pulled up the sheet and blanket, and as he looked down at the tiny body so trustingly cuddled against his, his heart was filled with tenderness. It was funny, really. He'd spent his life avoiding commitments that involved women and children. He'd always believed that they would be too demanding, that they would distract him from the really important things in life—like his work. But since arriving in St. Genevieve, he'd been forced to rethink that opinion, reexamine his priorities. He now had a woman *and* a child in his life, both of whom seemed achingly vulnerable and so in need of love. This little one in his arms was totally dependent on him.

And Rebecca...well, she didn't need him in the sense Isabel did, to provide food and shelter and the day-to-day necessities of life. But she seemed to need him in other ways. He'd come to the conclusion that for reasons he had not yet discovered, her heart was being held prisoner. But he also believed that it yearned to be free. He could see it in the wistful longing reflected in her eyes. Somehow he felt the key to her freedom was in his hands, that if he was patient he would find a way to release her captive heart.

And so, in different ways, he felt responsible for both Rebecca and Isabel. That sense of responsibility to another person was never something he'd wanted. But the odd thing was, now that he had it, he *liked* it. Caring about them, being committed to their well-being, didn't seem like a burden at all. It seemed like a gift. Because both of these special ladies had already enriched his life in countless ways.

"Pete...I'd like to see you for a minute."

The tall, lanky youth looked at Zach nervously, then shot a glance at his buddies, who were waiting in the hall. Zach noted the direction of his gaze, and as the last student filed out of his classroom, he very deliberately moved over to the door and firmly closed it.

"I have to go or I'll miss my ride," the boy said, trying for defiance but not quite pulling it off.

"How far away do you live?" Zach asked, keeping his tone casual.

"About three miles."

"No problem. I'll take you home when we're finished."

"Finished with what?" the boy asked suspiciously.

"Let me ask you something, Pete," Zach replied, ignoring the question as he propped a shoulder against the door and folded his arms across his chest. "Why did you take this class?"

Pete stared at him. "What do you mean?"

"Why did you take this class?" Zach repeated.

The boy shrugged. "It sounded better than another year of English lit."

"You did realize that in a creative writing class you'd be expected to write, didn't you?"

He gave Zach a sullen look, but remained silent.

Zach held his gaze steadily, and finally Pete's wavered, dropping to the floor as he shoved his hands in his pockets and shifted nervously from one foot to the other.

"I'll tell you what," Zach continued conversationally. "I'm new here, and as far as I'm concerned you're starting with a clean slate. You've only missed one homework assignment so far, and I'm going to let you make it up right now."

"Now?" Pete repeated, his dumbfounded gaze jolting up to Zach's.

"That's right. It shouldn't take you long. An hour at the most."

"But what if I don't want to?"

Zach pushed himself away from the door and walked toward the boy, hesitating in surprise for a brief second when Pete took a startled step back, almost as if he expected to be struck. Zach resumed his advance more slowly. "I think you do want to, Pete," he said quietly, his eyes locked on the youth's. "I've heard you're quite a student when you put your mind to it. And Mr. Carr said you have a real talent with words. I'd like to see what you can do."

"Why?" Pete asked suspiciously.

Zach considered his answer carefully, sensing that whatever he said could make or break his relationship with this boy. "Well, I happen to admire good writing," he said frankly. "There's a magic in being able to put words on paper in a way that brings a story to life, whether it's an investigative article or a short story. I think it's a very special gift, and people who have that gift should be encouraged to develop it. One of the best ways to do that is by writing as much as possible. So if you have the gift, I'd like to do what I can to help you develop it."

Pete stared at him for a moment, then looked down and shuffled his feet. "I'm not that good."

"Why don't you let me be the judge?" Zach suggested. "Would a laptop help?"

Pete gave him a surprised look. "Yeah."

"Good thing I brought mine along, then," Zach replied, flashing the teenager a grin. "You okay with Word Perfect?"

"Sure."

Zach retrieved the computer from underneath his desk and zipped open the case. "I'll print your work out at home," he told Pete as he set up the computer on a desk and plugged it in. "You ever work on one of these before?"

"No."

"Let me show you a couple of things, then."

With minimal instruction, and after asking a couple of astute questions, Pete was comfortable with the computer. The boy was sharp, Zach thought, just as the other teachers had said. "Okay, have at it. I'll be up front correcting papers. No hurry."

Fortunately he'd already told Rebecca of his plan, which she enthusiastically endorsed, and so she knew he would he late picking up Isabel tonight. He glanced at Pete, who sat slumped in front of the computer, staring at the screen, his fingers still idle. Suddenly, though, the boy leaned forward and started to type, and Zach settled back to finish reading the papers that had been turned in on Monday. So far so good.

He lost track of time as he made his way through the stack, writing both compliments and constructive criticism on each paper. The students were creative, he had to give them that. But there was plenty of room for improvement in terms of style, grammar and punctuation. Had the school ever considered a journalism class? he wondered. Or an editing class? Both would be excellent ways for students to polish the basics, as well as develop tight writing styles. They would be fairly easy to institute, he mused. It would just require...

"I'm finished."

Zach glanced up at Pete, who stood with his shoulders slouched, hands in his pockets, on the other side of the desk. Zach glanced at his watch—just over an hour. At least he'd made some sort of effort and not just blown the assignment off, he thought in relief.

"Great. Go ahead and shut down the computer while I gather up these papers. Then I'll drive you home."

"You don't have to do that. I can hitch a ride."

"A promise is a promise," Zach replied firmly as he stood up and slid the stack of papers into his briefcase.

Pete silently retreated to stow the computer, and by the time he returned Zach was waiting. "So how long have you lived in St. Genevieve, Pete?" he asked conversationally as he led the way to his car.

Pete shrugged. "Too long."

Zach looked at him. "You don't like it here?"

"It's okay, I guess. For a small town."

"You like cities better?"

"Yeah. I'm going to move to Chicago or New York or maybe even L.A. when I get out of school. Someplace where there's more action." He turned to look at Zach. "Are you really an investigative reporter?"

"That's right."

"So what are you doing here? Teaching must be pretty boring after that."

"Depends on how you define *boring*," Zach countered. "Let me tell you something, Pete. I've seen my share of action, and believe it or not, it isn't all that glamorous," he said frankly. "Teaching may not look exciting, but it can be very satisfying. That's why I double majored in college. As for why I'm here…it was timing, I guess. I was ready for a break from the fast life in St. Louis, and with Mr. Carr out, it was a good chance for me to get back into teaching, even if it's only for the rest of the semester." Zach glanced over at Pete, in time to catch a fleeting—but grudging—look of admiration in his eyes. "So now tell me about you."

Pete was reticent at first, but under Zach's casual but targeted probing he revealed a great deal. Some things Zach learned by the words Pete said; others, by the words he didn't say.

He came from a broken home, and apparently there had been a great deal of bitterness in the divorce seven years before. His father was awarded custody simply because his mother didn't want him. Zach got the distinct impression that there was no love lost between father and son. It seemed Pete had had a couple of minor run-ins with the law, which had alienated father and son even more. Even in the best of circumstances, however, Frank Cramer did not sound like the nurturing type, Zach thought grimly. He apparently didn't care how Pete did in school, didn't place much value on education, figured if a plant job was good enough for him it ought to be good enough for his son. He especially didn't think much of Pete's interest in writing and literature. In fact, it didn't sound like he thought much of Pete, period. Given that environment, Zach was surprised Pete showed up at school at all.

When they pulled up in front of the tiny house on the outskirts of town, Zach turned to Pete. "I expect you to finish today's assignment on time, Pete," he said, his gaze direct, his tone no-nonsense.

Pete half opened the door, then turned back to look at Zach. "Are you gonna make me stay late again if I don't?"

"Yes, I am."

Pete hesitated, then climbed out of the car. "Thanks for the lift."

"No problem. See you tomorrow."

As Zach pulled away from the curb, he glanced in the rearview mirror. Pete was still standing there, staring after the car, his hands in his pockets, his posture slouched. Zach wasn't sure how successful he'd been with the boy. His plan had been to be firm, to set the ground rules, as Rebecca had suggested. At the same time, he wanted to appear approachable and caring. And it appeared that Pete needed someone like that in his life.

Zach sighed. This teaching business was a whole lot more complicated than he'd expected. He'd always thought of it as classroom work—lecturing, grading papers, that kind of thing. He hadn't expected to get drawn into the lives of his students outside of class. But he now realized it was impossible to separate the two. One influenced the other.

Zach wasn't sure if he'd gotten through to Pete. But someone needed to. Because if what the other teachers said about his intelligence was true, it could very well be his ticket to the larger world he craved.

The challenge was to convince him of that.

"Well, I'll be," Zach said softly as he read the final line.

Rebecca looked up curiously from the board game she was playing on the floor with Isabel. "What's up?"

Zach glanced over at her and shook his head. "I just read Pete's paper."

"And?" she prompted.

"This kid can write," he replied, shaking his head in amazement. "I mean really write. Not high-school-level stuff, either. And this is just something he whipped off in an hour," he added incredulously. "If I hadn't been sitting there while he wrote it I wouldn't believe this was his work."

"Can I see?" Rebecca asked.

"Sure. I'd appreciate a second opinion. I was hoping he'd have talent, so maybe my judgment is jaded. Maybe I'm seeing more here than there really is."

Rebecca took the sheets of paper and reached over to smooth back Isabel's hair. "I'll be right with you, okay, sweetie?"

"Okay. Can I have another cookie while I wait?"

Rebecca smiled. "I think that would be all right."

Isabel jumped up and scampered toward Zach's tiny kitchenette as Rebecca scooted toward the couch and leaned against the front. Zach settled back into the cushions, content for the moment to enjoy the view of her long, shapely legs stretched out in front of her, to leisurely trace the enticing curves of her toned, firm body, to appreciate the endearing way she chewed her lower lip as she read, a frown of concentration on her brow.

When she'd appeared at the door earlier in the evening with a plate of chocolate chip cookies, he'd been taken aback. He'd been desperately searching for an excuse to invite her over, increasingly frustrated by their brief hellos and goodbyes at the restaurant when he dropped Isabel off and picked her up. He wanted to spend time with Rebecca, but neither of their schedules had allowed for that this week. Except for Monday night, when they'd had dinner together, he'd barely had a chance to say more than a dozen words to her. Tuesday night she'd driven to St. Louis to teach a cooking class at a gourmet shop. Wednesday night she had a church function. He'd thought about asking her to have dinner with them tonight when he picked up Isabel earlier in the afternoon, but when he'd arrived Rose told him that Rebecca had gone to the bank. So he'd written off this evening. To say he'd been glad to see her at the door was an understatement. He enjoyed spending time with Isabel, was grateful that she had warmed up to him, but he was desperately in need of some adult company. Preferably of the female variety. And preferably someone named Rebecca.

As he gazed down at her bent head, he thought about how much his life had changed in the past five weeks. He'd gone from hotshot investigative reporter to high school English teacher, from swinging single to pseudo family man. And he liked it. A lot. It was as if a missing piece in his life had suddenly fallen into place. If he didn't know better, he'd think...

"Wow!" The single word, spoken in a hushed tone, reassured Zach that he wasn't off base in his assessment of Pete's work.

"So I was right?"

Rebecca turned to look at him, her eyes incredulous. "This is amazing! It's written with such sensitivity, such pathos...how old is Pete?"

"Seventeen."

She shook her head. "Incredible. All I can say is, he has a future ahead of him if this is any sample of his ability."

"Can we finish our game now, Rebecca?" Isabel asked.

"Sure thing, sweetie. Then it's off to bed for you." She turned once more to Zach. "It would be wrong to waste this kind of talent. I hope you can get through to him," she said earnestly.

"I hope so, too."

"Hi, Rebecca. How's it going down there in the boonies?"

Rebecca smiled as she recognized the familiar voice of her wise-cracking, heart-of-gold sister-in-law. "Hi, Sam. I hear tell we're going to get running water next week," she replied in an exaggerated country-folk accent.

Sam chuckled. "Touché," she conceded. "But you do seem far away. We never get to see enough of you."

"Well, right now I should think company would be the last thing you'd want. Don't you have your hands full with a little bundle of joy named Emily?"

"She does keep me hopping," Sam admitted cheerfully, clearly not minding in the least.

"So how are you feeling?"

"Tired. But isn't that the story of all new mothers? Otherwise, great."

"How's Brad?"

"Tired," she echoed. "But loving every minute of being a daddy."

"Why am I not surprised?" Rebecca said affectionately.

"Listen, Rebecca, speaking of Easter..."

"Were we?" Rebecca asked with a smile, used to Sam's

conversational gymnastics—one direction one minute, another the next.

"As long as you mention it, no. But we are now. So what are you doing?"

"Now, or on Easter?" she teased.

"Easter, of course. Stay with me here, Rebecca."

"I'm trying," Rebecca replied with a laugh. That was one of the things she loved about talking to Sam—the other woman always made her laugh. She'd never met anyone with quite as much life and energy as Sam, and her sister-in-law made Brad incredibly happy. Which meant that as far as Rebecca was concerned, Sam was the greatest.

"So? What are your plans?"

"I don't have any yet," she admitted.

"Good. Because we'd love to have you up for the day. Henry is coming to visit for about a week, and we could all go to church together, have a nice dinner. It would be a great chance for us all to catch up."

"That does sound good," Rebecca agreed. But what about Zach and Isabel? she wondered, biting her lip. She hated to leave them alone on the holiday.

"And you're welcome to bring Isabel," Sam added, as if reading her sister-in-law's mind.

"Oh, I think she'd like that!" Rebecca replied with a relieved smile. "She hasn't had a chance to do much since she's been here. We've just been too busy to take her anywhere."

"Zach is welcome, too, by the way," Sam threw in with an air of casual indifference that didn't fool Rebecca for a minute. Rebecca had made it a point to downplay her relationship with Zach, saying simply that she was helping out a friend. But Sam's invitation clearly implied that she suspected it was more than that. Which left only one explanation. Henry.

"What has Dad been telling you?" Rebecca asked suspiciously.

"Oh, not much," Sam replied airily. "Not much at all. Just that you brought a really hot-looking guy down there to pick up the furniture. An *interested* hot-looking guy. No, I stand corrected. Make that a *very* interested hot-looking guy. And that the feeling seemed to be mutual. Of course, this is all secondhand information, you understand. We're only the brother and sister-in-law. Why should you tell us anything?''

The chiding was good-natured in tone, but Rebecca was immensely grateful that Sam couldn't see the crimson color that nevertheless flooded her face. She should have figured Henry would freely offer information—and opinion. She'd better set things straight right now. ''I would have been glad to tell you—if there was anything to tell,'' she pointed out, congratulating herself on her matter-of-fact delivery. ''Zach is just an acquaintance, like I've told you all along.''

''So then I guess you don't want to bring him along for Easter, this being a family gathering and all,'' Sam countered innocently.

Rebecca squirmed on her chair, tucking a leg under her. She'd backed herself into this corner, now she had to find a way out. ''Well, I hate for him to be alone on a holiday,'' she hedged.

''That would be a shame,'' Sam agreed.

''It might be the kind thing to do, to invite him to spend the day with us.''

''Yes, I suppose it would.''

''Well, I guess I could ask, anyway.''

''I guess you could.''

''All he can do is say no.''

''That's right.''

She took a deep breath. ''Okay. I'll ask.''

''Good. We'll expect you all then. We can meet at church, if that's okay. We'll save you a seat. Look for the redhead with the squalling baby.''

Rebecca grinned. ''Okay.''

''And, Rebecca, one other thing.''

''Yes?''

"If this guy is even close to the way Henry describes him, go for it!"

Rebecca's face flamed again. "Sam, I told you that—"

"I know, I know," she interrupted. "But listen, kiddo. I've been there. I was into this let's-be-friends-because-nothing-else-could-possibly-work-between-us mode for a long time with Brad. I fought the attraction as hard as I could, but fortunately your brother persevered. In the end I listened to my heart, and look where I am now? My version of paradise—at least as close as you can get on earth. All I'm saying is that if you're interested, give it a chance. Don't let fear hold you back." She paused for a moment, and when she spoke again her tone was noticeably lighter. "Well, enough lecturing for one day. We'll see you on Easter, okay?"

"Okay."

As Rebecca slowly replaced the receiver, she thought about Sam's words of advice. Rebecca was definitely interested. And she wasn't hiding it very well, either, if her father had picked up on it so quickly. But her fear—that was something else again. How did one control something that was irrational, that had no basis in reality, that was an instinctive response? she cried in silent despair. But no answer was forthcoming. And until one did, the situation was hopeless.

"Pete? I'd like to see you for a minute."

The boy looked at Zach defensively. "I turned in my homework."

"I know. I want to talk to you about something else. Go ahead and sit down."

Pete hovered uncertainly for a moment, then folded his long frame into a convenient desk, assuming his familiar slouch position. Zach waited until the last student exited, then shut the door and joined Pete, sitting down in the desk beside him. "I wanted to give you your paper back."

He took the assignment out of a folder and held it out to Pete. A look of trepidation quickly swept over the boy's eyes before being replaced by defensiveness. "I had to rush," he protested, his chin jutting out defiantly. "I didn't have a chance to—"

"Look at the paper, Pete," Zach interrupted quietly.

Pete sullenly reached for the paper, his eyes widening in surprise when he glanced at it. "You gave me an A?" he asked incredulously, staring at Zach in amazement.

"You deserved it. Go ahead, read over my comments." He settled back in his seat, waiting as Pete worked his way meticulously through the paper, carefully reading each of the constructive—and complimentary—remarks written in Zach's scrawling hand. When he reached the last one, the teenager read it once, then again, before looking up speechlessly, his face flushed.

Zach leaned forward and folded his arms on the desk. "That is a fine piece of work. You should be proud of it. And it confirms what Phil Carr told me. You do have talent. Very great talent. And I don't want to see it go to waste." He opened the folder again and removed two items, handing them to Hank one at a time. "This is some information on a national short story contest that I think you ought to consider entering. There are monetary prizes involved, but even more important, it would look very impressive on a college application. It would also give you a chance to be published. And this is a brochure about a writing camp being held in Michigan this August. It's for gifted writers, and I think you qualify. Look them both over, and we'll talk about them next week."

Pete stared in stunned silence at the brochures in his hands, then back at Zach. There was a new eagerness, an excitement, in his eyes that transformed his expression from sullen rebelliousness to youthful optimism.

"Do you really think I could do these things?" he asked.

"Absolutely. I wouldn't have given you the brochures if I didn't."

Zach saw the boy's Adam's apple bob, as if Pete was having difficulty swallowing. "Well, thanks," he said, rising suddenly, his face averted. "I'll read them this weekend. See you Monday."

He made his escape quickly, and Zach didn't try to detain him. He knew Pete was overcome by emotion, a tricky situation for a teenager trying to be cool and macho who didn't know quite how to handle such sentiment. He understood. But he also understood something else.

Pete had just been waiting for someone to care, to take an interest, to encourage him. Now that he'd found such a person in Zach, there was a chance he might shape up, might rethink the importance of education, might begin to consider the possibilities that it offered.

Zach knew people's lives didn't change overnight. Fifteen years of investigative reporting had taught him that. But lives *could* change, if people made an effort and learned to believe in themselves. And he had a feeling that Pete had just taken a step in the right direction.

Rebecca added a dollop of whipped cream to the final piece of chocolate torte, deposited the three servings on a tray, then paused, fidgeting nervously. She'd been trying to work up her courage to ask Zach about Easter ever since Sam's phone call two days before, and she still hadn't decided on the right approach. It was a family gathering, after all, and she didn't want him to get the wrong impression. Yes, she was interested. And yes, she hoped at some point she'd find the courage to give dating him another try. But she wasn't at that point yet. And she didn't want him to think she was. She had to find a way to let him know the invitation was only a friendly gesture, that—

"My goodness, Rebecca, that whipped cream is going to deflate if you stand there staring at it much longer!" Rose declared, planting her hands on her ample hips. "Just go ahead and ask the man. I guarantee he'll say yes."

Rebecca was sorry now she'd even mentioned the Easter invitation to Rose and Frances. She had done it in a moment of weakness, and she'd been paying for her lapse all morning. The sisters had been all for it, of course. They'd fallen in love with Isabel, coddling her and loving her like grandmothers, and the little girl had thrived on their attention. And of course they'd been enamored with Zach ever since he sent Rebecca that bouquet of roses. So their employer's reluctance to issue a simple invitation bewildered them.

"I'll ask him for you if you want me to," Frances offered helpfully.

"No! I mean, that's very kind, Frances, but it really should come from me. I was just going in." She lifted the tray and marched determinedly toward the door to the dining room, faltering only when she safely reached the other side and her gaze fell on Zach and Isabel, conversing very seriously and intently at a corner table. She paused to watch their interaction, glad that most of the Saturday lunch customers had departed. He looked great, she thought wistfully, appreciatively noting how his worn jeans and off-white cotton sweater enhanced his rugged good looks.

Just then he reached over to tousle Isabel's hair playfully, and she giggled, the sound of childish pleasure bringing a smile to Rebecca's face. She knew Isabel continued to miss her home and her parents. She talked about them often, excitedly relaying to Rebecca the messages she and Zach received on E-mail from Josef. But at least she seemed comfortable in her new environment, no longer withdrawn and uncertain as she'd been for the first few days.

As Rebecca watched them chatting, she let her eyes rest admiringly on Zach's strong profile. She knew that a child was the last thing he wanted in his life at this particular time. Yet he'd welcomed her without question, honoring a fifteen-year-old promise without hesitation, then constructed his life-style to accommodate her. Few men would behave that unselfishly, she knew. He truly was a rare find. Which made it all the harder for her to hide her feelings. But she had to, she told herself resolutely. Because she wasn't yet ready to face anything more than friendship. So, drawing in a deep breath, she put on her best "friend" smile and hoisted the tray into a more comfortable position.

The movement caught Zach's eye, and he turned. His mouth curved up into a lazy smile as he looked at her, and the simmering heat in his eyes was impossible to ignore as his gaze swept her lithe form. When his eyes reconnected with hers she could feel the sizzle of electricity between them, and she knew one thing with absolute clarity. Zach was not thinking friendship.

Flustered, Rebecca blushed, and his smile broadened. It was as if he sensed her discomfort, knew the reason and was pleased. So much for hiding her feelings, she thought wryly. But she had to keep up the pretense. For now.

"Well, are you two ready for dessert?" she asked, moving forward gamely, her voice determinedly cheerful.

"I always like something sweet after a meal," Zach replied, the husky tone in his voice and the look in his eyes implying he had another sort of treat in mind as he rose to pull out her chair.

"Chocolate cake! Oh, goodie!" Isabel exclaimed, reaching for hers eagerly and diving in enthusiastically.

Rebecca no longer had to wonder if Zach's interest in romance had died as a result of her rebuff the night of her birthday dinner. It was alive and well, she realized, suddenly finding it difficult to breathe as she sank down into her chair. Obviously he'd just been distracted during the last couple of weeks. Which wasn't surprising, given all that had been going on in his life. But he wasn't distracted now, she thought, venturing a glance at him as he snagged a piece of torte on his fork, then looked at her. The ardent light in his eyes left absolutely no doubt about his interest. Rebecca literally stopped breathing, her gaze riveted to his.

"This is good!" Isabel pronounced. "I like dessert."

"That makes two of us," Zach seconded, his eyes never leaving Rebecca.

The front door opened, and only when Ben strolled over did Zach finally release her gaze.

"Hi, there," Ben said cheerfully.

"Hi, Ben," Rebecca replied, her voice strained.

Ben looked at her worriedly. "You gettin' a cold?"

She shook her head, a delicate flush tinting her cheeks. "No. I'm fine. What brings you here? Do you want to join us for dessert?" she asked hopefully, thinking Ben's presence might dispel the present mood, which was fraught with overtones she didn't seem able to handle.

"No, thanks. Just taking a break for a few minutes. Thought Isabel might like to take a stroll with me. What do you say, little lady?"

"Can I, Uncle Zach?" she asked eagerly.

"I don't see why not," he agreed.

"We'll be back in a few minutes," Ben promised, taking Isabel's hand. As he turned to leave, Rebecca saw him glance quickly toward the kitchen door, where Rose and Frances were watching the proceedings with interest. As she caught their eyes, however, the sisters turned away guiltily, and the light suddenly dawned. This was a conspiracy. She should have known that Ben's arrival was too well timed to be a coincidence. The sisters and Ben had conspired to give Zach some time alone with her. The question was, had he been in on it?

She turned to look at him suspiciously, but he held up his palms in protest. "I know what you're thinking. But I had nothing to do with this. Although I can't say I mind too much," he added with a smile, reaching over to cover her hand with his. "I've missed you these past two weeks."

She swallowed, acutely conscious of his hand resting protectively and caringly over hers. "You see me all the time," she protested faintly, knowing that wasn't what he meant.

Don't push, he told himself. *Remember:* Patience *is the operative word here.* Play it cool and casual until she's ready for something more.

"True," he said easily. "But we've both been so busy

we've hardly had a chance to say more than a few words to each other. And as much as I enjoy being with Isabel, I could do with some adult company.''

Had she jumped to the wrong conclusions? Rebecca wondered suddenly. Misread the spark in his eyes earlier? Maybe he was just glad to have an adult to talk to. She didn't have enough experience with men to know for sure in situations like this whether they were pursuing or platonic.

''So I thought maybe you might join Isabel and me on a few outings now and then,'' he finished.

''Outings?'' she repeated curiously.

''Sure. You know, the state park, the zoo and science center in St. Louis, that sort of thing.''

''Oh.'' Those kinds of things sounded safe enough, she thought. ''Sure.''

''Great! How about a picnic tomorrow?''

''I can't tomorrow,'' she declined with honest regret. ''I promised to help out at the church supper.''

''That's too bad,'' he said disappointedly. ''And next Sunday is Easter, so I'm sure you have plans then.''

This was her opening. Now was the time to issue the invitation. She looked down at her uneaten cake, the whipped cream rapidly deflating—as was her courage. *Just ask*, she told herself sternly. *Stop trying to second-guess how he'll interpret the invitation. Remember what Sam said: don't let fear hold you back.*

''You're right, I do have plans,'' she confirmed slowly. ''I'm going up to St. Louis to spend the day with Brad and Sam. Dad will be there, too.''

''Sounds nice.''

''Actually, Sam said it would be okay if I brought Isabel. And she...she said you were welcome, too, if you wanted to come,'' Rebecca finished in a rush.

Zach tilted his head and eyed her speculatively. His first inclination was to accept immediately. But if it was going to make her uncomfortable with her family, he was reluctant to infringe. "How do you feel about that, Rebecca?" he asked quietly.

She hesitated, trying to frame her answer in a way that wouldn't make him think the invitation was too personal, even if she did want them both to come. "Well, I hate for you two to be alone on a holiday," she hedged.

"So you're inviting us out of sympathy?"

She squirmed in her chair. "No. I...I like you both. And it would be a nice change for Isabel."

"You could just take her."

He was putting her on the spot, calling her bluff. He was going to make her admit that she wanted him to come. Or maybe he was being considerate, giving her an out in case having him along would make her uncomfortable. Which it no doubt would, to some extent. But still, she'd like to spend the holiday with him, and she might as well admit it.

"I'd like for you to come, Zach, if you want to," she said softly, keeping her eyes downcast.

He reached for her hand, and when she looked up, she thought she detected a look of relief in his eyes. "I most definitely want to," he assured her with a smile.

She returned the smile tentatively, but a moment later it changed to a frown.

"What's wrong?" he prompted.

"I just remembered... You know Brad's a minister, and we're all going to meet at his church for the service when we arrive. But I know churchgoing isn't exactly on your Sunday schedule."

"That's true. But it won't kill me to go on Easter," he replied easily. "In fact, that reminds me. I've been meaning to ask if you would mind taking Isabel to church with you on Sundays. I know Josef would want her to go."

"Not at all," she assured him.

"Thanks. And Rebecca..."

"Yes?" She looked at him curiously.

"I want you to know that..."

"We're back!" Isabel announced, settling herself in her chair once more.

"We had a nice walk, didn't we, little lady?" Ben remarked.

"Yes. It was fun."

"Well, I'll see you two later," Ben said with a little salute before exiting.

"Rebecca! You didn't eat your cake!" Isabel pointed out in a horrified voice.

"No. I...I guess I didn't," she admitted.

"Can I have it?"

"But sweetie, you already had a piece."

"I'm still hungry."

Rebecca glanced at Zach with a helpless look.

"How about if I give you half?" Zach suggested, reaching over to divide Rebecca's neglected cake with his knife. Their eyes met, and she tried to read the end of his interrupted sentence in his eyes. What did he want her to know? But whatever he'd been intending to say, he had clearly decided to save it for another time.

And maybe that was better, she consoled herself. She had a feeling that whatever revelation he'd almost disclosed would only make her nervous. And she was nervous enough already.

Chapter Nine

When Rebecca opened the door on Easter morning, her breath caught in her throat as she drank in the sight of Zach, handsome and distinguished in his dark gray suit, crisp white shirt and blue-and-silver tie, his hair still slightly damp and darkened from the shower. He had such…presence, that was the word, she decided. Not to mention charisma and an almost tangible virility. All of which meant he could turn her to mush with just a glance. Especially a glance like the one he was giving her now as his gaze swept over her swiftly but comprehensively, lingering for just a moment on her loose, flowing hair. His smile of greeting remained unchanged during that quick glance, but the warmth in his eyes erupted into a white-hot blaze.

Zach reached up to run a finger around his suddenly tight collar, swallowing with difficulty. He had seen Rebecca in a variety of outfits, but none seemed to capture her essence as well as this one. Zach didn't know much about women's clothes, but for some reason Rebecca's attire gave her an old-fashioned beauty that made him think of afternoon tea or a garden party. From the gracious sweetheart neckline visible beneath the fitted, short-sleeved bolero jacket, to the full skirt that flared out from the tightly cinched waist, the style was eminently flattering to her trim, utterly feminine figure. And the pastel floral cotton fabric seemed to echo the spring hues of the lavender redbuds and pink flowering apple trees now blooming in profusion throughout the countryside.

But the crowning glory—literally—was her hair. Freed from the constraints of her usual French twist, the soft, unfettered waves cascaded past her shoulders, the glorious russet strands glinting in the golden morning sun as they framed her classic features. The wide-brimmed straw hat, adorned with a cluster of silk flowers in the back, was the perfect final touch.

Though Zach had adeptly avoided long-term romantic entanglements throughout his dating career, he was by no means immune to feminine charms. But he was usually drawn to savvy, sophisticated women. The girl-next-door type usually sent him fleeing in the opposite direction, away from all the things she represented—namely, commitment and responsibility and the constraints of a white picket fence.

But despite the fact that Rebecca was definitely of the girl-next-door variety, he wasn't running now—much to his surprise. In fact, just the opposite. There was something about her innate goodness, her straightforward honesty and innocence, that drew him in a way that the sophisticated qualities of the other women of his acquaintance never had.

As he looked at her in the gentle light of morning, his senses suddenly went haywire, and he was tempted to reach over and pull her into his arms, to kiss her sweetly tender lips, to run his fingers through her burnished tresses. It was only with a supreme effort that he restrained those impulses. But there was no way he could disguise the hunger in his eyes. That was out of his control.

Despite her limited experience with men, Rebecca knew desire when she saw it, and she gripped the edge of the door, her legs suddenly shaky. Apparently the Easter outfit she'd splurged on, in an uncharacteristic display of self-indulgence, was a hit. A pulse began to beat in the delicate hollow of her throat, and like a homing pigeon, Zach's gaze dropped to that sensitive area and rested there, the color of his eyes darkening even as Rebecca's mouth went dry.

"Happy Easter, Rebecca," Isabel piped up, her thin, childish voice interrupting the throbbing, electric connection that crackled between the two adults. "Look what Uncle Zach gave me!" She held up a large, stuffed white rabbit for inspection, and Rebecca dragged her gaze away from Zach's mesmerizing eyes, bending down to hug the little girl.

"Isn't that nice!" she exclaimed, her voice as uneven as her pulse. "And don't you look pretty!"

Isabel smoothed the crinolined skirt of her sashed cotton floral dress, touched the lace-edged ruffle at the hem, then reached up to adjust her white straw hat. "I never had a dress like this before. Or a hat, either," she said reverently.

"Well, I think you'll be the most beautiful lady at church today," Rebecca declared. Then she forced herself to take a deep, steadying breath. "Come in for a minute while I get my purse," she suggested breathlessly, backing up to give them access, her eyes touching Zach's briefly before skittering quickly away to escape the heat still radiating from them. "I think there's something on the coffee table for you," she told Isabel with a shaky smile, transferring her gaze to the little girl.

Isabel's eyes widened. "Really?" She scampered into the living room, pausing with a reverent "Oh!" at the sight of the giant basket of goodies, covered with clear yellow cellophane and topped with a big lavender bow. She turned to look at Rebecca, who had followed her and now stood just inside the room. "Is this mine?"

"It sure is, sweetie. Happy Easter."

"Oh, thank you!" she exclaimed, clapping her hands in delight. "Can I open it?"

"Of course."

As Isabel bent down to carefully free one side of the cellophane so she could peer inside, Rebecca felt Zach move behind her, his nearness almost palpable.

"That was very nice of you," he observed quietly.

She turned to find him in the doorway, one shoulder propped against the frame, his arms folded across his chest. She was grateful to discover that the fire in his eyes was now banked to a more manageable smolder.

"What's Easter without a basket—or a rabbit?" she replied, striving for a light tone but not quite succeeding.

"Or an Easter bonnet, as the old song goes," he added lightly, his eyes flickering to her hat for a moment. "By the way, thanks for taking her shopping for the outfit," he added, nodding toward Isabel. "I wouldn't have known where to start. But you were wrong about one thing, you know."

She tilted her head quizzically and frowned. "What do you mean?"

He dropped his voice, and when he spoke, his tone was intimate, caressing. "Isabel isn't going to be the most beautiful lady at church." He reached over and ran a gentle finger down Rebecca's cheek, lifted her soft hair and let it drift through his fingers, then drew an unsteady breath as he rested his palm tenderly against her cheek, his thumb stroking her silky skin, his eyes locked on hers. "I'm looking at the lady who will have that honor," he declared, his voice suddenly husky.

Rebecca's heart stopped, then raced on, her whole body quivering at the heat generated by Zach's unexpected touch—and by the need it inspired. She swallowed with difficulty, surprised to discover that she desperately wanted him to gently claim her lips as he had the night of her birthday, the tender pressure of his kiss stoking the fire in her heart that had languished, reduced to only a few embers, for so many years. She sensed that if any man could coax those embers of passion back to life, this one could. Because while he'd initially struck her as the fast, no-nonsense type who went after what he wanted with aggressive, single-minded determination, he had surprised her by exhibiting a touching gentleness and patience with Isabel. Could he bring those qualities to a relationship with her? she wondered, allowing herself a soaring moment of optimism.

But she stifled the hope quickly and firmly. A child and a woman were two different things, she reminded herself resignedly. And the expectations were entirely different. From a woman he would want responsiveness and satisfaction, and even under the most patient and nurturing conditions, Rebecca wasn't sure she could ever meet the needs of a man like Zach. There was one way to find out, of course—let the relationship progress. But that, unfortunately, involved risk—on a couple of fronts.

There was the risk of a second humiliation, of course—an extremely unpleasant prospect. But even if she could overcome the physical obstacles—and that was a big "if"—there was another, even greater, risk to consider. Zach's sojourn in St. Genevieve was just that—nothing more than a brief interlude. When it was over, he would return to his life in St. Louis, leaving her alone once more, her emotions tattered, her heart aching. It wasn't that he would intentionally hurt her, she knew. It was just that he was probably used to relationships that lasted only as long as the circumstances were convenient.

But a cavalier attitude about involvement wasn't Rebecca's way. She had been raised with solid, traditional values that clearly defined dating behavior and, as a result, had never believed in so-called casual intimacy. For her, kissing and touching were only appropriate in the context of a long-term relationship based on mutual respect and, if not love, certainly deep affection.

Rebecca already felt a deep affection for the man whose gaze now held hers so compellingly. And it wouldn't take much for her to feel even more. In her heart she sensed that her feelings for this man could deepen with very little additional encouragement. Because although Rebecca was uncertain about many aspects of her relationship with Zach, she was absolutely sure about one thing. He drew her in ways no other man ever had, stirring to life the almost cold embers of a long-suppressed passion. But she also knew that if she ever gave her heart to a man, it would be completely and for always. It would be his to cherish—or to break. And the latter possibility scared her to death.

Zach's eyes scanned Rebecca's expressive face. He didn't want to make another mistake with her, but he couldn't handle a strictly platonic relationship much longer. The more he got to know about her, the more he wanted to know. But he had to move slowly, he reminded himself firmly. So he held back, searching her eyes as objectively as he could, trying to discern her feelings. There was uncertainty in them, he acknowledged. And fear. But there was also desire. In fact, unless he was way off base, her eyes were now inviting him more eloquently than words ever could to claim her lips. And it was an invitation simply too tempting to refuse.

He changed his position slightly, a subtle shift that angled his body out of Isabel's view, his thumb still stroking Rebecca's cheek in a manner at once both sensuous and comforting. Slowly, carefully he leaned toward her, making no secret of his intent. He watched her eyes, gauging her reaction, ready to back off at the slightest withdrawal. But he saw only a soft yearning in their depths as he closed the distance between them, his hand moving to her nape to draw her close as her eyelids drifted shut.

"Rebecca, can I eat a chocolate egg?"

Rebecca's startled eyes flew open, connecting with Zach's as Isabel's innocent question short-circuited the electrically charged moment. A flash of frustration, coupled with dismay, swept over Zach's face, and he paused, hovering a mere whisper away from her lips. She could feel the tension radiating from his body, could sense the battle he was waging with his self-control. But in the end he sighed and backed off, giving her a smile that was clearly forced.

"I guess I'll just have to wait until later to finish this conversation, won't I?" he murmured, his voice strangely hoarse.

"Can I, Rebecca?" Isabel repeated.

Rebecca tried to swallow past the lump in her throat. "Yes, that would be fine," she replied breathlessly, her eyes still locked on Zach's, not even sure whose question she was answering.

Zach reached over and trailed his finger down her cheek once more, and his eyes darkened at her sharply indrawn breath. She thought his hand was trembling, but she was such a mass of vibrating nerves herself that she couldn't be sure. In fact, at the moment she was sure of only one thing.

Zach intended to kiss her later.

That realization sent a surge of excitement—and uncertainty—ricocheting through her. She wanted him to kiss her. That wasn't the question. The question was, should she let him? Because one kiss could lead to another, and gentleness would eventually give way to passion. She'd already humiliated herself once with this man. That he was even willing to give it another try seemed like a miracle. But she doubted whether any man's ego would be able to handle that kind of reaction—and rejection—twice. She couldn't count on a second miracle. Just like she couldn't count on her response.

And what of her concerns about the transitory nature of his appearance in her life? And the heartbreak that could result if she let herself get involved with him? Was it worth the risk—or should she just retreat to safety?

Rebecca didn't have the answer to her questions. But maybe in the Lord's house she would find guidance, as well as relief for her deep-seated doubts and insecurities, she thought hopefully. After all, He had always come through for her before, in His own time and way, when she turned to Him for direction with a problem that was too difficult to tackle on her own.

And this one certainly fell into that category.

Rebecca stepped out of the car and gazed up at the deep blue sky with a smile. "Isn't it a gorgeous day?" she exclaimed.

"Gorgeous," Zach agreed, his eyes never leaving her face as he shut the door behind her.

She blushed and reached for Isabel's hand, knowing that his comment wasn't directed at the weather but deciding for the moment it was safer to pretend it was. Although their conversation on the ride to St. Louis had been casual and impersonal, it had still taken her quite a while to recover from those few emotionally charged moments in her apartment. And the look in his eyes right now was stirring up all those unsettling feelings again.

"I always think it's such a shame when Easter is rainy or cold," she chattered nervously as Zach took Isabel's other hand and they made their way toward the church.

Zach gave her a lazy smile that would have warmed her all the way to her toes even if the day had been dismal, and the pink in her cheeks deepened. Sensing her discomfort, reminding himself that he needed to move very slowly, he changed the subject. "I'm looking forward to meeting your brother and sister-in-law," he remarked conversationally.

They were looking forward to meeting him, too, she thought ruefully. Especially Sam, whose imagination had been working overtime. Rebecca's goal today was to convince everyone that she and Zach were just friends. Whether that was true or not was beside the point. She just didn't want her family jumping to any conclusions. Especially when she hadn't reached any herself.

Zach didn't help matters, though, by draping an arm around her shoulders and leaning close to whisper in her ear as they paused in the back of church. "There's your dad," he noted, inclining his head toward the left rear.

Rebecca's head swiveled in that direction, just in time to see Sam and her father exchange a knowing look, and her heart sank. This friendship business was not going to be an easy sell, she thought in dismay. Henry had already formed his opinion, and from the smug look on Sam's face hers had just been cemented. Maybe Brad would be the voice of reason, she thought without much hope.

Rebecca deliberately moved out of Zach's grasp and walked toward Sam, leaving him to follow with Isabel.

"Rebecca, you look absolutely gorgeous!" Sam declared without preamble when her sister-in-law was within earshot. "Doesn't she, Henry?"

"Glowing, that's what I'd say," he pronounced. "You been taking vitamins? Or is there another explanation?" he asked with a twinkle in his eyes.

Sam's gaze flickered behind Rebecca. "This might be the explanation right here," she observed in an undertone, giving Rebecca a grin and an approving wink. When Rebecca blushed furiously, Henry nudged Sam.

"What did I tell you?" he asserted.

"Did I miss something here?" Zach interrupted smoothly, smiling down at Henry.

"No!" Rebecca replied quickly, giving her father a "don't you dare say one more word" look. "It was just…just a family joke," she explained lamely.

"Well, are you going to introduce me to this handsome man or not?" Sam asked pertly, when her sister-in-law made no move to do so.

Rebecca turned in time to see Zach's neck redden even as he smiled down at Sam. At least she wasn't the only one being embarrassed today, she thought wryly. She just hoped he hadn't heard the initial exchange between her father and Sam.

"Sam, Zach Wright. He's the *friend* I mentioned," she said pointedly. "And this is Isabel," she added more gently, drawing the suddenly shy little girl forward. "Zach, Isabel, my sister-in-law, Sam. Zach, you already know my father. Isabel, sweetie, this is my papa," she explained.

Zach shook hands with Henry, and Rebecca sat down to peek at Emily's tiny face, framed by a pink bonnet edged in lace. "Oh, Sam, she's so much bigger already!"

"She is growing fast," Sam agreed. "Listen, I hope you

don't mind sitting in the back, but I need to be close to the exit in case Emily decides to exercise her vocal cords. I'm afraid to say that I think she's inherited her mother's big mouth,'' Sam declared with a grin.

"This is fine," Rebecca assured her.

Isabel reached over and tugged on Rebecca's skirt. "Can I sit by the baby?" she asked softly, her fascinated gaze locked on Emily, who was sucking on her fist and watching Isabel with big, round eyes.

"Sure," Sam said. "Emily likes an audience. And that way we can get to know each other better. Just change places with Rebecca," she instructed.

Rebecca wasn't fooled by the apparent innocence of Sam's suggestion. It was clearly a setup. But there was no way out. Left with no choice but to comply, she moved next to Zach. Being only inches away from him wasn't going to help her emotional state in the least, however. Especially when he draped an arm across the back of the pew behind her and proceeded to brush his fingers lightly across her shoulder.

"How've you been, Zach?" her father asked, his sharp eyes missing nothing as he leaned forward to talk around Sam and Isabel.

"Just fine, Henry," Zach replied, his breath warm on Rebecca's temple as he spoke across her. "How's that rose garden coming along?"

"Great! The new shoots are bursting out already. You'll have to come back down and see it in bloom."

"I'd like that," Zach replied with an easy smile.

"So what do you think of my granddaughter?" Henry asked, turning his attention to Isabel.

"She's little," Isabel replied, her tone serious, her face thoughtful. Then she tilted her head and looked at Henry. "Are you really her grandfather?"

"Yep."

"I never had a grandfather," she told him regretfully.

"Well, then, why don't you just pretend I'm your grand-father today?" he suggested. "I could use the practice."

"Really?"

"Sure."

The service started then, putting an end to the conversation—much to Rebecca's relief. Her plan to convince everyone that she and Zach were just friends was already in shambles, and she needed some time to regroup and think about a new approach. Sam and her father clearly had their minds made up about the relationship. Most likely Brad did, too, she thought, watching as he entered, impressed as always by his com-manding appearance in clerical garb. Sometimes, when she saw him in this setting, it was hard for her to remember that he was the same big brother who had teased and bullied and protected and encouraged her from her earliest memories to her adolescent years, when he'd left for the seminary. Their relationship changed after that, matured, and in the intervening years the bond between them had grown even stronger.

Rebecca was immensely grateful that Brad now had Sam and the family he'd always wanted. He deserved all the good things the Lord chose to bless him with. In fact, his only "family" worry these days seemed to be her. She knew that he had never understood why she chose to live a solitary life. In his gentle way, he let her know on a regular basis that he was willing to listen if she wanted to talk about it. But even after all these years, her secret was still too painful, too fraught with humiliation and guilt, to discuss.

Rebecca supposed that someone with a less-sensitive nature would have been able to move on, to overcome the shame and embarrassment. But she'd been born tenderhearted, prone to emotional hurt. And so the incident continued to haunt her, leaving her powerless to overcome the debilitating fear that had deprived her of the rich dimension that love could add to her life.

Yet somehow, deep in her heart, Rebecca sensed that there was a chance she could find love with the man at her side.

The possibility was there, dangling alluringly just out of her grasp, like the golden ring on a carousel. All she had to do was reach for it. Or, in this case, simply offer some encouragement. But she was so afraid of failure! What if she freaked out again? Or worse yet, what if she didn't, what if she allowed their relationship to develop, only to have Zach reject her in the end as inadequate? How would she ever be able to go on after that?

Rebecca was torn, her heart pulling her one way, her intellect another. But now was not the time to work out her personal dilemma, she told herself resolutely. It was Easter Sunday and she was here to worship, not agonize over her problem. She would simply put it in the Lord's hands, ask for guidance and hope that He would show her the way. In the meantime she should be listening to Brad's sermon. Determinedly she forced herself to focus on her brother's words.

"And so I believe that the real message of Easter is one of renewal—of new life, of hope, of trust, of a promise fulfilled.

"In our society, Christmas has become the biggest holiday of the year. And it is, indeed, a wonderful event to celebrate. But without today, without Easter, Christmas would have no meaning. Because this is the day when the Lord gave us the legacy of everlasting life. And it is this legacy that gives Christianity its meaning.

"It seems to me that as Christians we can learn much from this day. Certainly it forms the foundation of our beliefs, gives us an incentive to live our lives based on the principles that the Lord taught. And it offers us great hope. Because of Easter, we know that anything is possible with God.

"I believe that the themes of this day—renewal, rebirth, hope, trust—are beautifully symbolized in nature. Consider the tulip. In the fall, when it is placed in the ground, the withered bulb appears to be dead. It lies dormant through the long, cold winter, wrapped in icy fingers. But in the spring it finds new life as the gentle warmth of the sun patiently coaxes it to grow and blossom into a glorious flower.

"In many ways I think the story of the tulip bulb is a good analogy not only for Easter but for a heart that longs for love. All of us here today know from personal experience that the heart is a very fragile thing. We know that it can be easily hurt, it can wither away, it can appear to be dead and empty. But I believe that with warmth and patient nurturing, most hearts can bloom again.

"On this Easter day, as we celebrate the promise of eternal life, let us also celebrate the earthly life given to us by the Lord. Let us resolve not to waste this precious blessing, in all its infinite dimensions. And as we thank God today for the gift of love He gave us through his Son's death and resurrection, let us celebrate that gift by nurturing the love in our own lives. Let us find the courage to seek love if we do not have it, and the wisdom to cherish it if we do. For despite its inherent risks and heartaches, it is still the greatest gift the Lord can bless us with in this life.

"Let us pray...."

As Brad finished his sermon, Rebecca felt her hand being taken in a gentle grasp. She looked up at Zach as he entwined his fingers through hers, and her vision blurred with tears at the tenderness in his eyes and the memory of the pink tulips he'd given her. She didn't know if Brad had intentionally directed the last part of his sermon to her, but it had certainly hit home, she thought, averting her eyes and blinking rapidly to dispel the tears. And he was right. Love was a gift. And the Lord seemed to be offering her a chance for love with the man now holding her hand. Hadn't she promised herself on Valentine's Day that if the right man came along, she would take the risk of pursuing a relationship? Well, the opportunity was being offered. Now it was up to her to take it.

Rebecca knew that she wasn't going to be able to overcome her fear overnight. But maybe, if Zach was patient and understanding, they could find a way to work through it together. It was a long shot, she knew. But for the first time in years she allowed a tender seed of hope to sprout and send out a tentative root.

"Rebecca! Sam! Wait up!"

Rebecca turned at the familiar voice, smiling as Laura and Nick walked toward them hand in hand.

"Don't worry. Brad's still gabbing," Sam replied with a grin. "That's one of the downsides of being the preacher's wife—you're always the last to leave."

"Are you complaining?" Laura asked with a smile.

Sam's face softened. "Hardly. He's worth waiting for any day."

Laura looked up at Nick, her own face softening with love as they exchanged a tender glance. "I know what you mean," she replied. With an obvious effort she tore her eyes away from Nick's and turned to Rebecca, reaching out to take her hand. "It's good to see you, Becka. And this must be Isabel—and Zach," she said, looking from one to the other.

"That's right. Brad, this is Laura and Nick. Isabel, sweetie, these are friends of mine."

While the two men shook hands, Laura studied Zach, frowning slightly. "Have we met before?" she asked. "You look very familiar."

"Not formally," he replied with a smile. "But you two were having dinner at Rebecca's a few weeks ago the same night I was there. I noticed you when Rebecca brought your dessert out."

"That's right!" Laura acknowledged, her frown evaporating as memory returned. "You and Rebecca had coffee together after she talked to us. Remember, Nick?"

Nick grinned sheepishly. "I have to admit I don't. I only had eyes for you that night."

Laura blushed with pleasure as their eyes touched briefly. "Anyway, it's nice to meet you formally," she told Zach.

"The pleasure is mine," he assured her.

"You mean you two had dinner together weeks ago?" Sam asked, eyeing Zach and Rebecca with new interest.

"Not dinner. Coffee," Rebecca clarified.

"But dinner would have been better," Zach interjected with an engaging grin. "Coffee was all I could manage to waylay her for that night, though. And even that was under duress," he admitted candidly. "But fortunately things have improved since then." His eyes sought, held and mesmerized hers.

Rebecca knew that the four adults were watching the two of them with unabashed interest, could sense their rapt attention. She ought to look away, make some flippant remark, carry on the charade that she and Zach were just friends. But she was fighting a losing battle, and she knew it.

"Well, I'm glad to hear it," Henry declared. "Rebecca could use some male companionship."

"Dad!" Rebecca turned to him, her face horrified.

"What's he done now?" Brad asked, his voice laced with tolerant amusement as he came up behind her. But after one look at her crimson face he slipped an arm around her shoulders comfortingly. "Never mind. Don't tell me. I can guess. I have a feeling it has something to do with Zach. And I take it this is Zach?"

"Guilty," Zach replied with a grin.

Brad held out his hand, and Zach took it promptly, realizing that the other man was assessing him even as he smiled. Zach was also aware of Brad's arm protectively around his sister's shoulders. Consciously sent or not, the message was clear: treat my sister with care or you'll answer to me.

Zach respected that, admired it even, and he returned Brad's gaze steadily. "Rebecca's spoken very highly of you. I'm glad we finally have the chance to meet."

"So am I. I try to keep up with the events—and people— in her life. She's very special to me."

"She's very special to me, too," Zach replied candidly, his gaze direct and honest.

Brad held Zach's eyes a moment longer, and when he released the other man's hand there was a satisfied expression on his face.

"Well, we're going to take off," Laura said. "Happy Easter, everyone."

She and Nick left to a chorus of best wishes, and then Brad squatted down beside the silent little girl who clung to Rebecca's hand. "You must be Isabel," he said quietly with a smile. "I'm Rebecca's brother."

"I know. She told me," Isabel replied in a small, timid voice.

"Well, we're glad you came to visit us, Isabel. What do you think of my new little girl?"

"She's pretty," Isabel stated shyly. "And soft."

"Yes, she is," he agreed. "Maybe later you'd like to hold her."

"Could I?" she asked, her eyes growing big.

"I think we could arrange that. You just remind me if I forget, okay?"

"Okay."

"I'd say it's time to head home," Sam declared, shifting Emily in her arms. "This little lady is getting hungry."

Brad stood up. "We'll meet you there, okay?" he said to Rebecca and Zach.

"Sounds good," Zach replied.

As they made their way to Zach's car, he turned to Rebecca with a smile. "You have a nice family."

She smiled ruefully. "Thanks. I love them all dearly. But they can be a little too outspoken at times. Except Brad, of course. He's very diplomatic."

"And very protective."

She looked at him curiously. "What do you mean?"

He shrugged. "He obviously cares about you very much. And he was clearly concerned about my...intentions."

She stared at him curiously as he opened the back door and leaned in to buckle Isabel into her seat belt.

"How in the world could you pick that up from such a brief conversation?" she asked when he emerged.

He straightened up and grinned as he shut Isabel's door and opened Rebecca's. "It must be a man thing. But the message was clear, trust me."

As Rebecca slipped into her seat, she frowned thoughtfully. She wasn't sure how Zach had picked up so much when only a dozen words had been exchanged, but she wasn't going to argue with him. Brad *was* protective. He knew her feelings were easily bruised and always did everything in his power to make sure she wasn't hurt. So of course he would be concerned about a man who suddenly appeared out of the fog, admittedly for a brief stay, and who could disappear just as quickly. Because a man like that could easily leave a broken heart in his wake. Her heart. Given the circumstances, it was natural that Brad wondered about Zach's intentions.

As a matter of fact, so did Rebecca.

"Happy birthday!" Sam, Henry and Nick chorused as Sam entered the dining room with a decorated cake topped with flickering candles.

"Is it your birthday?" Isabel asked, turning to Rebecca in surprise.

"No, honey. My birthday was a month ago," she explained, frowning in confusion at the three grinning faces. "What's this all about?"

"Well, you didn't think we'd forget to celebrate your birthday, did you?" Sam asked. "Okay, so it's a little late. Blame it on the little gal now sleeping soundly down the hall."

Rebecca shook her head and smiled. "You guys are too much. I'm going to be spoiled after this year, with two birthday celebrations!"

"Two?" Sam repeated, raising her eyebrows questioningly.

Rebecca didn't even try to sidestep the question. She'd given up the "just friends" pretense hours ago. "Zach took me out for a dinner a couple of days after my birthday," she explained.

"Good for him," Sam asserted promptly. "The fun factor in your life could use a boost. You need to work on that with her, Zach," Sam declared as she deposited the cake in front of Rebecca.

"I try, but she's a pretty hard sell," he admitted.

"Be persistent," Henry advised firmly. "Persistence pays."

"I'll remember that," Zach replied with a chuckle.

"Will you all stop?" Rebecca protested, her face flaming. "I make time for fun!"

"When?" Henry countered.

"Dad." Brad's quietly authoritative voice put an end to the inquisition. "Go ahead, Rebecca, make a wish and blow out the candles," he suggested, turning to her with an understanding smile.

She sent him a grateful look before complying and was rewarded with a round of applause as the last candle was extinguished.

"What did you wish for?" Isabel asked.

"It won't come true if I tell, sweetie," Rebecca replied with a smile.

"Oh." Isabel's face fell. "Well, was I in it?" she asked hopefully.

"In a way," Rebecca hedged.

"Was Uncle Zach?"

Again Brad came to the rescue. "Isabel, how would you like a piece of cake with a big rose on it?" he asked, earning Rebecca's gratitude once more.

Her attention effectively diverted, she nodded her head eagerly, supervising as Sam cut a generous piece with a huge rose in the middle.

When the last bite of cake was consumed a few minutes later, Sam leaned back and groaned. "I'll never lose the rest of the weight I put on with Emily if I keep this up," she lamented good-naturedly.

"You look exactly the same to me as you did before," Rebecca insisted.

"Thanks. But I've still got five pounds to go," Sam admitted ruefully.

"Speaking of new babies...have you ever seen a real baby bunny up close, Isabel?" Henry asked.

"No."

"Would you like to?"

"Do you have one?" she asked, enthralled.

"No. But I know where there's a nest, and if we're real careful, I don't think the momma rabbit will mind if we take a quick look."

"Can I, Uncle Zach?" Isabel asked eagerly.

"I don't see why not."

Isabel scrambled to her feet, and Henry stood up and reached for her hand.

"Some fresh air sounds like a good idea," Sam remarked as she also rose. "Why don't you two take a little stroll to the park down at the corner while Brad and I clean up?" she suggested.

"We can't leave you to deal with this mess!" Rebecca protested. "I'll help."

She started to rise, but Brad placed a hand on her shoulder. "Go ahead, Becka. You deal with kitchen work every day. We can manage here. I know we're all fascinating company, but I'm sure Zach won't object to spending part of the day just with you." He looked at the other man and smiled.

"You're right," Zach replied, relieved by the approval he saw in the other man's eyes. Apparently Rebecca's brother had decided that Zach could be trusted with his sister.

"But it doesn't seem right," she protested once more.

"Rebecca, for heaven's sake, just go!" Sam insisted. "You're our guest today. Plus, it's a belated birthday celebration. So you are *not* going to do dishes. Period. End of discussion. That's final." She paused and looked at Brad.

"Should I be a little more forceful, do you think?" she asked innocently, her eyes twinkling mischievously.

He chuckled. "I think you made your point. Go ahead, you two. We'll still be here when you get back. And Henry will keep Isabel entertained."

Rebecca looked at Zach. They'd had almost no time alone together since Isabel's arrival, and this opportunity might not come again soon. If she was going to let this relationship progress, now was as good a time as any to start. Besides, things couldn't get that...involved...in a public park in broad daylight. Or could they? she wondered in sudden alarm, noting the eager, ardent light in Zach's eyes.

"What do you say, Rebecca?" he asked, the casual tone of his voice at odds with the intensity of his gaze.

With sudden determination she stood up. "It sounds like a good idea to me," she agreed, her voice slightly breathless. She turned to look at Brad, whose expression was thoughtful, and Sam, who was grinning like the Cheshire Cat. "We won't be gone long."

"Don't hurry on our account," Sam declared. "You two just have fun."

"We will," Zach promised, smiling down at Rebecca as she joined him in the doorway.

She forced herself to smile back, but as her nerve endings started to tingle, an unsettling question suddenly came to mind. How, exactly, did Zach define *fun?* she wondered nervously.

Chapter Ten

Zach would have reached for Rebecca's hand immediately when they left the house—except that she hid hers in the deep pockets of her full skirt. He knew she was nervous, knew she was probably thinking about the last time they were alone together, and he was determined to put her at ease. He'd just let her take the lead, give her the time she needed to get comfortable.

"I had a note from Josef this morning," he told her conversationally as they strolled along.

"How is everything?" she asked, turning to him with a worried frown.

"No better, unfortunately. Maybe worse. He's not a complainer, so it's hard to tell. But one thing is clear. He misses Isabel desperately."

"I'm not surprised." She sighed and looked up at the canopy of flowering trees above her, the peaceful stillness broken only by the call of the birds. "It's hard to believe on a day like this that somewhere in the world a country is torn apart with strife and terror," she said softly, her voice troubled. "Isabel's only been here a short time, but already I'm dreading the day we have to send her back to that environment."

"I know what you mean," he admitted.

"Does she talk about her home very much when she's with you?" Rebecca asked.

"Only casually. Usually at night, when she's going to bed. How about with you?"

Rebecca nodded slowly, her face thoughtful. "She tells me quite a bit. Enough to give me a pretty clear picture of her everyday life. I know her family didn't have much in a material sense, but it seems they made up for it with love. And she obviously misses her parents. I try to keep her busy at the restaurant, giving her little jobs to do or books to read or puzzles to work on, hoping that will keep her from dwelling on her homesickness. It seems to work most of the time. Actually, I'm amazed at how smoothly she's adapted to such a different environment."

"I think you can take a lot of credit for that," Zach remarked quietly. "Isabel has grown very fond of you—which is easy to understand."

She looked up at him, noted the tender light in his eyes, and averted her glance quickly. "Do you hear from Josef often?" she asked, diverting the spotlight from herself.

"As often as he can get access to a PC, which is every couple of days. Isabel and I check morning and evening for messages, and we send him a note every day when I get home from school."

"Speaking of school, how's your problem student doing?"

"Pete Cramer? He's not a problem anymore. In fact, I heard some teachers in the lounge talking the other day, speculating on why he's suddenly buckled down and gotten serious about his studies."

Rebecca smiled. "I could clear up that mystery in one word—you."

Zach shrugged. "All I did was offer a little encouragement. And some discipline. Very good advice, by the way," he acknowledged with a smile. "Anyway, I think he's going to apply for that week-long writing camp this summer in Michigan that I told you about. The only problem is funding. Which brings me to a subject I've been meaning to raise. Do you hire any extra wait staff in the summer, high school kids?"

"Yes. Do you think he might be interested?"

He nodded. "It would give him something constructive to do, and he could earn the money for camp. Would you consider talking to him?"

"Absolutely. Have him come over someday after school."

Zach gave her a grateful smile. "I appreciate it, Rebecca."

She waved his thanks aside. "I need the help, anyway. And if I can give a job to someone who will really benefit, that's even better."

They reached the end of the block and paused to gaze at the small, deserted park.

"Would you like to sit for a few minutes?" Zach asked, nodding toward a convenient bench.

Rebecca thought about the last time they'd sat on a bench together, and her stomach clenched at the memory. A wave of panic washed over her, and she started to refuse. But as her gaze fell on a bed of colorful tulips in the center of the park, the flowers waving encouragingly to her in the gentle breeze, the words died in her throat. She recalled Brad's sermon, as well as her own promise to herself, and took a slow, steadying breath.

"Yes. That would be nice."

Zach took her elbow as they made their way across the uneven ground, then sat beside her on the wooden bench. "Nice spot," he remarked.

She forced herself to lean back, then folded her hands primly in her lap and glanced around. "Yes. Sam and Brad were glad there was a park close by, with swings and all, so Emily will have a place to play near home when she gets older. Of course, they didn't buy the house because of that. They didn't know then there would even be an Emily. They just liked the house. And that contemporary ranch style suits them, don't you think?" she rattled off breathlessly.

"Mmm-hmm. And I like them a lot. They seem like good people," Zach replied, acutely aware of her unease yet determined not to let that deter him from broaching the subject that had been on his mind for days. "But let's talk about us for a minute, okay?"

Rebecca glanced down, twisting her hands nervously in her lap. After a long pause she spoke softly. "Is...is there an 'us'?" she asked, her voice quavering slightly.

"I'd like for there to be."

"Even...even after what happened the night you...you took me to dinner?" Her voice was tentative, uncertain.

"Let's talk about that, too."

Rebecca forced herself to look up at him, and the caring and kindness—and concern—she saw in his eyes made her throat tighten. She swallowed with difficulty, searching for an explanation that would be enough to satisfy him but not enough to expose her darkest secret. "I-I'm not a woman who likes to be touched very much." Her voice was so soft he had to lean close to hear her.

The obvious question hovered on his lips, but he refrained from asking it. He doubted whether she would tell him why, anyway, not at this point in their relationship. So he'd have to approach her reply from a different direction.

"In general—or just by me?" he asked, striving for a teasing tone.

"In general."

There was silence for a moment, and when he spoke his voice was gentle. "Touching is part of a relationship between two people who like each other, Rebecca."

She was aware of that. It was the source of her fear. "I know."

"Do you like me?"

"Yes." Her voice was a mere whisper.

"Then maybe you should define what you mean by touching," he suggested quietly. He reached over and took her hand, lacing his fingers through hers, stroking the side of her hand with his thumb. "Does this kind of touching bother you?"

Her heart began to pound in her chest as she looked at his strong hand linked with hers, and she drew a shaky breath. "Yes." His thumb stilled, and she hurried on. "B-but not in the way you mean. I...I like that."

He resumed the gentle stroking motion, then reached over with his other hand and tipped her chin up, forcing her to meet his eyes as he traced a gentle finger down her cheek. "Do you like this kind of touching, Rebecca?" he asked, the timbre of his voice deepening.

She closed her eyes as his caress sent a shiver of excitement rippling through her. "I...yes, I like that," she whispered.

He leaned over then, slowly, and pressed his lips to her forehead, letting them travel gently down the bridge of her nose to her lips. "How about this?" he asked huskily, his breath warm against her face.

Even though it was Easter, the fireworks that suddenly erupted all around her made Rebecca feel like it was the Fourth of July. "I...I like that, too," she replied unsteadily.

Zach pulled back then, far enough to look into her dreamy eyes filled with unbridled yearning and ran his fingers through her hair, brushing it back softly from her face. "Well, I don't see much of a problem here, Rebecca. You like me, and I like you. And you also like being touched, whether you realize it or not. So here's my suggestion. We'll have one simple rule. If I touch you in a way you don't like, tell me and I'll stop. How does that sound?"

She swallowed, deciding that she might as well be honest with him up front. "Zach, I...touching like this is...it's nice. But I...I can't handle the...the heavier stuff."

He looked at her speculatively. "Is that why you don't date?"

She nodded mutely, her face suddenly forlorn and sad. "I have dated a little. But whenever things got...close, I...I freaked out. I scared the men to death and embarrassed myself.

Needless to say, they never came back. And I wouldn't have gone out again if they had."

He frowned, the unspoken question again hovering between them. What on earth had made her so paranoid of physical closeness? She was not a cold woman. Far from it. She was loving and warm and kind, and he could see the repressed passion in her eyes, struggling for release even now. Something had frightened her at some point in her life—badly enough that she'd denied her desires all these years, given up her dreams of a husband and family. But what? Again he almost asked the question. And again he decided that patience would serve him better. She would tell him when—or maybe *if* was a better word—she felt comfortable doing so. Forcing the issue would only make her close down.

He drew a deep breath and took both her hands in his, angling his body to face her, his eyes intense and serious. "Do you know what I think?" he asked. She shook her head mutely, and he continued. "I think you've never had a real chance to find out whether you can handle the heavier stuff."

She frowned. "But I told you, I—"

"Rebecca," he stopped her gently. "Let me finish. I'd be willing to bet that none of the men you dated went out with you long enough to give you a chance to feel comfortable with them, to establish a trust level. They probably got into the so-called heavy stuff right up front. Sort of the same mistake I made the night I took you out for dinner," he admitted with a disarmingly rueful grin.

She flushed and bit her lower lip. She'd never really thought about that before. "You might be right," she admitted slowly.

"Well, I'm in no hurry," he assured her, even as he silently acknowledged that those words weren't quite true. But he cared enough about this woman to let the relationship progress at whatever pace she set. "We'll just take it a day at a time, okay?"

Rebecca stared at him, finding it hard to believe that at last a man had come her way who not only had integrity, but patience. It seemed too good to be true. Yet the tender touch of his hands and the warmth of his eyes were real enough. How could she refuse?

"All right, Zach. If you're sure."

A smile spread across his face. "I've never been more sure of anything in my life. And by the way…"

"Yes?" She looked at him quizzically when he paused.

He touched her nose with the tip of his finger. "You really were the most beautiful lady at church today."

"So did you have a nice day?" Brad asked, coming up behind Rebecca as she stood at the window watching Isabel show Zach the baby rabbits.

She turned, her face filled with a soft radiance that reflected both her new hope and the feeling of being at peace with her decision. "Yes. It was lovely. Thank you."

Brad stuck his hands in his pockets, then gazed out at Zach and Isabel for a moment before turning again to his sister. "I like him," he said simply.

She smiled, and a faint blush colored her cheeks. "So do I."

"Rebecca, I…" He paused and expelled a long breath. "Look, I don't want to interfere in your life. Dad does enough of that for both of us," he observed with a quick grin. "But I want you to be happy. I don't know why you've never married, although I'm sure you have your reasons. But I also know that you *should* be married. You have so much love to give, and you'd make a wonderful wife and mother. I hope you…well, I hope you give things a chance when the right man comes along."

Rebecca reached over and laid a hand on his arm, her throat constricting. "Thank you for caring so much, Brad. And I— I'm working on it."

"Well, speaking from personal experience, I can only say that the rewards are great when you find the right person," he replied with a gentle smile.

"I can tell," she assured him. She turned to watch Zach and Isabel making their way back toward the house, her tiny hand trustingly tucked into his powerful one. "I guess I'll just have to ask the Lord to guide me on this one."

He put an arm around her shoulders and gave her a quick hug. "I can't think of anyone better to ask," he agreed. "And I'll do the same."

Rebecca poured Zach's coffee, then sat down at her dinette table.

"This is good cake," Isabel declared, digging into the large rose on top of her piece.

"Well, I'm just glad I could share the rest of it with two of my favorite people," Rebecca said warmly, her eyes meeting Zach's across the table. She'd been floating on a cloud ever since she and Zach had talked in the park yesterday. He gave her a lazy smile as he sipped his coffee, and her pulse lurched into overdrive.

"My birthday is next month," Isabel informed them as she polished off the rose.

Rebecca forced her gaze back to the little girl. "So I hear. And I think we should plan something very special. Don't you, Zach?"

"Absolutely."

"A party?" Isabel asked hopefully, her eyes lighting with anticipation.

"Of course. You can even pick the menu for dinner."

"Spaghetti. And French fries. And corn on the cob. And...and chocolate cake!" she declared, ticking off the list without hesitation.

Rebecca laughed. "Well, that's not the most nutritious menu I've ever heard. But it is your birthday, so I suppose we can eat like that for one day."

"Let's see," Zach reflected, reaching for his calendar. "Your birthday is on a Monday. Maybe we could have a picnic Sunday, too. That way we can celebrate for two days."

"I like picnics," Isabel declared. "Mama and Papa and I used to go on picnics sometimes."

Her face clouded, and Rebecca's heart ached for her. She tried desperately to think of something to distract the suddenly solemn little girl. "A picnic would be great," she agreed. "In fact, why don't we have a slumber party, too?" she suggested with sudden inspiration.

"What's a slumber party?" Isabel asked curiously.

"Well, you bring your pajamas over on Sunday night and sleep here with me. We'll make cookies and watch movies and stay up late."

"That sounds like fun!" she exclaimed enthusiastically. "Can Uncle Zach come, too?"

Rebecca almost choked on her coffee, and her gaze flew to Zach, who grinned at her engagingly.

"Can I?" he asked innocently, his eyes twinkling.

"There's room in the bed," Isabel said, her voice eager as she turned to Zach. "Rebecca has a big bed," she told him.

"Is that right?"

By now Rebecca's face was flaming, but Zach ignored the pleading glance she sent him. He actually seemed to be enjoying the situation, she thought in dismay. It was clearly up to her to get out of this. "Isabel, sweetie, slumber parties are…they're just for girls," she stammered.

"Oh." Isabel's face fell. "I wish Uncle Zach could come."

He chuckled. "So does Uncle Zach. But Rebecca's right, honey. The kind of slumber party she's talking about is just for girls," he explained, giving Rebecca a wink that made her nerve endings sizzle.

"We'll still have lots of fun," Rebecca promised, her voice slightly uneven.

"Well…okay," Isabel capitulated.

They moved on to other, less volatile subjects, and it wasn't until Zach and Isabel were leaving that the situation heated up again. She walked them to the door, wondering how Zach would say good-night, knowing that their options were extremely limited with Isabel there. Which was really for the best, she told herself, though for some strange reason it didn't seem so.

When they reached the door, she glanced at him expectantly, and although she thought she saw a flame flare suddenly in his eyes, he simply leaned over and kissed her forehead. Rebecca tried to stem the tide of disappointment that swept over her, forcing herself to smile and wave as she watched them climb into the car. Not until she closed the door and leaned against it did her lips droop. It was true that she wanted to move slowly, but at this rate she wouldn't even get a proper kiss until Isabel left. At which time Zach might very well leave, too, she reminded herself, her spirits taking a sudden nosedive.

She was just sliding the second lock into place when a soft knock sounded on the door. Frowning, she opened it to find Zach smiling at her from the other side.

"I told Isabel I forgot my wallet," he explained.

"Oh. Come on in," she said, turning toward the living room. "I didn't see it, but—"

"Rebecca." He cut her off and reached for her arm, restraining her as he slipped inside and shut the door behind him. "I lied."

She turned to him in surprise. "Why?"

Gently he took her hands and urged her toward him, looping his arms loosely around her waist. "Because that brotherly peck on the forehead didn't quite cut it for me as a good-night kiss," he admitted huskily.

Rebecca swallowed and stared up at him, her hands flat against his chest, the pounding of his heart vibrating beneath her fingertips. "Oh," she breathed softly.

"I'd like to kiss you properly, if that's okay."

She swallowed with difficulty, as delicate color suffused her face. "Y-yes. I think that would be n-nice," she murmured.

Zach stared down at her, telling himself to be slow and gentle and attuned to every nuance of her response. Which was extremely difficult, when what he really wanted to do was pull her close and capture her lips in a kiss so thorough that she would be left breathless. But he knew that impulsive approach would end up killing, not creating, desire.

So instead he left one hand resting lightly at her waist while he cradled the back of her head with his other, his eyes burning into hers as he slowly lowered his head to claim her lips.

Rebecca was frightened—frightened of her reaction, frightened of what would happen if things started to move too fast, frightened at the prospect that he might lose control and forget his promise to go slowly. But as his lips closed over hers— gentle, warm and coaxing, demanding no more than she was willing to give—she slowly began to respond. Her kiss was shy, tentative, cautious, but it was given freely. Her hands crept around his neck of their own volition, and she buried her fingers in the hair at the base of his neck. A soft sigh escaped her lips, and she felt the pressure of his hand at her waist tighten ever so slightly. But she wasn't frightened. He seemed in control, and she could handle this level of intimacy.

When at last Zach released her lips, he drew a long, shuddering breath and pressed her cheek against his chest, his chin resting on top of her head. He held her like that in silence for several long moments, his hand rhythmically stroking the small of her back. Never in a million years would he have believed that he could be so moved by just a simple kiss. But Rebecca's shyness, her inexperience, her sweet response just about undid him. He needed a few moments to compose himself. When he'd blithely made the promise to let her set the pace, he'd had no idea how difficult it would be to keep. If nothing else, he would come out of this experience with better mastery of his self-control, he though wryly.

When at last he spoke, his voice was hoarse and unsteady. "I have to go."

"I know."

"Were you okay with this?"

She nodded. "Mmm-hmm."

"I'm glad. Because I intend to repeat it—as soon as possible. That is, if you're willing." He backed up slightly and looked down at her, his eyes probing.

Rebecca drew a long breath, her lips already tingling with anticipation. "Yes. I—I'm willing," she whispered.

He smiled then, a smile filled with promise and tenderness—and relief. "How about tomorrow night? We'll take Isabel out for ice cream. And I'll think of something else to conveniently forget."

She smiled. "Okay."

He leaned down and brushed his lips across hers once more, then quickly slipped out the door.

She closed it behind him, a dreamy smile on her face. Isabel would enjoy the ice cream tomorrow. But Rebecca was looking forward to a different kind of dessert.

The phone rang, and Rebecca glanced at the clock in surprise. Since Easter, almost a week and a half before, Zach had taken to calling her every night after Isabel was in bed. She looked forward to those long, rambling, end-of-the-day conversations, but he was a little early tonight. Usually he called about ten, and it was only nine-thirty. Maybe he was anxious, she thought with a smile.

"Rebecca? Zach. Listen, I know it's late, but can you come over?"

Her smile of pleasure changed to a frown of alarm at his taut, tension-filled voice. "What's wrong?"

"It's Isabel. She was just drifting off to sleep when a couple of kids set off some fireworks right outside her window. I guess she thought it was gunfire or something. Anyway, she just freaked out. I can't seem to get through to her," he said, his voice touched with desperation.

"I'll be right there."

As Rebecca dashed for her purse and fumbled for her keys, she sent a silent prayer racing heavenward. *Please help me find a way to comfort this little child! I have no experience with this kind of trauma. But I love her so much! Please show me how to use that love to console her,* she pleaded.

Less than ten minutes later Rebecca stood at Zach's door, her finger impatiently pressed to the bell. Within seconds it was pulled open, and the lines of concern etched on Zach's face made her stomach clench. She stepped into the eerily quiet apartment, then turned to face him as he shut the door.

"Tell me what happened," she said quietly.

He sighed and raked his fingers through his hair. "Like I said, fireworks. I heard her cry out, and by the time I got in there she was huddled on the floor with her doll, shaking. I think she's in shock or something. I tried talking to her, but it's like she can't hear me. She's kind of crying, but there's no sound. I'm sorry to bother you, Rebecca, but I just didn't know what else to do."

"It's okay," she said, placing a hand reassuringly on his arm as she tossed her purse onto a convenient chair. "But I'm no expert at this, either. I just hope I can help."

She moved quickly toward the bedroom, pausing on the threshold. The scene was exactly as Zach had described it. Isabel was huddled against the wall, her knees pulled up, her face pale. Her frail shoulders were shaking, and she clutched Raggedy Ann tightly against her chest. There was a glassy look to her eyes, and although she made quiet crying sounds, there were no tears. Rebecca's heart ached for the frightened, vulnerable little girl, and she moved into the room, dropping to her knees beside her.

"Isabel, sweetie, it's okay. You're safe," she comforted her gently, reaching over to brush some stray strands of hair back from the wan face. She could feel a shudder run through the little body, but Isabel continued to stare straight ahead, as if unaware of Rebecca's presence. "Isabel, would you like me to hold you?" Rebecca asked. Still no response.

Rebecca tried to quell her own growing panic. Zach was right—Isabel appeared to be in shock. She glanced up at him in the doorway, her own worried frown a mirror of his. "Well, how about if I just sit here right next to you?'' she asked, turning back to Isabel. "Uncle Zach will sit with us, too, okay?''

She turned again and motioned for Zach to join her, and the two of them sat beside Isabel on the floor. Rebecca looked over at Zach and mouthed the words "touch her" even as she began stroking Isabel's arm. Zach followed her example. "Remember that song I sang to you the first night you were here, Isabel?'' Rebecca said gently. "How about if I sing it again?'' Without waiting for a reply, Rebecca began to softly sing the words of the familiar hymn. She sang all the verses, and as she neared the end she thought she detected a slight softening in Isabel's rigid muscles. "Would you like to hear another?'' she asked, and again she began to sing without waiting for a response.

Rebecca sang for almost twenty minutes, never breaking physical contact with Isabel, and gradually she felt the little girl's muscles go limp, until finally the sobs became more pronounced and the tears began to flow. Suddenly Isabel reached for her, and Rebecca pulled her onto her lap. The thin arms went fiercely around her neck and Isabel buried her face in Rebecca's shoulder. Rebecca closed her eyes and slowly expelled a shaky, relieved breath. Then she gazed at Zach over the little girl's shoulders, rocking her gently.

"I think we'll be okay now,'' she told him softly.

He nodded, the relief evident in the sudden slackening of his strained features, and he rose slowly. "I'll get her a glass of water,'' he offered quietly.

Rebecca nodded, then turned her attention back to Isabel, who clung to her tightly.

"I want my m-mama and p-papa,'' she sobbed.

"I know, sweetie,'' Rebecca consoled her. "I'm sorry they can't be here with you. But Uncle Zach and I love you very much. And we promised your papa we'd take care of you until it was safe for you to go home.''

"S-sometimes it was s-scary at home, when the guns went

off,'' she choked out. ''Mr. Ptasnik, who lived on the f-first floor, got shot once. I saw it happen from our window. A-after that my papa would make me get d-down on the floor whenever there was trouble. He told me that there wouldn't be any shooting here, but t-tonight I thought I heard guns.''

''It was just fireworks, sweetie, like Uncle Zach told you. You don't need to be scared. We promised your papa that we'd keep you safe, and we will.''

Zach reentered and silently handed Rebecca the glass of water, squatting down beside her.

''Would you like a drink, Isabel? Uncle Zach brought this for you.''

Isabel turned in Rebecca's arms and looked at Zach. He reached over and touched her cheek.

''Rebecca's right, Isabel. We won't let anything hurt you.''

She took a gulp of water and silently handed the glass back to Zach. ''I wish my papa was here,'' she sniffled softly.

''I do too, honey. He misses you just as much as you miss him. But just think of all the stories you'll have to tell him about America when you go home.''

She considered that for a moment, and a ghost of a smile flickered across her face. ''Just like he used to tell me stories about America.''

''That's right.''

Suddenly she yawned, and Rebecca smiled. ''I think it's way past somebody's bedtime.''

Zach reached for Isabel, lifting her easily, then extended a hand to Rebecca, pulling her up in one smooth motion.

''Rebecca, will you stay with me for a little while, please?'' Isabel pleaded as Zach tucked her into bed.

''Sure. I'll just lie here right beside you until you go to sleep, okay?''

''Okay.''

Rebecca looked up at Zach. ''I'll stay for a little while,'' she said softly.

He nodded. ''I've got some papers to read, anyway.'' He

kissed Isabel good-night and walked toward the door, shutting it halfway as he exited. He paused to take a deep breath and massage the tense muscles in his neck. It had been some night, he thought tiredly. Isabel had adapted so well he'd almost forgotten the trauma she'd endured, the terror she'd lived with every day. But tonight's episode brought home very clearly the kind of environment she and Josef coped with on a daily basis.

Zach walked over to the window and stared out into the darkness, shoving his hands into his pockets. What was Josef doing right now? he wondered. Missing Isabel, of course. And mourning Katrina, certainly. He was truly alone now, with only his God and his faith to comfort him.

But maybe that helped more than he realized, Zach acknowledged. Ever since the Easter service, Zach found himself thinking more and more about his abandoned faith. He'd even gone with Rebecca and Isabel to services last Sunday, much to her surprise—and delight. Oddly enough, it gave him a sense of…stability and…connectedness. He couldn't explain why. But for some reason those worship services seemed to fill a gap in his life, offer him a new kind of hope. Maybe Josef felt the same.

Zach fervently hoped so. Because despite the fulfillment Josef found in his work, despite the commitment to his cause that gave his life so much meaning, he must be struggling right now to hold on to his hope and to deal with his loneliness. *Watch over him, Lord,* Zach prayed silently. *Let him know that we care and that he is in our thoughts and prayers.*

Zach pushed the last paper aside and glanced at the clock, his eyebrows rising in surprise. Eleven-thirty. He stood up quietly and moved silently toward Isabel's door, pausing on the threshold to glance toward the bed.

Rebecca lay on her side, one arm protectively around Isabel, her hair splayed on the pillow behind her. Isabel's back was cuddled against Rebecca, and she still clutched Raggedy Ann.

Zach's throat tightened with tenderness as he gazed at them. They both looked so fragile and innocent and vulnerable. And they looked right together, he thought, like they belonged with each other.

Suddenly, with an insight that took him completely by surprise, he wished they belonged with him. Having these two special people in his life these past few weeks had given him a taste of family life. Okay, so it was only temporary. It was just pretend. But despite the fact that he'd spent his life studiously avoiding that kind of commitment, he realized he liked it. A lot.

Rebecca shifted slightly, emitting a soft sigh, and he suddenly wondered what it would be like to have her in his life permanently. That thought had never entered his mind about any of the other women he'd dated. But then again, he hadn't loved them.

Zach frowned. Love? He didn't love Rebecca. At least, not yet. Did he? How did a person know when they were in love?

Zach didn't have the answer to that question. All he knew with absolute certainty was that he cared about Rebecca deeply. And it was becoming harder and harder to imagine his life without her.

Chapter Eleven

Rebecca stretched her jeans-clad legs out in front in of her, closed her eyes and tilted her head back to let the warm, mid-May sun caress her face. The capricious breeze gently ruffled the long russet waves of her hair, and she smiled contentedly, looking more relaxed than Zach had ever seen her.

He watched her quietly across the remains of Isabel's pre-birthday picnic, strewn between them on the large, flat boulder where they sat. Since the fireworks incident, their relationship had grown slowly but steadily. Rebecca had become comfortable with his physical expressions of affection, letting her hair down with him—literally and figuratively—as her trust level grew. And as their relationship developed, Zach found the answer to his question. He was definitely falling in love with Rebecca.

It was odd, he mused. He'd been closer to other women physically. But he'd never felt as connected on a deeper, more emotional, level than he did with the woman beside him. Her innate simplicity, warmth and goodness brought a new, rich dimension to his life, and he said a silent prayer of thanks for the blessing of her friendship which he hoped, in time, would evolve into love.

As if sensing his gaze, she opened her eyes and turned to him, tilting her head questioningly at his enigmatic expression. "What are you thinking?"

He considered the question for a moment, debated the merits of telling her how he felt, and decided the time was not yet right. He couldn't risk scaring her off. Waiting was hard, but it was far preferable to losing her by laying his cards on the table prematurely.

"I had some good news this morning," he told her.

"What?"

"My editor called. They're going to run the series on government corruption. One of my sources came forward voluntarily—with plenty of documentation to validate my story."

For the briefest moment, Zach though he detected a look of anxiety on Rebecca's face. But it was replaced so quickly by a smile he couldn't be sure.

"That's great, Zach! You should be very happy."

He nodded thoughtfully. "Yes, I should be. But strangely enough, I don't feel much of anything…except vindication. When the phone rang I was getting Isabel ready for the picnic—and looking forward to seeing you—and the call seemed more like a nuisance, an unwanted distraction. I've hardly thought about it since." He paused and glanced at Isabel, playing happily at the edge of the stream. "The rat race in St. Louis seems so far away sometimes…almost like another lifetime."

Rebecca studied Zach's pensive profile, trying not to read more into what he was saying than was intended. It *sounded* like he was implying that he'd found something better in St. Genevieve. But he hadn't actually said that. And as far as she knew, he still intended to return to St. Louis when his leave was over and Isabel was gone. Until—or unless—he told her otherwise, she would be wise to remember that this interlude was just an unexpected detour in Zach's life.

"Isabel seems to be having fun," he remarked.

Rebecca looked over at the youngster, who was trying

vainly to catch minnows in a plastic cup, and smiled. "Yes. I'm glad you thought of the picnic."

He turned to her then, his eyes thoughtful. "Remember the last time we were here?"

Rebecca nodded. It was the day after their disastrous dinner, the same day he'd told her about Josef's request and she'd offered to help with Isabel. "It seems like a long time ago," she remarked quietly.

"Yeah, it does," he agreed. "But thank God our paths crossed that day! I don't know how I would have managed Isabel without your help. You've been really great with her."

She waved his praise aside. "You would have done just fine. You're obviously good with kids, Zach. You're a hit at the high school, and Isabel took to you right away. I can see why Josef trusted you with her. You make a good uncle."

He turned to look at his young charge again. She'd filled out since arriving, and her cheeks had taken on a healthy glow. Gone was the solemn, wary look that had so often haunted her eyes when she first arrived. Now she seemed like any other carefree almost-eight-year-old. And oddly enough, instead of being the burden he had anticipated, she'd added an unexpected spark to his life. He was going to miss her—a lot— when she went home.

"Believe it or not, I really feel like Isabel is family now," he said slowly. "When I agreed to this arrangement, it never occurred to me that I'd actually grow to love her. I just expected to be sort of a caretaker—keep her fed, clean, safe and as happy as possible under the circumstances. But now..." He gazed at the little girl again and sighed, his eyes troubled. "Now I dread the thought of sending her back into that turmoil, even though I know Josef will do his best to protect her." He raked his fingers through his hair and expelled a frustrated breath. "God, why does the world have to be in such a mess?" he said helplessly.

Rebecca swallowed past the lump in her throat, knowing the question was rhetorical, knowing also that there was no answer. She, too, had been thinking more and more about Isabel's impending departure. In three weeks they would put her on a plane and send her home to an uncertain future. It would be the hardest thing Rebecca had ever done in her life.

"I guess we always want to protect the people we love," she reflected softly, "even though it's not always possible. We'll just have to put her in the hands of the Lord and pray that He'll watch over her."

"Uncle Zach! Rebecca! Come see the fish I caught!" Isabel called, hopping from one foot to the other in her excitement.

Rebecca forced herself to smile. "Okay, sweetie." She stood up, then spontaneously held out her hand to Zach. She had been initiating physical contact more and more often lately, he realized with gratitude. He knew that her willingness to reach out to him spoke far more eloquently than words of her growing trust and deepening feelings.

He stood up and laced his fingers with hers, his mouth quirking into an apologetic smile. "Sorry to be so melancholy. I didn't mean to put a damper on the party."

"It's okay. I've been having the same thoughts lately myself. It will be so hard to let her go." Her voice faltered, and she took a deep breath. "I just never realized I could care about someone so much this quickly."

Zach gazed at her, and his eyes grew tender and warm. "Neither did I," he concurred huskily.

He wasn't talking about Isabel anymore, Rebecca realized, her heart soaring at his intimate tone. But before she got carried away she reminded herself that while Zach might care for her, she had no idea just how deeply his feelings ran. She suspected that he was used to casual relationships, where each partner took what they needed and then moved on. And that wasn't her style at all.

But even if he was serious, she still had another obstacle to overcome. In the past few weeks she'd grown comfortable with the gradual introduction of physical contact into their relationship. She welcomed his kisses, waited eagerly for his tender touch. But always she sensed a simmering passion just below the surface, firmly held in check for the moment but clearly seeking release. And when he did give expression to that passion, she was terrified that he would find her inadequate or, worse yet, too frightened to respond with anything but panic.

Even that, however, wasn't her greatest fear. For Zach, these few weeks represented a promise kept, a fling at teaching, a change of pace from his hectic life in St. Louis. He hadn't intended the situation to be permanent. As far as she knew, he still didn't.

And so her greatest fear, the one that haunted her dreams, was that bidding farewell to Isabel wouldn't be the only good-bye she would have to say in the very near future.

"Which present would you like to open first?" Rebecca asked, arranging the colorfully wrapped packages on her coffee table. "Or are you too full?" she teased. Much to the amazement of Rebecca and Zach, Isabel had polished off a plate of spaghetti, a pile of French fries, an ear of corn and two pieces of chocolate cake.

"I think she has a hollow leg," Zach declared, reaching over to tickle her.

"I do not," she told him, giggling as she squirmed out of his grasp. "I was just hungry. And I'm not too full to open presents," she informed Rebecca, eyeing them with delight.

"Then how about if you start with Uncle Zach's?" Rebecca suggested.

"Okay." She reached for it eagerly, quickly tearing the paper off. Her eyes sparkled at the child-sized backpack, decorated with characters from a popular animated children's movie, and she threw her arms around Zach's neck. "Oh, thank you, Uncle Zach! Wait till all my friends at school see this next year!"

Rebecca handed her the next gift, two boxes tied together with ribbon. The first contained a ballpoint pen with Isabel's name engraved on it. "For when you start writing," Rebecca told her. The other held a pink sweater with a smiling teddy bear face on the pocket.

"This is the one we saw in the store the other day," Isabel declared excitedly as she held it up. "I love it! Thank you so much!"

"You're very welcome, honey," Rebecca replied. "Here's your papa's present, sweetie." She reached for the package, which had arrived just a few days before, and handed it to Isabel.

The little girl cradled it in her hands for a moment, then carefully tore off the paper to reveal a beautifully carved wooden box. "I bet my papa made this," she speculated softly, running her fingers reverently over the intricate handiwork. "He's a real good carver." She lifted the lid slowly, and inside, on a red velvet lining, rested a folded sheet of paper and another, smaller package.

Isabel removed the package first and unwrapped it, fishing through the tissue to extract a delicate filigreed gold brooch. The front was hinged, and she flipped it open to reveal a photograph of Katrina and Josef. "This was my mama's," Isabel said, her voice subdued. "She always told me someday it would be mine."

Rebecca blinked rapidly, trying desperately to keep her tears at bay. *Don't cry,* she told herself fiercely. *It will only make Isabel feel worse.*

Isabel withdrew the single sheet of paper in the case and unfolded it, frowning at the words before looking up at Zach. "I'm not very good yet at reading, especially handwriting," she told him. "Would you read it to me?"

Zach took it and smoothed back her hair. "Of course, honey." His voice sounded strained, and Rebecca knew he was struggling with his emotions, just as she was.

"My dearest Isabel," he began. "I am so sorry that I cannot be with you to celebrate your eighth birthday. But I will be thinking of you all day, and hoping you have a good time with

Uncle Zach and Rebecca. Wasn't it nice of them to have a party just for you?

"I made you this treasure box, which I hope you will keep always and fill with special things that are important to you. I have given you the first treasure to put in it, the brooch your mama loved so much. Remember how she always wore it close to her heart? I hope you will do the same, my child, to remind you that your mama and I will always be close to your heart, even when we are far away.

"I miss you, little one, more than words can say. You are my sunlight and my joy. Your mama always used to say that God gave us a touch of heaven when He sent you to us, and I believe that she was right. You are a precious gift, and I love you with all my heart. I am counting the days until you are home with me again.

"Happy birthday, Isabel. And may God be with you."

Zach's voice was grave by the time he finished, and he cleared his throat as he slowly refolded Josef's heartfelt note. Rebecca wiped away the tear that suddenly spilled out of her eye, then reached over to hug the suddenly subdued little girl at her side.

"Your papa loves you very much, Isabel," she said, her voice choked. "You're a very lucky girl to have such a wonderful father."

"I know," Isabel replied in a small, quavering voice. She fingered the delicate brooch and stared at the photograph of the smiling young man and woman. "I miss him. And I miss my mama. She was very pretty, wasn't she?"

"She was beautiful," Rebecca agreed. "I think you have her lovely smile, as a matter of fact."

Isabel looked up at Rebecca. "Really?"

"Really."

"Maybe someday I'll look like her," Isabel said hopefully.

"I think that's a very good possibility. Would you like me to pin the brooch on for you?"

Isabel nodded, and Rebecca reached over to secure it firmly on Isabel's sweater.

"They're right by my heart now, aren't they?" she said wistfully.

"Yes, sweetie, they are." She had to get away for a minute, Rebecca thought desperately, or she was going to lose it completely. "Zach, let me get you some more coffee," she offered, reaching for his nearly full cup, fleeing to the kitchen before he could respond.

Even before she reached that sanctuary, the tears were trickling down her cheeks. She leaned against the refrigerator and closed her eyes, her heart tattered, her emotions raw. How on earth could they send this poor child back to the danger and turmoil in her country? And yet she belonged with Josef, who clearly loved her more than anything else on earth. She thought about all the lonely nights he'd spent since Isabel's departure, painstakingly creating the treasure box for her in his silent and empty apartment, and her heart ached. Another tear traced its way down her cheek, and she struggled to stifle her sobs, the back of her hand against her lips. Josef needed Isabel—desperately. But could he protect her? Dear God, what are we to do? she cried silently. How can we ever let her go?

Rebecca suddenly felt two strong arms encircle her, and then Zach pulled her close, smoothing her hair tenderly as he held her. He pressed her cheek against his chest and stroked it soothingly.

"I put a video in," he said softly, his lips against her forehead. "She'll be occupied for a few minutes, anyway."

"Oh, Zach!" Rebecca whispered brokenly. "She's so little. And so helpless. Just thinking about sending her back..." Her voice choked.

"I know." His own voice sounded none too steady.

"I'll worry about her constantly."

"So will I." He pressed her even closer, and she hugged him tightly as they tried to draw strength from each other. "I was beginning to think I might enjoy having kids someday, but I'm not sure I can handle the emotional turmoil and worry that goes with that responsibility," he said heavily. "Isabel isn't even my daughter, and yet this whole thing is tearing me up inside."

"I guess that's part of what loving is all about," Rebecca replied tearfully. "Just by caring we expose ourselves to hurt and risk. And yet...Isabel has added so much to my life. I wouldn't have wanted to miss that."

As Zach stroked her back comfortingly, Rebecca realized that she felt the same way about him. Even if he left next month, as he very well might, he had given her a precious gift. With patience and gentleness, he had helped her to believe that she could overcome her debilitating fear of physical intimacy and ultimately realize her dream of having a husband who would also father her children.

The only problem was, she couldn't imagine anyone in that role but Zach.

The sound of shattering dishes—for the second time in an hour—brought a frown to Rebecca's face, and she glanced up from the computer in her tiny office at the restaurant. She didn't usually come in on Sunday, but she'd been trying to spend as much time as possible with Zach and Isabel, and so she'd gotten behind on paperwork. Two of her high school wait staff had also volunteered to come in and set up for a special party she was doing tomorrow. But it sounded like her profits were going right down the drain.

She was about to investigate when a tentative knock sounded on her half-closed door and Pete Cramer stuck his head in. "I'm sorry to bother you, Ms. Matthews, but I think there's something wrong with Melanie," he told her, his face a mask of concern. "She looks kind of...funny. I asked her if she was sick, but she said no."

Rebecca studied the lanky youth with a frown. He'd only been on the staff for a week, but already she could see that he was a hard worker. He was also very sensitive to people.

If he said something was wrong with Melanie, she believed him.

"Are you two about done?" she asked.

"Yeah. We just finished."

"Great. Thanks a lot for coming in, Pete. And ask Melanie to come back for a minute, would you? Just lock the door behind you as you leave."

"Okay."

He disappeared, and a couple of minutes later she heard the front door open and close. Moments later a pale, drawn Melanie appeared in the office doorway, biting her lip nervously. The sixteen-year-old looked nothing like her usual cheerful, smiling self, Rebecca noted worriedly.

"I'm really sorry about the dishes, Ms. Matthews," the girl apologized. "You can just take it out of my pay. I don't mind."

"Don't worry about it, Melanie," Rebecca reassured her. "I'm more concerned about you. You've been working for me for nine months, and I don't think you've ever dropped a plate or glass, let alone a tray. Is everything all right?"

Melanie lowered her eyes and rubbed the palms of her hands nervously against her jeans. "Yeah. I...I guess so."

Her tentative tone negated her words, and Rebecca stood up and impulsively put her arm around the girl's shoulders. "I have a feeling that's not quite true," she said gently. "Would you like to have a soda and talk for a few minutes? I'm a good listener."

Melanie considered the offer for a moment, again nervously biting her lip. Finally she nodded her head jerkily. "Okay."

"Go ahead into the restaurant. I'll grab the sodas."

By the time Rebecca joined her, Melanie's eyes were suspiciously moist and her shoulders were hunched miserably. She was obviously deeply upset, but she remained silent, so Rebecca decided to do a little probing.

"Have you had some bad news, Melanie?" she asked quietly. She knew the plant where her father worked was downsizing. Perhaps he was being laid off, which would certainly disrupt the whole family.

The girl shook her head. "No."

Rebecca glanced at Melanie's hand as the girl toyed with the straw, noticing the bruise on her arm for the first time.

"What happened here?" Rebecca asked, laying her finger gently against the purple area. Melanie flinched and her face seemed to grow even paler. Rebecca realized that the bruise was a clue to her present emotional distress. "When did you do this?" she prompted gently.

"L-last night. I went to the end-of-the-school-year dance."

"Well, I've had a few bruised toes from dancing, but never a bruised arm," Rebecca commented, trying unsuccessfully to induce the girl to relax a little.

"It didn't happen at...at the dance. It happened later."

A niggling suspicion suddenly put Rebecca on alert. She reached over and took the girl's hand.

"Melanie, honey, who did you go with?"

"J-Jack Simpson."

"Did he do this?"

Suddenly the girl broke down, no longer able to keep the tears in check. Between choked sobs, she told Rebecca what happened—the excitement of being asked out by one of the most popular boys at school, the fun she had at the dance, the drive to lookout point...and the increasingly aggressive, suddenly frightening, advances that she'd fought off as fear had given way to panic. Only the arrival of another car of laughing teenagers had halted the terrifying attack. But the incident had left Melanie shaken and deeply upset.

Rebecca hugged the shaking girl, trying to control her seething rage. "Did you tell your parents?" she asked, struggling to maintain an even tone.

"N-no," the girl sobbed.

"Don't you think you should?"

"I...I don't know," she replied helplessly.

"Would it help if I called? Asked them to come over here?"

"I...I think so."

"Then that's what we'll do."

An hour later Rebecca stared at Melanie's parents in disbelief after sending Melanie out of the room. "You mean you aren't going to do anything about this?" she demanded, her eyes blazing.

John Lewis rubbed a hand wearily across his face. "Look, Ms. Matthews, Melanie is a good girl and we want to protect her. But Jack is the son of the plant manager, and my job is already in jeopardy. Betty here has medical expenses, and I have four kids to support. I can't afford to take any risks. Besides, it worked out okay. Nothing happened."

"Nothing?" Rebecca's voice was outraged. "Mr. Lewis, Melanie was traumatized last night. An incident like that can leave emotional scars that never heal. And retribution in the workplace is illegal."

"Yeah. So they say. But that doesn't stop it from happening," he replied wearily. "We'll do our best to keep her out of situations where something like this could happen again. And we'll keep her away from that boy. That's all we can do."

Rebecca knew it was useless to press the point, and she watched in helpless frustration as they left, their arms around their daughter. She knew they loved Melanie, knew they meant what they said about doing their best to protect her. But she also knew it was wrong to let that boy get away with what bordered on criminal behavior. What if that other car hadn't driven up and prevented him from finishing what he started? Melanie was lucky. She'd escaped with her virtue intact. But Rebecca knew she could easily carry the emotional scars for the rest of her life.

Rebecca prowled around the restaurant restlessly, too angry to even think straight. She needed to do something to work off her anger, release some of the hyper energy coursing through her veins. Cooking always helped, she thought, heading for the kitchen. A glance at her watch told her she had three hours before Zach and Isabel were scheduled to pick her up for dinner. Hopefully by then she would calm down.

As he passed Rebecca's restaurant, Zach eased his foot off the accelerator in surprise. She'd mentioned at church that she planned to stop by for a little while, but that was hours ago. Why was her car still here?

He pulled up to the curb and parked, then hesitated. He'd been on his way to her apartment, knowing he was an hour early, hoping she wouldn't mind. A friend of Isabel's from Sunday school had unexpectedly invited her for dinner, a movie and a slumber party, and Zach had agreed. He was happy Isabel had made some friends her own age. And, on a more selfish note, he was also grateful for the unexpected opportunity to see Rebecca alone.

Frankly, he was beginning to worry about the lack of progress in their relationship. While Rebecca seemed comfortable with small intimacies, his attempts to get closer to her emotionally made her tense. He could feel her withdraw, close down, put up a No Trespassing sign. And he'd promised not to push. He'd kept that promise, but it grew more difficult daily.

Rebecca had said once that she wasn't a woman who liked to be touched. And he knew, somewhere in her background, there must be a good reason for that. She hadn't chosen to share it with him, which was her right. But he'd hoped that his patience and consideration would eventually make her comfortable enough to trust him, to reveal the secrets of her heart that made her wary.

So far that hadn't happened. And he was running out of time. Isabel was leaving in two weeks. His leave was over a week after that. He had some important decisions to make, and a lot of those decisions hinged on Rebecca. He couldn't wait any longer to discuss their situation. He'd held off too long already, hoping things would progress in their relationship, but the status quo persisted. Now it was time to find out why.

Rebecca stirred the soup, banged the lid on the pot and then let the spoon clatter to the stainless steel counter. For some reason, making noise helped her vent the anger that still consumed her, even after two hours.

She slammed a pan on the stove and turned on the heat, then paused as an insistent knocking penetrated the other noises in the kitchen. She glanced toward the back door with annoyance, then wiped her hands on her apron and strode over to yank it open.

Zach's smile faded to a frown as his sweeping glance took in her flushed face, clenched jaw and the lines of strain around her rigid mouth. "Are you all right?" he asked without preamble.

"Of course I'm all right," she snapped, glancing irritably at her watch. "What are you doing here, anyway? I thought you were going to pick me up at six. At home. And where's Isabel?"

His frown deepened at Rebecca's uncharacteristic bad humor, and a tingle of alarm raced along his spine. "What's wrong, Rebecca?"

She pushed some loose strands of hair back from her face and glared at him. "What makes you think anything's wrong?" she demanded tersely. "And where's Isabel?"

"A friend from Sunday school invited her to spend the night and go to a movie."

"I thought we were all having dinner together."

"She wanted to go, Rebecca. I'm glad she has a friend. I didn't think you'd mind."

Suddenly Rebecca wrinkled her nose. She turned in dismay and, with a muttered exclamation, dashed toward the smoking pan on the stove. Zach followed more slowly, propping a shoulder against the wall and folding his arms across his chest as he watched her. He'd never seen her this upset. Anger was seething out of every pore in her body.

She dropped the pan into the sink, then turned to the carrots lying next to the cutting board and began to chop them viciously. When Zach remained silent, she looked up at him irritably. "I don't need an audience," she declared crossly.

"I was just trying to give you some time to cool down," he said, striving for a mild tone even as his nerves grew taut. "Do you want to talk about it?"

In reply she gave him a smoldering look, then went back to the carrots.

"Are you angry at me, Rebecca?" he asked quietly.

"No."

"You could have fooled me."

"Sorry," she said shortly, continuing to chop.

"Well, you're obviously angry about something. So do you want to tell me what's wrong?"

There was silence for several long seconds, and Zach began to think she was going to ignore this question, too. But finally she spoke.

"Do you know Melanie Lewis?" she asked curtly. "One of my waitresses?"

Zach frowned. "Yes. She's in one of my classes, as a matter of fact. Why?"

"She went to the end-of-the-school-year dance last night with the son of her father's boss, and he attacked her."

Zach straightened up abruptly, his eyes narrowing. "What do you mean, he attacked her?"

"Exactly what I said." She gave him a cursory account of the incident, her voice shaking with anger. "And if another car full of students hadn't come by that boy might be facing criminal charges right now," she concluded bluntly.

"Is she okay?"

"Physically, yes. Emotionally, I'm not so sure. I talked to her parents about it, but they're not going to do anything. Can you believe that?" she demanded irately.

"I don't know how much they *could* do," he replied thoughtfully. "Those situations are very sticky. We really don't know all of the circumstances. Maybe it was just a misunderstanding."

"A misunderstanding!" Rebecca stared at him disbelievingly, so angry she could barely choke out the words. "She was practically raped!"

"That's a serious charge, Rebecca," he replied gravely.

"It's true!"

"We haven't heard his side."

"I don't need to! I heard Melanie's! I saw her eyes! I know her!"

"I'm not saying she wasn't frightened," Zach tried to placate her. "But maybe she just got in over her head. Maybe he misinterpreted her cues."

"Or maybe he just decided to add another notch to his belt," she replied with cold fury.

"Rebecca, all I'm saying is that we don't know the whole story," he pointed out. "A charge like that could ruin a young boy's life."

"Well, what do you think it does to the victim's?" she shot back.

The conversation was getting way too emotional for Zach. "Look, Rebecca, calm down. You did everything you could. You talked to Melanie. You talked to her parents. They made their decision. There's nothing else you can do."

She finished the carrots and reached for the celery, pausing only to glare at Zach in silence.

"Rebecca, there's a real stigma attached to a charge like this, whether it's true or not," he tried again. "I did a series on date rape a couple of years ago, and it's a murky issue."

She looked at him, her eyes blazing. "Oh, so Mr. Journalist thinks he's an expert just because he wrote a few articles," she retorted sarcastically.

"It was an in-depth series," he replied defensively. "As a matter of fact, it won several awards."

"Well, excuse me. I guess that qualifies you as an expert," she said derisively.

His own temper was beginning to flare. Planting his fists on his hips, he faced her across the counter. "And you are? What makes you such an expert on the topic?" he flung back at her.

She stopped and glared at him, one hand clenched around the knife, the other white-knuckled as it gripped the edge of the counter. When she spoke, her voice was low, but it contained a harsh undertone of bitterness, and it shook with barely controlled rage.

"Because when I was Melanie's age, I came this close," she held up one trembling hand and measured a meager half-inch gap between her thumb and index finger, "to having it happen to me."

Chapter Twelve

For several eternal seconds of quivering, shocked silence they stared at each other across the room, Zach stunned by Rebecca's words, she equally stunned that she'd spoken them.

In a two-second explanation consisting of one simple sentence, Zach finally had an answer to the question that had troubled him for weeks. Now he understood why Rebecca was so afraid to let anyone close. The traumatic experience she'd endured as an impressionable young girl had apparently convinced her that accepting a date carried serious physical risks or, at the very least, expectations of physical closeness. But Rebecca didn't even engage in casual displays of affection, let alone intimacy. With her sensitive nature, that frightening early dating experience would have been a nightmare, one that had pursued her relentlessly through the years. It had taken what should, in the right context, have been a beautiful experience and made it an act of aggression, totally devoid of tenderness or even consideration. No wonder she rarely dated after that, was still so fearful when even a hint of passion surfaced.

As these thought raced through Zach's mind, his shock rapidly gave way to anger. How could anyone have hurt this warm, vulnerable, caring woman? he railed silently. His jaw clenched as a cold fury enveloped him and a surge of protectiveness swept over him, so fierce it took his breath away. For the first time in his life he felt capable of doing serious damage to another human being.

Rebecca was aware of Zach's changing expressions, but only on a peripheral level. She was too busy trying to cope with the fact that she'd just revealed her most closely guarded secret. Melanie's story had brought back her own experience with a shattering, vivid intensity that tilted her world out of alignment. The anger she'd vented on Zach had been directed not at him, but at the boy who had scarred her indelibly so many years ago. And it was also directed at herself, for allowing his despicable behavior to ruin her life all these years. It was almost as if a release valve had been flicked open, and all the anger and hurt she'd bottled up inside for almost twenty years had finally burst forth.

As she stared at Zach across the room, trying to decide what to do next, his figure suddenly wavered before her eyes, and the room tilted strangely. She groped for the edge of the counter, then grasped it tightly as she tried to take a deep breath. But her lungs refused to cooperate.

Zach saw the sudden look of disorientation in Rebecca's eyes, took in her white-knuckled grip on the edge of the counter and moved rapidly around the work area, praying he would reach her before she nosedived against the unforgiving edge of the stainless steel work space.

Despite the fuzziness in her brain, however, Zach's movement registered, and a surge of panic swept over her. In a triumph of will over body she fought off the sudden attack of vertigo, backing away from him unsteadily even as she rode the waves of blackness that crashed over her. "Don't touch me," she whispered, wrapping her arms around her body, staring at him with frightened eyes as she willed herself to remain upright.

He stopped a few feet away, sensing that she needed the

safety of distance for the moment but poised to reach out to her instantly if she started to pass out. She looked so alone, so vulnerable, so in need of being held. It took every ounce of his willpower to honor her plea when his overriding instinct was to pull her into his arms and hold her until she felt safe and protected and loved.

He saw a shudder ripple through her, and he swallowed convulsively, his gut clenching as burning rage once more consumed him. But comfort and compassion, not anger, were what she needed now, he reminded himself. If she wouldn't let him go to her, maybe he could get her to come to him. Slowly, nonthreateningly, he lifted his hand and held it out to her.

"Let me help, Rebecca," he murmured softly.

She shook her head jerkily. The dizziness was gone, but now she felt oddly weak—and weary. "It's too late," she told him, her voice flat and lifeless.

"I don't think it is. Talking about things can help a lot, and I'm a good listener." When she didn't respond, he took a tentative step forward. "At least take my hand," he coaxed.

She looked down at the strong but gentle hand he offered, then up into his compassionate, caring eyes. Maybe she *should* talk about it. Her secret was out now, anyway. Perhaps the Lord had let her make that slip as a sign that it was time to share her story, to open her heart to this special man. Perhaps by doing that, she could truly begin to heal.

Slowly, hesitantly, she reached out and took his hand, and he enfolded her cold fingers in his warm, reassuring clasp. Gently he urged her toward him and wrapped his arms around her trembling body, stroking her back.

He held her like that for a long time, murmuring soothing words, telling her over and over again that everything would be all right, until finally her trembling subsided. Then, his arm around her shoulders, he led her into the restaurant, to a roomy booth in the corner. As they sat down, he pulled her close, into the protective curve of his arm. Silently he handed her his handkerchief, and she took it gratefully, dabbing at her red-rimmed eyes.

"I—I'm sorry for the way I treated you just now," she apologized tremulously. "It wasn't fair."

"A lot of things in life aren't fair," he said, his voice rough with emotion. "Rebecca, I'm so sorry! I wish I could just erase that whole ugly experience from your life."

"I've wished the same thing thousands of times through the years," she admitted, the catch in her voice tugging at his heart. "But you can't change the past."

"No. All you can do is move on and try not to let it ruin your future."

"That's easier said than done, Zach," she told him wearily.

"I know that, sweetheart," he replied sympathetically. "Sometimes, though, talking it out helps to put it to rest. Do you want to tell me about it?"

She sighed. "I guess I can try. I just don't know where to start."

"Then how about if I play journalist and ask a few questions?" he suggested.

"Okay."

"You said you were the same age as Melanie?"

"Yes. Sixteen. I guess that's why her experience hit so close to home."

"Who was the boy?" Whoever he was, and wherever he was, Zach fervently hoped he'd been made to pay in some way for what he'd done to Rebecca. Maybe that was wrong. But it was the way he felt.

"H-he was the high school football hero. Everyone wanted to go out with him. I couldn't believe it when he asked me to the spring dance, which was the big social event of the season. I thought I was so lucky, to be asked out by the big man on campus on my very first date."

"You mean...this happened to you the very first time you ever went out?"

"Yes."

She heard him mutter something under his breath. Though she couldn't quite make it out, she knew from his tone that it wasn't pretty. She inched closer and let her hand rest lightly on his thigh, almost in a gesture of comfort, he thought, a muscle in his jaw twitching. Even in the midst of her own pain, she was attuned to the needs of others. But that was Rebecca. He reached over and covered her hand with his own as she continued.

"We had fun at the dance. And afterward, when he asked me if I wanted to go for a drive, I said yes. I assumed he wanted to…well…do a little kissing, and I wasn't opposed. I thought it was pretty exciting to have a first date and a first kiss all in the same night. Except…except he had a lot more than that on his mind."

Zach squeezed her hand, and she drew a long, shaky breath.

"We drove to Miller's Point. It wasn't the usual make-out place, but I wasn't suspicious. I just figured, being an 'experienced' guy, he'd found a few places that were off the beaten path. I just didn't realize how 'experienced' he was."

She swallowed convulsively, and Zach felt her muscles tense as she continued.

"He had a bottle of wine in the car. I only had one glass, but it was my first experience with wine, so it didn't take much to make me a little 'floaty,' you know? After the wine, he said he knew a great spot that overlooked the river, and would I like to sit there for a while and enjoy the view? I said yes."

She was starting to shake again, and Zach reached over and stroked her cheek, his eyes holding hers compellingly, reassuringly. "It's okay, Rebecca. It happened a long time ago. It can only hurt you now *if* you let it."

"I know." He was right. She had to get through this, deal with it once and for all, so she could move on. "For…for a few minutes it was fine. He kissed me, and it was…nice. But all of a sudden he got…he got really…aggressive. It was like he became a different person. His kisses weren't…simple…anymore. They were…rough. I started to get scared, and I tried to pull away. But he pushed me down and just kind of fell across me. He was big...and...and strong. My arms were pinned down and I—I couldn't move.''

Her words were choppy now, her breathing uneven. Zach wanted to tell her to stop, to bury the terrible memories so deeply they would never resurface again. But he knew they would never be put to rest until she dealt with them. The best thing he could do for her was let her talk through the terror and remembered pain, until it no longer had the power to dominate her life. And so he remained silent, stroking her hand comfortingly as she spoke.

''I had long hair, and he...he twisted it so I couldn't move my head. The more I struggled, the harder he pulled.'' She stopped and squeezed her eyes shut. A tear trailed down her cheek and she drew in a harsh breath. ''I fought as much as I could, but it was useless. I tried to scream, but he never took his lips off of mine. There wouldn't have been anyone to hear me, anyway. The only thing I could do was pray.

''Then all of a sudden I felt him p-pulling up my dress, and I heard a zipper. I...I knew what he was planning to do. Oh, God!'' She let out an anguished cry, and Zach pulled her close, his gut twisting painfully.

''It's okay, Rebecca. It's okay,'' he repeated helplessly, knowing it wasn't but unable to find any adequate words of comfort. Her whole body was shaking, and he could feel her tears soaking through his cotton shirt. All he could do was hold her until she was ready to continue and try to control the rage that burned in his heart.

After a couple of minutes, she drew in several ragged breaths and spoke again, her voice raw with pain, her fingers clutching his shirt convulsively. ''I think I...I was hysterical by then, because I d-don't even remember clearly what happened next. Except that out of the blue it started to rain. It was a downpour, as if the heavens had opened—almost like a miracle. In any case, it dampened his enthusiasm—and his determination. He took off for the car.

"For the longest time I just lay there. I guess I was in shock or something. But finally I got up and stumbled back to the car. He was waiting for me, none too patiently, aggravated about his rented tux getting wet. He told me to get in. We were out in the middle of nowhere, and I guess I sensed that at that point it would be more dangerous to wander the back roads on foot in a storm than ride back to town with him. Besides, I could tell his ardor, if that's what you'd call it, had cooled. So I got in and he took me home. Can you believe that he...he asked me out again, two weeks later?" she said brokenly, the tears still streaming down her face.

Zach muttered another unflattering comment and pressed her cheek more closely to his chest. She could feel the hard, rapid thudding of his heart, could sense his anger in the rigid lines of his body. Oddly enough, her own simmering rage, so tightly coiled all these years, had eased.

Finally Zach drew back slightly and cradled her tear-streaked face with his hands, his thumbs gently erasing the evidence of her tears. "Have you ever told anyone about this, Rebecca?"

"N-no."

"Why not?"

"Because I...I was too ashamed. I felt like maybe it was my fault, that I'd done something wrong, encouraged him in some way."

"You don't still think that, do you?"

She shook her head. "No. But it took me a long time to get past that. And I never did get over my fear of being alone with men. That's why the few dates I went on turned into such disasters. I just assumed every time a man kissed me that it would evolve into an attack. I know that's irrational, but I can't seem to control the panic. It just...overwhelms me."

"Have you ever thought about counseling?"

"Yes. But I—I've always been too embarrassed to talk about it. And I figured eventually I would get over it. Only...I never did."

He stroked her back in silence for a few seconds, then reached up and fingered a few loose tendrils that had worked free of her hairpins and now lay curled softly at her nape. "That's why you always wear your hair up, isn't it?" he asked with sudden insight. "Because he used your long hair against you that night."

She hesitated, then nodded. "Yes. I like long hair, but it seemed…safer…to wear it up. And this style suits my profession. But I let it down around family and close friends. Like…like you," she said, her voice suddenly shy, her eyes downcast.

He studied her for a moment, then decided to risk the question. "Is that all I am, Rebecca?" he asked softly. "A friend?"

He felt a shudder run through her as she drew in a shaky breath. "I…I like you a lot, Zach," she replied cautiously. "But I have a major problem with…with intimacy. I break into a cold sweat just thinking about it. Touching makes me feel fear, not desire. And no man's ego can take that forever." Her voice suddenly sounded resigned and defeated.

Zach didn't believe for a minute that Rebecca was incapable of desire. He'd seen it flashing in her eyes on any number of occasions. But *she* believed it, and only patience and understanding would convince her otherwise.

"Can I tell you something, Rebecca?" he asked quietly. "I don't think the right man's ego would *have* to take it forever. I've seen the way you look at me. I know in your heart you feel more than just liking for me. You're just too afraid to let those feelings out. But my ego is strong enough to handle your fear until you feel comfortable enough to move forward. I think we could have something very special, you and I. And I also think you owe it to yourself—to both of us—to give this thing a chance."

Rebecca bit her lip as she considered his words. How much progress could she make in three weeks, before Zach left? And the real question was, how much did she want to make? Zach never talked about leaving, or what would happen when he did. Maybe he just wanted to help "cure" her out of compassion and genuine caring. It didn't mean he loved her. But to let the relationship progress and then have him walk out—could she deal with that?

Rebecca wanted to believe that Zach cared enough about her to find a way to keep her in his life once he left St. Genevieve. St. Louis wasn't that far away, after all. If he wanted to continue their relationship, they could manage it.

She closed her eyes, seeking guidance. *Please, Lord, give me a sign. Show me what to do. Do I take a chance on this wonderful man, trust that he cares enough about me to make me part of his life, or do I throw away the possibility for love, let him walk away, out of fear?*

No answer was immediately forthcoming, and she sighed. But when she opened her eyes, her gaze fell on a painting of tulips she'd recently added to the restaurant. It spoke eloquently of spring and hope and new life. And suddenly she knew what she was going to do.

"All right, Zach," she said quietly. "Let's give it a chance."

Zach gathered up the final papers from his desk and shoved them into his briefcase, snapped the clasp shut and glanced around the deserted classroom. It was hard to believe that the last day of school had arrived already.

"Mr. Wright?"

Zach glanced toward the door and smiled. "Hi, Pete."

"Hi. Do you have a minute?"

"Sure. Come on in. I thought everyone had cleared out by now."

"I was just cleaning out my locker." He shuffled in self-consciously, his hands stuck in the pockets of his jeans.

Zach eyed him speculatively, noting the slight flush on his cheeks and the spark in his eyes. He could feel an…excitement…radiating from the youth. "What's up?" he asked mildly.

Suddenly Pete grinned, unable to keep the good news to himself any longer. "I won the short story contest!" he blurted out, his voice tinged with pride.

Zach's lips curved into a smile of pleasure. He strode toward the boy, taking his hand in a firm grip as he laid his free hand on Pete's shoulder. "Congratulations! Are you the national winner?"

"Yeah. The story will be published next fall. And there's a thousand-dollar prize!"

Zach grinned. "I knew you could do it. You're one of the most talented writers I've ever met."

The boy blushed and looked down. "Well, I just wanted to say that if it hadn't been for you, this would never have happened."

Zach waved his thanks aside. "It's hard to hide talent like yours, Pete. Sooner or later you would have found your voice with or without me."

The boy frowned and shook his head slowly. "I don't think so, Mr. Wright. I was at kind of a low point in my life, getting involved in some things that weren't…well…very good. I think you came along at just the right time. You made me believe in myself. I wouldn't even have known about the contest if it hadn't been for you, let alone entered it. And so I just wanted to…to say thanks for making such a difference in my life. And to ask if it would be okay for me to keep in touch when you go back to St. Louis."

Zach smiled and squeezed Pete's shoulder. "Absolutely." He reached over to the desk, jotted down his address and handed it to the boy. "I'll be in town for at least another two weeks, though."

"Maybe I'll run into you at Rebecca's," the boy said hopefully.

Zach smiled. "You can count on it."

"Well…see you around."

Zach watched him amble out, filled with a sense of deep contentment. Never, in all his years of reporting, had he been aware of making such a direct impact on a single life. And it felt good, he realized. Very good.

Zach propped his hip on the edge of the desk, folded his arms across his chest and gazed pensively out the window at the lush foliage. When he'd arrived in St. Genevieve, in mid-February, the world was gray and dead and cold. Now, at the end of May, it was bright and alive and warm. Much like his heart, he realized. Here, in this small rural town, as a high school teacher, he'd found work that energized him in a way journalism no longer did. He'd found, through Isabel, a new outlook on the world and discovered a surprising paternal side to his personality. And he'd found, in Rebecca, a woman to love.

He thought about the past two weeks, since she'd revealed the trauma that had scarred her heart. He couldn't believe the progress they'd made in just that short time. One by one, Rebecca's emotional defenses had begun to drop away. She was relaxed around him, lighthearted, even affectionate at times. Finally, the scars of the past had begun to heal, and they grew closer day by day. When she faltered, he held fast, and with infinite patience, helped her past the hurdle. It hadn't always been easy, he admitted. He wasn't, by nature, a patient man. At least, he never had been before. But he'd learned a lot about patience this spring, both from Isabel and Rebecca. And patience was the key to winning her heart, he knew.

It was hard to believe his time in St. Genevieve was almost over. The weeks had flown by. He'd learned a great deal, been challenged in countless new ways, discovered an unexpected capacity for love and new dimensions to his personality. The break from reporting had definitely been worthwhile and satisfying on many levels, both personal and professional.

The question now was whether to make that break permanent.

As of this morning, he had the perfect opportunity to do so.

When the principal called him into his office before class, Zach assumed it was simply to say thanks and good luck. Instead, he'd offered him a permanent job. Phil Carr would return in the fall, but another English teacher was leaving unexpectedly. Zach had been flattered—and taken aback. The principal had asked him to think about it for a couple of weeks, and then, if he was interested, they could discuss the details.

Zach was definitely interested. Professionally, it would be a good change for him. But ultimately his answer depended on the answer to another, far more personal question: would Rebecca agree to marry him?

Zach hadn't planned to propose just yet. She was only now beginning to feel comfortable with him. But he knew her self-confidence was still at a low ebb, knew she still harbored tremendous doubts and worries about their physical relationship.

Personally, he had no such doubts. He was convinced that in the context of marriage, of a "till death do us part" vow, she would learn to respond, to give full expression to the passion he knew was in her heart. But with the job offer now to consider, he needed to pose the question sooner than planned. Because if he made a commitment to stay in St. Genevieve, he wanted her by his side—permanently.

Zach stood up and reached for his briefcase, his thoughts turning to Ted Larsen's request for a meeting tomorrow in St. Louis. Zach assumed it was to discuss his return to work and his next assignment. Obviously he'd have to put his editor off. But at least the trip to St. Louis would give him a chance to take care of one very important piece of personal business— a trip to a jewelry store.

Zach stared at Ted, his mouth literally dropping open in surprise.

The managing editor smiled at the younger man's dumbfounded reaction. "Don't look so shocked, Zach. You're a top-notch reporter. You deserve this promotion."

"But...Washington Bureau chief?" Zach said incredulously, his face still stunned. It was the most coveted job on the newspaper, a chance to mingle with the movers and shakers in Washington, to do in-depth coverage of the events that shaped the nation. "What about Joe?"

"He's decided to take early retirement. I guess he figured that after fifteen years on the Washington beat he's pretty much seen it all. We're sorry to see him go, to be honest. He's done a fine job. But new blood won't hurt, and we're all confident you'll do a terrific job."

Zach felt a surge of adrenaline shoot through his veins. Washington! Press conferences with the president. Interviews with the secretary of state. Access to the most powerful political figures in the world. It was heady stuff. "To say I'm overwhelmed would be putting it mildly," he admitted, shaking his head.

"Then you'll accept?"

Accept? He hadn't even fully absorbed the offer yet. His first instinct was to say yes. But the weight of the ring box in the pocket of his sports coat, resting lightly against his heart, made him hesitate. If he accepted the position, all the plans he'd been making for a far different life would have to change dramatically. Zach knew intuitively that Rebecca wouldn't like the fast-paced, glitzy life in Washington, even if she loved him enough to go. The quieter, simpler style of small-town life suited her. And until a couple of minutes ago he thought it suited him, too, especially if she was by his side.

When Zach didn't respond immediately, Ted placed his elbows on the arms of his chair, steepled his fingers and leaned back, eyeing the younger man speculatively. "I can see this isn't quite as simple a decision for you as I expected, Zach. Would you like to take a few days to think it over?"

Zach nodded. "Yeah. There are some…complications."

"Well, just give me a call when you reach a decision." Ted stood up and extended his hand, his grip firm and warm. "Think it through carefully, Zach. Opportunities like this don't come along very often."

As Zach rode down in the elevator, then strolled aimlessly along the street, Ted's words kept replaying in his mind. His editor was right. Some opportunities were rare. Like the offer of Washington Bureau chief. But others came only once in a lifetime. Like winning the love of the most wonderful woman he'd ever met.

Zach detoured into a convenient sidewalk café and mulled over his options as he sipped a cup of coffee. The Washington job certainly offered excitement and the chance to do some of the best reporting of his life. But to take it, he'd have to give up a number of things: satisfying work that he knew, from personal experience, had a direct, positive impact on young people's lives; a life-style that gave him time to breathe; and most important, the woman he loved and the chance to create with her a warm and loving family that would sustain him all the days of his life. That was something Washington couldn't offer. Eventually the excitement there would fade. In the end all he would have to show for his adventure in the nation's capital would be a dusty scrapbook of stories, perhaps a couple of awards to hang on his wall. And those tangible reminders of "success" would be bought at a high price—the price of the life he could have had in St. Genevieve.

Suddenly Zach wondered why he'd even hesitated. Yes, the job offer meant a lot to him. But it meant even more to win one of Isabel's smiles or to feel Rebecca's hand in his or hear the sincere thank-you of a student who had turned his life around. Maybe small-town life didn't have the glitz and glamour of Washington. But he knew with absolute conviction that it was what he wanted.

Zach tossed some bills on the table and rose. "Is there a phone close by?" he asked a passing waitress.

"Sure. Inside. By the rest rooms."

"Thanks."

Zach located it quickly, dialed Rebecca's restaurant, then waited impatiently.

"Rebecca's."

"Rose?"

"No. It's Frances."

"Frances, it's Zach. Is Rebecca there?"

"Of course. Isn't she always? Hold on and I'll get her."

Zach heard her say, "It's your young man, dear," before Rebecca came on the line, and he smiled.

"Zach? Where are you?"

"Still in St. Louis."

"How did it go with your editor?"

"Fine. In fact, are you ready for this? He offered me the job of Washington Bureau chief!"

There was a momentary hesitation, but when Rebecca spoke her voice was bright. "That's wonderful, Zach. When are you supposed to go?"

"I haven't even given him my answer yet."

"Why not? It's a great opportunity, isn't it?"

"Yeah. But…"

"Hang on a second, Zach."

He could hear Rebecca conferring with Rose, something about a customer complaint.

"Sorry, Zach," she apologized, sounding frazzled. "It's a zoo here."

"I can tell." He paused, debating how to proceed. He was anxious to talk with her, explain how he felt, but this was clearly not the best place or time. They needed somewhere quiet, where neither would be interrupted. "Listen, I'll tell you all about it when I see you. I guess you'll be pretty swamped until Sunday morning, won't you?" The Friday lunch rush was barely over, and she was probably already gearing up for the dinner crowd. It would be the same tomorrow.

"Yes. You know how Friday and Saturday are."

He sighed. "Yeah. Okay, how about a picnic on Sunday? Just the two of us. Isabel is going right from church to that pool party with her friend from Sunday school. I'll even bring the food."

"That sounds nice, Zach."

Her voice seemed oddly subdued, and Zach frowned. "Is everything okay?"

"Of course."

"You sound...funny."

"Just tired. It's been crazy around here."

"Well, try not to work too hard. How about if I stop by for lunch tomorrow?"

"I'll look forward to it. Have a safe drive back, Zach."

"At least I won't have to worry about fog this time," he teased. "Although I can't complain too much. Without that fog, I might never have met you."

"That's true. Listen, I've got to run. I—I'll see you tomorrow."

"Rebecca, I—" The line went dead and Zach frowned, a puzzled expression on his face. Her voice had sounded shaky at the end, like she was upset. Maybe it was just a really rough day at the restaurant, he told himself. Maybe it had nothing to do with him. But for some unsettling reason he had a feeling it did.

As Rebecca replaced the receiver, she forced herself to take a calming breath. She'd always feared the day when Zach would begin making plans to return to his old life. Only she hadn't expected those plans to take him to Washington. Maintaining a long-distance relationship between St. Louis and St. Genevieve was manageable. It was much less feasible if he lived a thousand miles away.

"Is everything all right, dear?" Rose asked, pausing as she bustled by to give Rebecca a concerned look.

"Yes," Rebecca assured her, summoning up a bright smile. "I think I'll go out and talk to that customer who was complaining."

"Oh, he's happy now," Rose assured her. "It wasn't that he didn't *like* the soup. He just didn't understand that it was *supposed* to be cold. But I explained it nicely, and he's happy as a clam now. Even ordered a second bowl."

"Well, that's good news. Thanks, Rose."

Rebecca moved back to the stove and automatically went through the motions of preparing the sauce for the chicken Madeira, that evening's entrée, even while her mind drifted far away.

Rebecca knew why Zach had invited her on the picnic. He was going to tell her that he was leaving. He would say that he cared about her, but explain that this was too good an opportunity to pass up. And she couldn't blame him. Washington offered glitz, glamour, prestige, recognition, a higher profile for his work. What did she have to offer? Her love, certainly. But no guarantee about the ability to give physical expression to that love.

It was true that under Zach's gentle, infinitely patient nurturing, she had made great strides in a very short time. She felt closer to Zach and trusted him more than any man she'd ever known. The bud of her long-dormant passion had begun to unfurl. There had been moments when she really believed that she would overcome her problem.

But even though Zach had never pressed for more than tender kisses there were still moments when the familiar, unreasonable panic response kicked in.

Rebecca sighed. She already knew that Zach was a man of deep passion, who would approach the physical component of love with joy, giving affection freely and without inhibition. And he would rightly expect the same from a partner. She just wasn't sure she was up to the task.

So given a choice between the guaranteed excitement of Washington, the challenge of working in the nation's capital in a prestigious position, versus taking a chance on a woman who might never be able to express love fully, she couldn't blame Zach for choosing the former.

It was, quite simply, no contest.

Rebecca tiredly removed her apron and brushed some stray strands of hair back from her face. It had been a very long day. Saturdays were always busy, but today had been absolutely crazy. She was one server short at lunch, and Rose was out sick. So Rebecca found herself doing all the cooking, while Frances filled in for Rose as hostess. She'd hardly had a chance to say ten words to Zach during lunch before dashing back into the kitchen. Dinner hadn't been any less hectic.

She was just about to grab her purse and switch off the lights when the sudden ringing of the phone startled her. She glanced at her watch, noting the time with a frown. Eleven-thirty. No one ever called the restaurant this late. She dropped her purse on the counter and reached over to pick up the receiver.

"Hello?" she said tentatively.

"Rebecca?"

She frowned. It sounded like Zach—sort of. "Zach?"

"Yeah. Listen, I know it's late, but can you come over."

A rope of tension coiled tightly in her stomach. "Is Isabel okay?"

"Yes. She's asleep. I just had an E-mail from a friend of Josef's. He's—" His voice choked, and Rebecca tightened her grip on the receiver as a feeling of foreboding swept over her. When he spoke again she hardly recognized his voice, it was so raw with emotion. "Rebecca, Josef is dead."

Chapter Thirteen

Rebecca stared unseeingly at the wall as her whole body went numb. "What?" she said uncomprehendingly.

"Josef. He...he's dead," Zach repeated in a choked voice.

Suddenly the reality of his news slammed home with a force that sent her reeling, and she groped for the stool, sinking down as her legs turned to rubber. Hot tears stung her eyes and she squeezed them shut, her stomach curling into a tight ball. "Oh, Zach!" she cried, her voice anguished, her heart aching.

"Can you come over?"

It wasn't a question. It was an SOS.

"I'll be there in five minutes," Rebecca promised.

She hung up the receiver and rose, but reaction kicked in with a vengeance. She began to shake, and every nerve ending seemed to be vibrating. She was in no condition to stand, let alone drive, she realized. Even though every instinct told her to get to Zach's side as quickly as possible, she forced herself to sit back down and remain there for a full sixty seconds while she took a dozen deep, steadying breaths. Only then did she grab her purse and run for the car.

As she traveled the short distance to Zach's apartment, she

tried to sort through the jumble of incoherent thoughts racing through her mind. What had happened to Josef? Did Isabel know yet? What would become of the little girl now? She was scheduled to go home in less than a week. And how was Zach coping with the news? He sounded bad on the phone. Shocked. Shattered. Lost. Which wasn't surprising. Josef was his best friend. Closer than a brother, he'd once told her. He must be consumed with grief and pain. Rebecca pressed harder on the accelerator. She had to get to him as quickly as possible! *Lord, please help us through this!* she prayed desperately.

Zach was obviously watching for her, because the minute she pulled up he flung open the door. She jumped out of the car and dashed toward him, catching only a quick glance of his grief-ravaged face before he took her hand and pulled her inside. He pushed the door shut with his foot, then silently buried his face in her shoulder, holding her against him so tightly she could hardly breathe. She felt a shudder run through him, and the sound of his ragged breathing made her eyes flood with tears yet again.

For a long time neither spoke. Zach seemed to need the tactile reassurance, the solace, that only her arms could provide. And so she just held him, stroking his back, feeling his desolation as if it was her own.

When at last he drew back, he left one hand resting at her waist while he wiped the back of the other across his eyes. Rebecca was so used to Zach's rock-solid strength and confidence that it tore at her heart to see him so vulnerable and devastated. She reached up to lay a hand against his cheek.

"Zach, I'm so sorry," she whispered, her eyes echoing the pain in his.

"Me, too." His voice still sounded choked, and he shook his head. "He was such a good man. The kind the world needs more of. Caring, compassionate, committed. And now…" His words trailed off and he looked down at her helplessly. "Why did this have to happen?"

She tried to think of something to say that would comfort,

but nothing came to mind. In the end, she just shook her head. "I don't know," she admitted, her voice breaking.

He sighed, then took her hand and drew her to the couch, pulling her down beside him.

"Have you told Isabel?" she asked.

He shook his head. "No. She's been asleep for hours, and I only got the message about twenty minutes ago. She's one of the reasons I asked you to come over. I hoped that together we could think of a way to tell her. Besides, I just needed you with me. When I got that message, it was like…like I had to reassure myself that the other person I care most about in the world was okay. I just needed to touch you," he said with simple candor as he squeezed her hand.

Rebecca looked at him wonderingly. That was the closest Zach had ever come to revealing the depth of his feelings for her. Was he saying that he…that he loved her? He hadn't used those words, yet what else could he mean? But her feelings, and their relationship, were a low priority at the moment. She would deal with them later. For now, there were other questions to be asked, decisions to be made.

"Do you know what happened, Zach?" she asked gently.

He nodded. "Josef apparently asked a colleague named Stefan to notify me if—" He drew a shaky breath, unable to say the words. "Stefan said that Josef was working late at their makeshift office, and that a bomb went off. He was…killed instantly."

Rebecca shut her eyes and tried to swallow past the lump in her throat. Never before had she been so closely touched by the horror of senseless violence that resulted in the loss of life. A tear trickled down her cheek, and she felt Zach reach over and gently brush it away.

"Oh, Zach, it's so awful!" she whispered, opening her eyes to gaze with shock into his.

"Yeah." He drew a shaky breath, obviously fighting back his own tears, and nodded toward the coffee table. "I got that out of the closet, but I haven't been able to bring myself to open it."

Rebecca glanced toward the large envelope addressed in Josef's hand to Zach. It was the one that Josef had carefully packed in Isabel's luggage, with instructions to open it only if something like this happened. She looked back at Zach and took his hand.

"Maybe it will be easier if we do it together," she said quietly.

He hesitated, then leaned forward and picked up the manila envelope. With one quick motion he slit open the edge and slid the contents, which were held together with a large rubber band, onto his lap. He pulled Rebecca close, and together they scanned the letter on top.

My dear Zachary,

If you are reading this letter, it is because I have been called home to the Lord. Please do not grieve for me, my friend. I am happy now, at peace, and I am once more with my beloved Katrina. All is well with me.

It is Isabel, not me, who needs your sympathy now. In recent weeks, it has become clear to me that without her mother or me here to watch over her, my country will be an inhospitable place for her. It is filled with strife and terror, and while I still believe that things will change, I am resigned that it will not happen during her youth. So there is no life here, no future, for my precious child.

Therefore, Zachary, it is my final wish that Isabel remain in America, the country of her birth, which was always so good to me. I do not expect you to take on the responsibility of raising her. I would not stretch the bounds of our friendship that far. But I do ask that you find her a good and loving home. I have great faith that you will do your best to make sure she is happy and loved.

In this envelope you will find all of the necessary papers—records of Isabel's birth and baptism, of my marriage to Katrina and of her death, as well as letters from my family and my minister, concurring with my decision. Very soon Stefan will send you a record of my death as well. Should you need to obtain any other records or letters, he has agreed to assist you. I have enclosed his address.

I have also included some things that Isabel may find of interest later. Letters her mother and I wrote to each other, photos of her relatives and the house where we lived, some pages from my journal. I believe it is important that she make a new life in America, but it is also important for her to remember her roots.

My dear Zachary, you have my deepest gratitude for all you have already done for Isabel. I hope you will forgive me for placing this one last obligation on you. But I do so, believing that the bond we share will make my request less burdensome. You are my brother in everything but blood, my friend. And I could not have chosen a finer man to fill that role.

I know that this is a difficult time for you. Separation is always painful. But please do not grieve too deeply. I have had a good, full life. I have done satisfying, worthwhile work. I have known the great joy of fatherhood. And I have loved—and been loved—by a woman beyond compare. No man can ask for more.

So farewell, Zachary, until we meet again. And know that you will always be in my prayers.

They finished reading the note at the same time, and Rebecca raised her eyes to his in silence, her face a mask of grief. She watched him swallow convulsively, saw the glimmer of unshed tears in his red-rimmed eyes, found her own cheeks suddenly damp once again.

"He was a very special man, wasn't he?" she said softly, her voice uneven.

"Yeah." He swallowed again and looked down at the letter once more. "I respected Josef more than any man I've ever met. I know he accepted this possibility, made his peace with it. But I—I'll miss him. And so will Isabel. Dear God, how will we ever tell her that not only is her father gone, but now she has no home to return to?" he asked, his voice anguished.

The idea came to Rebecca suddenly, taking her momentarily off guard. Yet she knew instantly that it was right. She'd always wanted a husband and a family. The husband part still seemed like a long shot. But now, out of the blue, she was being offered the opportunity for a family, the chance to share her life with a child who desperately needed someone to love her.

"Zach."

He turned to her, then tilted his head curiously at the odd expression on her face. "What's wrong?"

"Well, I know this might sound a little off the wall, but…well…Isabel *does* have a home, because…because I'd like to take her," she said impulsively. "I know a single-parent household isn't ideal, but I promise I'll give her enough love to make up for it."

Zach looked into Rebecca's eyes—sincere, warm, loving, compassionate, generous—and his heart overflowed with love for this special woman who cared so deeply and gave of herself so freely. He couldn't have made it through this night without her. And he didn't want to face even one more day until he had her assurance that she would be with him always.

Zach knew the present setting wasn't ideal, nor were the circumstances. But suddenly he knew that this was the right moment to ask the question that would fundamentally affect all of their lives. He reached for her hand, cocooning it snugly between his palms, and drew a deep breath.

"Maybe it doesn't have to be a single-parent household," he told her softly.

She stared at him uncomprehendingly. "What do you mean?"

His lips tilted up into a rueful smile. It shouldn't surprise him that she failed to understand his meaning, he supposed. After all, he'd never told her that he loved her. But he intended to remedy that right now.

"Wait here." He rose and walked over to the desk chair, reached into the pocket of the sports coat draped on the back, and removed something Rebecca couldn't see. When he turned back to her, he held a small box in his hand, and he flipped open the lid as he sat down to reveal a solitaire nestled on a bed of dark blue velvet. "This is what I mean, Rebecca," he said huskily as he held it out to her. "Will you marry me?"

Rebecca looked from the ring to Zach's face, then back again to the ring. Was this a mirage, a dream? Zach had never even said he loved her and now...now he was asking her to become his wife? She transferred her gaze back to his face. "Are...are you serious?"

"I've never been more serious in my life. I planned to ask you on our picnic tomorrow, but suddenly the timing seems right."

"But...but I thought you were leaving. What about the job in Washington? You never said anything about...about love. I'm not even sure I'm wife material, Zach. I—I'm defective merchandise." Her words were disjointed, an almost incoherent jumble of thoughts.

He set the ring carefully on the coffee table and then turned to her, his eyes compelling, intense. He grasped her shoulders firmly but gently, so that she couldn't turn away.

"Let's deal with those issues one at a time, okay? First, I'm not leaving. At least, I'm not if you agree to marry me. I was offered a permanent teaching job at the high school, which I'd like to accept. Second, I'll admit that the Washington offer was flattering. And a year ago I would have jumped at it. But since then I've found something even better. I found a satisfying job here, a life-style that suits me and, most important, a woman I love."

He paused for a moment and searched her eyes. "I haven't

told you that before, Rebecca, because I was afraid of scarin
you off. I know how you feel about intimacy. I know it fright
ens you. But as for being wife material, I can't think of anyon
who would make a better partner. And don't ever say you'r
defective merchandise,'' he told her fiercely, his eyes burnin
into hers. ''You're the most wonderful woman I've ever me
You're compassionate and caring and warm and sensitive an
kind and intelligent…not to mention drop-dead gorgeous.
know that the passion you're so afraid of is there, locked awa
in your heart, but yearning to be set free. I'm not afraid tha
you lack passion, Rebecca. My only fear is that I'll be over
whelmed by it when it's set free.''

A warm, glowing elation spread through her as she listene
to his words. She believed everything he said, unable to argu
with the honesty she saw in his eyes. At least, she believe
he believed it. And maybe he was right. Maybe she did hav
an abundance of passion. But she wasn't as convinced as h
seemed to be that she would ever find a way to fully expres
it.

''Zach, I…I want to say yes. But I'm so afrai
I'll…disappoint you,'' she admitted artlessly, her voice falter
ing.

''Rebecca, I have only one expectation if you agree to marr
me,'' he told her firmly. ''That you love me with all you
heart—and for all time.''

She felt her throat tighten with emotion. ''Oh, Zach, I do
I love you more than words can express! I have for a lon
time.''

His eyes filled with warmth and tenderness—and immens
relief. ''Then there's no problem,'' he said easily. ''The res
will come in time.''

''How can you be so sure?'' she persisted. ''I've lived wit
this fear for so long. It won't go away overnight, Zach.''

''I don't expect it to.''

''But…what if…if it never does?''

''Rebecca…'' He sighed and took her hand. ''I've finall

reached the point in my life where I understand what Josef knew all along. Love is the only thing that really matters in the end. I love you. I want to spend my life with you. The physical side of marriage is important. I won't deny that. But it's only a very small part of our life together. Most of the time it's just the everyday living, the sharing of small joys and sorrows—enjoying the first flower of spring, taking a long walk, even cleaning the house and shopping for groceries. In other words, just being there for each other in a thousand small ways. It's the everyday living that makes a marriage endure and grow stronger as the years pass."

Rebecca blinked back her tears, overcome with gratitude for the gift of love being offered to her by this wonderful, insightful, caring man. Marriage was a huge step, requiring a tremendous leap of faith on both their parts, given her background. But if Zach was willing, if he truly believed they could overcome her problem, how could she say no? He was offering her the life she'd always wanted, and she'd be a fool to walk away out of fear. She would just have to put her trust in him—and in the Lord—and take that leap.

Zach watched her, trying to discern her thoughts, praying that she loved him enough to commit herself to him—in every way. He'd done everything he could think of to make her feel safe and cherished and loved. Now it was up to her. He tried to remain calm as he waited for her answer, but it was a difficult task when his heart was banging against his rib cage, his respiration had gone haywire and his stomach was twisting painfully.

"Can I have a glass of water, Uncle Zach?"

Both heads swiveled in unison to the little girl who stood in the doorway, clutching her bedraggled Raggedy Ann. Rebecca's eyes flew to Zach's in sudden panic. They hadn't yet discussed how they were going to tell Isabel the news—or when. He seemed equally at a loss.

"Why are you here, Rebecca?" Isabel inquired, rubbing her eyes sleepily. "It's not morning yet, is it?"

"No, sweetie."

Isabel walked toward them, looking from one to the other
her face troubled. "Is something wrong?" she asked.

Rebecca turned to Zach and bit her lip, realizing, not fo
the first time since Isabel's arrival, that children seemed to
possess a sort of sixth sense that made them acutely attuned
to nuances of emotion. She lifted her eyebrows helplessly, in
a "What should we do?" expression.

With sudden decision Zach patted the sofa beside him, mov
ing far enough away from Rebecca to make room for Isabel.

"Come on in, honey. Rebecca and I have something to tel
you."

Rebecca wasn't ready for this, she thought in sudden panic
Her emotions were already in shreds. But delaying the inevi
table wouldn't make it any easier, she realized. They had to
tell Isabel sooner or later, and the little girl already suspected
that something was amiss. They might as well get it over with
she thought, trying to control the painful thudding of her heart

Isabel climbed onto the couch between them and looked
solemnly from one to the other. "Is my papa sick?" she asked
intuitively sensing the source of the gloom in the room.

Zach took her small hand in his and smoothed back her
flyaway hair, mussed from sleep. "A friend of your papa'
sent me a note on E-mail tonight. He had some bad news fo
us. Isabel, honey, it seems that…well, your papa, he—'
Zach's voice broke, and Rebecca stepped in.

"Sweetie, what Uncle Zach is trying to say is that the Lord
decided it was…it was time for your papa to go to heaven.'

Isabel stared at her with wide eyes. "You mean he died?'

Rebecca nodded. "Yes."

Isabel clamped her mouth shut and turned away, clutching
her doll more tightly to her chest. "I don't believe it. My papa
wouldn't leave me alone. He promised he'd always take car
of me."

Rebecca looked at Zach helplessly.

"And he will," Zach told her gently. "Remember the not

he sent you on your birthday? About always being close to you in your heart, even when he was far away? He still is, honey. He still loves you. It was just his time to go to heaven.''

Suddenly Isabel's lower lip began to quiver, and her eyes filled with tears. ''But why did he have to go now?'' she asked plaintively, her face bereft.

''I don't know,'' Rebecca confessed gently, blinking to hold back her tears. She slipped her arm lovingly around Isabel's slim shoulders. ''Sometimes it's hard to understand why God takes people when he does.''

''Maybe Mama was l-lonesome for him,'' Isabel offered, her voice quavering. ''Maybe God knew she needed him.''

''That might be,'' Rebecca agreed.

''But I need him, too!'' Isabel cried. ''I was supposed to go home next week. Where will I live now?''

Rebecca looked over at Zach. He was watching her carefully, his eyes filled with hope and tenderness and love. In the past few months he had become so much a part of her life that she could no longer imagine it without him. She loved him with all her heart. And she knew that together they could create a beautiful home for each other—and for the precious child that had been entrusted to their care.

Impulsively she reached across the top of the couch and took his hand. His grip was sure and solid and warm. In her heart she suddenly knew, with absolute conviction, that this was meant to be. Her eyes locked on his, reflecting the love and confidence and joy that suddenly overwhelmed her, and when she spoke, her voice was thick with unshed tears. But this time they were tears of happiness.

''You'll live with us,'' she said softly.

She pulled Isabel onto her lap, and Zach instantly closed the distance between them, his eyes never leaving hers as he draped his arm around her shoulders and pulled them both close. Finally he dragged his gaze from Rebecca and transferred it to the child she held.

"Would you like that, Isabel?" Zach asked, his voice gentle and unusually deep.

"You mean…stay here?" she asked.

"Yes. You see, Rebecca and I are going to get married. And we'd like it very much if you would be part of our family."

Isabel looked up at them. "Are you getting married because of me?"

"No, sweetie," Rebecca said quickly, before Zach could respond. She looked over at him. "We would have gotten married anyway." She needed him to know that her decision wasn't based on compassion for Isabel, but on deep, abiding love for him. A slow smile spread across his face, and she knew he'd gotten her message. "But it will be even better if you come to live with us," she continued, turning her attention back to the little girl.

Isabel grew silent for a moment. "I think my papa and mama would like me to do that," she said slowly at last, the tears still welling in her eyes as she turned to look up at Zach. "I heard Papa say once that he wished you had someone like Mama and me to come home to. He said that would make you very happy." Her eyes were serious as she studied his face. "Now you have me and Rebecca. Does that make you happy, Uncle Zach?"

Zach considered her question for a moment, thought about the odd twists and turns of life, with its jolting combinations of deep tragedy and great joy. In one day he'd lost his treasured friend, found a daughter and won the heart of the woman he adored.

Part of him was sad. Part was joyful. But under it all he suddenly felt a sense of peace, a deep contentment, a feeling of coming home. With a silent prayer of thanks, he reached down and touched Isabel's nose, then looked into Rebecca's beautiful, loving eyes and smiled.

"Yes, Isabel. It makes me very happy." He glanced over

at Rebecca, and her throat tightened at the love shining in his eyes. "And it feels good to come home at last."

"All right, all right, let's get organized," Sam declared, planting her hands on her hips as she surveyed the dressing room. "Henry, straighten your boutonniere. Isabel, do you need to go to the little girls' room? No? Okay. Rebecca, kindly descend from the clouds long enough to sit down so I can put your headpiece on."

Rebecca smiled dreamily at Sam and did as instructed. Thank goodness *someone* was in charge. She was too wrapped up in being a bride to be of use in any other capacity today.

Rebecca watched in the mirror as Sam securely anchored the wreath of baby's breath and stephanotis, then fluffed the yards of whisper-soft tulle that drifted down the back. When Sam was at last satisfied, Rebecca stood up, and her sister-in-law turned her to face the full-length mirror.

As she did so, Sam recalled a day two and a half years before when she'd done the same with her best friend, Laura. And she thought about the day two years ago when she'd looked at herself as a bride in this same mirror. Three happy endings in less than three years, she mused. Not a bad record, she concluded with a smile.

"So...what do you think?" she asked Rebecca.

The bride stared at her reflection in awe. Was that really her, that woman with the radiant face and shining eyes dressed all in white? It didn't seem possible. She gazed at the head-piece of fresh flowers and her cascading waves of russet hair, which tumbled loose and full past her shoulders; the beaded lace bodice of her gown, with its gracious sweetheart neckline; the quaint leg-of-mutton sleeves, which came to a point on the backs of her hands and added a delicate, old-fashioned touch to the gown; the full, satin skirt that swept into a dramatic cathedral-length train.

She truly was the epitome of the traditional bride, Rebecca thought in wonder. It was a role she'd never thought to play, and she relished it with joy and gratitude even as she said a silent prayer of thanks.

"Well?" Sam prompted.

"I guess it's real, isn't it?" Rebecca murmured softly, fingering the clouds of tulle that drifted past her shoulders.

Sam laughed. "Kiddo, you better believe it's real! If you have any doubts, go ask that handsome man who's anxiously waiting for you at the altar." She turned to the audience of two watching the proceedings and angled Rebecca toward them. "Ladies and gentlemen, I give you—the future Mrs. Zachary Wright," she pronounced.

Henry smiled. "I always knew you'd make a beautiful bride, Rebecca. Course, I just about gave up. But the minute I saw Zach, I figured he was the one for you."

"You look so pretty," Isabel said in awe, overwhelmed by the proceedings, reaching out a tentative hand to touch the billowing satin skirt.

"Thank you, sweetie." She nodded toward the brooch that Isabel held carefully in her hand. "Would you like me to pin that on for you?"

"Yes, please."

Rebecca knelt down. "I'm glad you thought about wearing this today," she said softly as she secured it to the front of Isabel's green satin, floor-length dress, an exact duplicate of Sam's. "It makes me feel like your mama and papa are right here with us." She gave the little girl a hug, pressing her close.

A sudden change in organ music sent a surge of excitement sweeping over Rebecca, and with one final, encouraging squeeze for Isabel she stood up.

Sam's discerning gaze swept over her once more, and she gave a satisfied nod. "Perfect," she declared, reaching for her bouquet and handing Isabel hers. "Do you remember everything we practiced the other night?" she asked the youngster.

"Yes."

"Good girl." Sam looked back at Rebecca with a grin and winked. "Knock 'em dead."

Rebecca watched them leave, then turned to her father with a tremulous smile. "Well, Dad, I guess this is it."

"Yep." He cleared his throat and looked down. "I'm mighty happy for you, Becka. Zach is a fine man. I'm only sorry your mother couldn't be here today."

"Me, too," Rebecca concurred softly, her eyes growing misty. "But I have a feeling she's here in spirit."

Henry nodded. "Yeah. I do, too. I know she'd offer you some words of wisdom if she could. I'm not much with words myself. But I hope and pray you and Zach have as wonderful a partnership as your mom and I did, honey. Just remember that marriage is like a roller coaster—lots of ups and downs. But if you stay on track, everything ends up just fine. And don't forget to enjoy the ride."

"I will, Dad. And thanks. For everything."

His eyes suddenly glistened suspiciously, and he sniffed. "Well, honey, you ready for the big walk?"

She took a deep breath and nodded. "It's time." She slid her arm through his and reached for her bouquet, smiling at the springlike combination of white roses and pink tulips. When she'd chosen her flowers, she'd known that tulips weren't traditional for a Thanksgiving wedding. Known they would be out of season. Known the expense would be outrageous.

Known, also, that she had to have them.

As Rebecca and Henry stepped into the vestibule and began the slow march down the aisle, she glanced around at the beaming faces. There were Rose and Frances, in their Sunday best, smiling happily—and just a touch smugly. And Ben, nodding sagely, his bow tie bobbing. Pete was there, too, with Melanie. And Laura and Nick, with their own new daughter, their smiles warm with remembrances of their own special day in this same place. Rebecca felt incredibly blessed to be able to share this day with so many dear family members and friends.

Her gaze shifted to the front. Sam and Isabel watched joyfully as she approached, Isabel looking proud in her "grown-up" dress, Sam giving her a knowing wink. Brad was there, too, waiting to perform the ceremony that would join his sister and Zach for life. He smiled at her now, a smile of understanding filled with deep affection and happiness. She returned it, thanking him with her eyes for all that he had been to her through the years—a brother, certainly, but even more than that, a friend.

And then her eyes went to the man who had become the center of her universe.

Rebecca's breath caught in her throat as she gazed at him. He looked incredibly handsome in his tux, she thought. Strong. Solid. Steadfast. He had the kind of looks that would make heads turn in any setting, she acknowledged appreciatively.

But it was his eyes that held her spellbound. As Henry placed her hand in Zach's, her husband-to-be smiled down at her. For a long moment they looked at each other, two hearts touching, joining in a timeless way that only those in love can understand. His eyes—tender, yearning, caressing, filled with love and warmth and joy—told her more clearly than words what was in his heart.

And as they stepped forward to recite the vows that would unite them as man and wife, she pledged in her heart to treasure and cherish this wonderful man all the days of her life. For he had already given her what the Good Book rightly described as the greatest thing of all—a deep, abiding love that would last for all time.

Epilogue

Six months later

Rebecca opened her eyes slowly, savoring the sensation of being totally relaxed and at peace. She sighed contentedly as she gazed out of the window at the lush May greenery, enjoying the gentle touch of the warm breeze that drifted lightly over her. Only the melodic song of a bird broke the stillness, and the early-morning light cast a golden glow over the landscape. Since Isabel was spending the Memorial Day weekend with Henry to celebrate the end of the school year, Rebecca had the whole day to share with Zach. Her lips curved into a smile, and a delicious tingle of anticipation swept over her as she turned toward him.

But his side of the bed was empty.

She frowned and rose on one elbow to survey the rumpled pillow, absently adjusting the spaghetti strap that had slipped down her shoulder. Where could he be? She'd been looking forward to a lazy morning in bed, perhaps even a late breakfast on the patio, just the two of them. But it seemed Zach had other plans, she thought disappointedly.

She was just about to swing her legs to the floor when a creaking stair caught her attention. She glanced toward the half-shut bedroom door, just in time to catch Zach peering carefully around the edge. He grinned when he saw that she was awake and pushed the door open with his shoulder.

"Good morning," he greeted her cheerily, smiling at her as he entered.

She stared at him. He was carrying a tray holding a bud vase that contained two pink tulips, a plate of croissants, butter, jam, a pot of coffee and various eating utensils. But what really caught her attention was his attire—shorts and a black tuxedo bow tie. Period.

"Aren't you going to say good morning?" he teased, depositing the tray on the nightstand.

"Good morning," she parroted automatically, her gaze quizzical as she tilted her head. "May I ask what this is all about?"

He stuck his head in the closet and rummaged around, removing two gaily wrapped packages before turning to her with mock chagrin. "I knew it! The magic is wearing off already. You forgot!"

Not likely, she thought with a soft smile. But it surprised her a little that he hadn't. "How could I forget our six-month anniversary?" she chided him gently. "I just didn't expect you to remember. Most men don't think about those things, you know."

His eyes—warm, filled with love, caressing—caught and held hers. "I guess I'm not most men—at least when it comes to you, Rebecca. I've treasured each moment of our marriage and counted my blessings every single day."

Rebecca's throat tightened with emotion as he stretched out beside her, propping himself up on one elbow while he reached over to play with the strap of her gown. As she gazed into his wonderful eyes, she knew in her heart that *she* was the one who had been blessed. She doubted whether many men would have exhibited Zach's infinite understanding and patience, both of which had been taxed to the limit over the past few months. She knew he had often wanted more than she was able to give, but he'd never pushed her. Instead, in his lovingly supportive way, he'd helped her take one step at a time until finally, oh-so-slowly, she'd learned to relax. He had loved her through it all, had never stopped believing and encouraging, even when her own optimism wavered. She owed him a debt of gratitude she could never repay. Except with love. And thanks to him, she had learned to joyfully give full expression to that emotion.

She glanced at the tray, the flowers, the gifts, and her throat constricted with tenderness once more at his thoughtfulness. If she lived a hundred years, she vowed never to take for granted this special man, who let her know every day in count-less ways that she was cherished and loved beyond measure. Impulsively she reached over and gave him a long, lingering kiss.

"Happy anniversary," she said huskily.

"Happy anniversary, sweetheart," he echoed, pulling her close to return the kiss. When at last he drew back, he took a deep breath then gave her a crooked grin. "Aren't you going to open your presents?" he teased.

She smiled and snuggled next to him contentedly. "Do I have to?"

He hesitated, then sighed deeply. "I think you'd better," he decided, reaching behind him to retrieve the two packages. "Otherwise I'm likely to forget all about them."

She scooted into a more upright position, reaching for the smallest package first. She tore the wrapping off and flipped open the lid of the jewelry box to reveal a gold tulip on a delicate chain. Her eyes misted as she looked over at him, and he gave her a tender smile.

"That will always be our flower—a symbol of new life and new beginning after a long, dark winter," he said quietly.

"You were my sun, you know," she told him softly. "Your warmth is what brought my heart to life." She reached over and touched his dear face, the tears glistening in her eyes. "Oh, Zach, I love you so much!"

His eyes held hers compellingly, and he reached for her hand, kissing the palm tenderly. "It's mutual, sweetheart," he seconded huskily. "Go ahead and open the other package."

This one was flat, and when she pulled off the paper it was, as she suspected, an envelope. Her gaze fell on the return address and she looked at Zach with eager anticipation. "Is this what I think it is?"

He nodded. "It came yesterday. But I decided to keep it for today."

Carefully, her hands trembling slightly, she opened the envelope and scanned the papers. A feeling of immense relief swept over her, and she closed her eyes, saying a silent prayer of thanks. She'd been confident this day would come, yet there had still been an underlying tension. She and Zach had kept their concerns from Isabel, knowing she'd already dealt with too much uncertainty in her young life. As far as she was concerned, she had belonged to them since the night Josef died. But now it was official. The red tape was finished. Isabel was theirs.

"I thought this would make the day even more memorable," Zach said, smiling at her tenderly.

She set the gifts carefully aside and stretched out beside him. "It makes things feel...complete," she reflected. "Like we're really and truly a family now."

"I know what you mean," he concurred, reaching over again to play with a strand of her beautiful hair.

"Zach."

"Mmm-hmm."

"I don't have a present for you. But I do have some news."

"I'm not in the news game anymore," he reminded her distractedly.

"I think you might want to hear this news."

"Actually, I have something else on my mind at the moment,'' he confessed, reaching down to drop a trail of soft kisses along her collarbone.

''Well, I guess it can wait. I just figured that when a man's wife was going to have a baby, he might want to know right away.''

His lips stilled, and then he lifted his head and stared at her. ''A baby?''

''Mmm-hmm. You know… Small. Pink. Cry and sleep and wet a lot?'' she teased.

''A baby? A baby!'' he repeated. His tone was incredulous, awed, joyous. ''Wow!''

''I just found out yesterday. I didn't want to say anything until I was sure. I hoped you'd be happy.''

''Happy? Happy doesn't even begin to describe how I feel! This is…this is awesome, as my students would say!''

She laughed softly, a delicious feeling of joy filling her heart. ''Yeah. Awesome.''

Zach's eyes softened with adoration as he leaned over her, tangling his fingers in her hair. His gaze caressed her, taking in every nuance of her beautiful, expressive face. ''Do you have any idea how much I love you?'' he asked, his voice catching in a way that tugged at her heart.

''Why don't you show me?'' she whispered, her eyes burning into his.

He complied readily, lowering his lips to hers in the silent but eloquent language known to lovers through the ages, and Rebecca gave thanks once again. For the joy Isabel had brought them. For the new life growing within her. And for the gift of this cherished man's love, whose patient nurturing had at last healed her heart.

Zach's heart was also filled with gratitude as he softly gathered Rebecca into his arms. He knew that without this special woman, he might never have discovered the one simple truth Josef had always understood: that love is the only thing that really matters in the end. And for a fleeting moment, just before he lost himself in the wonder of Rebecca's sweet love, he hoped Josef knew how things had turned out.

Because somehow he knew his friend would approve.

* * * * *

Dear Reader,

As I write this letter, I am sitting in my woodland garden watching the world reawaken after the long cold winter. It is a place of renewal, refreshment and enrichment, where the quiet is broken only by the lovely song of the birds. Here, in this special spot, the beauty of God's handiwork can be fully appreciated.

Eight years ago, however, when my husband and I bought this house as newlyweds, this garden was a dense thicket, overgrown and wild. Slowly, year by year, I cut and pulled and dug and planted, always working toward a vision of what it could be, always believing it could be transformed into a beautiful and tranquil oasis. My husband even caught the spirit, adding his own special touch—a meandering stone path. And now, at last, my vision is a reality. But as I have discovered, the garden is, and always will be, a work in progress, one that requires regular tending. Yet the rewards are great.

Love is much like my special place. It requires vision. And persistence. And faith. And attention. But it returns a hundredfold in joy.

All three of my heroines in the VOWS series made this discovery, each in her own unique way. In this, the final book in the series, Rebecca's heart finds new life (much like her cherished tulips) as she discovers the tremendous healing power of love. Writing this story uplifted and inspired me, and I hope it does the same for you as you read it.

This spring, may your life be filled with love—
and tulips!

Irene Hannon

Beginning in June from
Love Inspired™

SUDDENLY!

a new series by

Loree Lough

*Celebrate the joy of unexpected parenthood
in this heartwarming series about some very
unexpected special deliveries.*

In June, look for:

SUDDENLY DADDY

Ciara and Mitch were swept to the altar on a
whirlwind courtship. And all too soon Mitch's
dangerous job took him deep undercover, leaving a
lonely Ciara to hope and pray for his safe return. But
months later, when Mitch managed to make it back, it
was to find his wife expecting their baby...any minute.
Suddenly this daddy-to-be had some serious
explaining—and romancing—to do!

*And watch for SUDDENLY MOMMY,
available this August, only from
Love Inspired.*

Welcome to *Love Inspired*™

A brand-new series of contemporary inspirational love stories.

Join men and women as they learn valuable lessons about facing the challenges of today's world and about life, love and faith.

Look for the following June 1998
Love Inspired™ titles:

SUDDENLY DADDY
by Loree Lough

IN GOD'S OWN TIME
by Ruth Scofield

NEVER ALONE
by Lyn Cote

Available in retail outlets in May 1998.

LIFT YOUR SPIRITS AND GLADDEN YOUR HEART
with *Love Inspired!*™

Steeple
Hill™

1698

Take 3 inspirational love stories FREE!

PLUS get a FREE surprise gift!

Special Limited-time Offer

Mail to Steeple Hill Reader Service™
3010 Walden Avenue
P.O. Box 1867
Buffalo, N.Y. 14240-1867

YES! Please send me 3 free Love Inspired™ novels and my free surprise gift. Then send me 3 brand-new novels every month, which I will receive months before they appear in bookstores. Bill me at the low price of $3.19 each plus 25¢ delivery and applicable sales tax, if any*. That's the complete price and a saving of over 10% off the cover prices—quite a bargain! I understand that accepting the books and gift places me under no obligation ever to buy any books. I can always return a shipment and cancel at any time. Even if I never buy another book from Steeple Hill, the 3 free books and the surprise gift are mine to keep forever.

103 IEN CFAG

Name	(PLEASE PRINT)	
Address		Apt. No.
City	State	Zip

This offer is limited to one order per household and not valid to present Love Inspired™ subscribers. *Terms and prices are subject to change without notice. Sales tax applicable in New York.

ULI-198   ©1997 Steeple Hill